THE ALIAS AND THE ALTAR

LENA HENDRIX

Copy editing by James Gallagher, Evident Ink

Proofreading by Laetitia Treseng, Little Tweaks

Cover by Sommer Stein, Perfect Pear Creative Covers

For all of us who love a grump.

ABOUT THIS BOOK

The moment I kissed my wife, I knew I was in trouble.

A stoic, dangerous man with ties to the Mafia has no business keeping a gorgeous ray of sunshine like her, but she was scared, and I was desperate.

On the run, we land at a secluded ranch designed to protect federal witnesses. As long as everyone believes we're married, she won't have to testify against me for killing the man who put his hands on her.

But the longer we pretend, the more **the lines between fact and fiction begin to blur**. My eyes linger a second too long. My hands soften on her skin. My kiss, a little too demanding.

Before I can help it, our pretending extends behind closed doors, and our relationship begins to feel very, very real.

My plan is to hide out until I know she's safe—set her up for life and disappear. Still, I'm drawn to the way she breathes life into me without even trying. A better man would walk away.

But I never claimed to be a better man.

READER NOTE

This book contains adult material including references to substance abuse, child neglect (not on page), and discussions of violence and an attempted rape (on page).

It is my hope that I've handled these topics with the care and research they deserve.

ONE

SIENNA

"We have to leave. Now."

The words barely registered as I looked down at my shaking hands and tried to wipe away the streaks of blood across my knuckles. My heart was racing and my fingers numb. I couldn't stop staring at my hands. I started scooping up the overturned contents of my purse, smearing blood on the hard linoleum floor.

The man clasped my arm. His hand was so large it enveloped my biceps. His tug toward the back exit of the restaurant was gentle but insistent.

I looked up at him, my eyes going wide as the intense furrow in his brow deepened. I should run. I should be afraid of him.

"It's too late. They already know who you are," he insisted.

I swallowed hard and only nodded.

I trusted him.

After all, this was the man who came into the restaurant every Tuesday and Sunday. He sat in the darkest corner of my section every time and offered little conversation beyond his order. Once I'd realized he ordered the same thing—a meatball sub, extra marinara on the side—his conversation skills plummeted to a series of grunts and nods.

That man had also just saved my life.

～

A TWENTY-HOUR CAR ride from Chicago to the middle of nowhere hits different when it's done in near silence.

I'd learned that my mysterious stranger was *the* Parker Marino. I'd only gaped at him when he'd reluctantly revealed his identity. Working in a sub shop in Little Italy, I'd heard plenty of rumors about the Chicago Mafia and the ruthless business they conducted. It was best for everyone if you didn't ask questions, so I never did. My schedule was flexible and tips were amazing, so no matter who came into the restaurant, I'd serve them with a smile. My gift in life was that I could talk about everything and nothing with anyone.

Parker was notorious in the neighborhood for being intense. Ruthless. Driven.

Everyone forgot to mention he's also hot as fuck.

I adjusted in the seat beside him, angling my body even closer to the door.

Was I being kidnapped?

I spared a glance in his direction. His sharp blue eyes were laser focused on the road ahead of him. The long trip had a little scruff across his sharp jaw, and my stomach tingled at the closeness of him.

No. I definitely went with him willingly.

As flats of tall grasses sailed past, I longed for the familiar chaos of Chicago. I had never left Illinois, and as I looked out onto the horizon, I was overcome with the sheer *nothingness* of the landscape. In the distance, jagged mountains rose out of the golden plains, black against the riot of indigo and crimson that bled across the fading afternoon sky. I tucked my legs under me and wrapped my arms around my knees.

"Are you cold?"

Without bothering to wait for my response, Parker adjusted buttons and cranked up the heat.

Ignoring his question, I embraced his willingness to speak. "Do you know where we're going?"

He only nodded but I held my stare. Finally he continued: "I had a contact in the police department. I've been looking for someone, and it turns out we'll be safe where he's at."

It was more words than Parker had spoken to me in our entire relationship, and I still had no idea what he was talking about. I fought the urge to spew the onslaught of questions that bubbled inside me.

I gestured toward the window. "And where is that?"

Parker kept his eyes on the road and was silent for a moment. "Montana."

I looked outside again. The wide-open space started making a lot more sense. "Montana? There's *nothing* in Montana."

Parker shook his head, quietly mocking me with a gentle laugh. "Exactly."

Hours ago at a gas station bathroom outside of Minneapolis, I'd been tempted to run and hide. Find a way to leave Parker and never look back. Except I owed him more than that. I'd made a promise to a man I'd spoken only a few sentences to, but I wouldn't break my word.

Not after what he had done for me.

The sun sank lower beyond the mountain as small farm

buildings gave way to larger ones. Soon we approached a town, and a faded sign that read TIPP, MONTANA greeted us. As we drove across the main drag, it looked quiet. Peaceful. A banner hung across the road, advertising a fall festival. Despite the early evening hour, it looked as though shop owners were dimming the lights and locking their doors.

Parker checked his phone and skirted around Main Street to a dingy motel a few blocks from downtown.

He put the car in park and gripped the steering wheel. "We'll stay here tonight. Then I'll find Evan and get this sorted out. It'll be fine, Ray."

"Sienna."

"What?" How he made one syllable sound both sexy and dangerous was beyond me.

I fumbled for my words. "My name is Sienna."

The crease between his eyebrows deepened. "Your name tag said *Ray*."

I turned my palms up. "Old family joke, I guess."

A grumbling sound rumbled between us. "Let's go."

I stared at the motel door in front of me. It was dirty and dark, the flickering overhead light not helping make it look any less murdery. I chewed the inside of my bottom lip.

Parker gripped the steering wheel so hard his knuckles went white. I tried not to stare at his left hand and the fact it was missing a pinkie. "I can sleep in the car. You can have the room to yourself."

My head whipped around. "No freaking way. You're not leaving me alone in there." I pointed toward the motel. "You're my bodyguard now, champ."

Parker didn't find me cute or funny. He only muttered as he exited the car and strode toward the office. I jumped out of the car and walked as fast as I could to catch up to him. Parker's strides made it nearly impossible to keep pace without breaking into a jog. When we got to the door, I was breathless.

"You might not have noticed, but my legs are a little shorter than yours." I had to look up to see his reaction. He only held the door open for me and tipped his head toward the cramped lobby.

After checking in, I reached into the back seat. Everything I owned was now stuffed into an oversize duffel bag. My heart sank at the thought. As I was hoisting it over my shoulder, Parker caught it midair and slung it effortlessly across his back. Panicked and heartsick when I packed, I had no clue what was in the bag. I only hoped it was enough clothes to get me by.

I stood in the doorway to the motel room. It was clean . . . in a *nothing here is ever actually clean* kind of way.

I closed my eyes and focused on the positive.

Just be thankful it doesn't smell.

I smiled a little to myself. Ever since I was a little girl, I'd had an uncanny knack for looking at the bright side of things. As a baby, my dad had nicknamed me Lady Radiance—Lady Ray for short, which had morphed into Ray, and the name followed me into adulthood. Even the name tag on my uniform touted the name *Ray*. My chest pinched at the memory. I stared back at my hands as I remembered my uncle's blood smeared across them. It had taken an eternity to get it all off, and sometimes when I looked down, I could still see it.

Parker stormed through the motel doorway and dropped our bags onto the small table under the window. Parker claimed the bed closest to the door, and I breathed a sigh of relief.

He stiffened at my side and looked at me, questioning my obvious relief in his choice of bed.

"Thanks," I offered. "I like the bed farthest from the door. It feels less *rapey*." I shrugged.

He stared at me.

Nerves tickled my throat, and I couldn't stop myself from continuing. "You know . . . if someone were to come in . . . I'd be farther away."

A muscle ticced in his jaw, and he turned from me.

Back to silence. *Awesome.*

Exhausted, I plopped down across the bed and flipped off my shoes. Soul-shattering tiredness swept across me. My eyes burned with fatigue, and I closed them just long enough to let the hum of the television next door lull my nerves.

Hours later, I jolted awake. The room was pitch black, and my eyes took a moment to adjust. I lay in silence, steadying my breath. Looking down, I noticed that while I was still clothed and sprawled across my bed, Parker had covered me with the top comforter from his bed.

A strange warmth spread over me at the thought of him covering my sleeping body to keep me from getting a chill. I knew—just *knew*—deep down there was more to Parker Marino than he was letting on. I tilted my head to get a better look at him. Next to me, his rhythmic breaths filled the small room.

I can do this.

No matter how long it took, I would honor the promise I'd made to myself. The men who'd attacked us, knew who I was. He could have ran, but Parker had protected me. Now it was my turn to protect him in any way I could. I would find a way to make sure that he wouldn't be punished for what he had done.

Parker's body was turned away from me. The silhouette

of his massive shoulders rose and fell with every breath. His dark hair was inky in the low light of the motel room.

This man was a stranger.

This man was my protector.

This man was a murderer.

TWO

SIENNA

I LEANED FORWARD to look out the windshield. We crossed a small creek via a bridge with a huge wooden sign overhead —LAUREL CANYON RANCH.

"What is this place?"

Parker's eyes swept across the land as he followed the dirt-and-gravel path toward a large building. "It's a cattle ranch that also happens to house federally protected witnesses. My brother is here."

Witness protection? A brother?

"Okay, great!" I chirped and smoothed my sticky palms down my thighs.

Parker shifted beside me. "He's going to be less than thrilled to see me."

I swallowed my excitement and sank lower in the seat. Between the silent treatment and the general lack of conversation, any hopes of this brother of his being a strong conversationalist were dashed.

After wary glances and three separate, scary-looking men asking us questions, I was deposited onto the couch of the living room inside the large lodge. A man stood across from me, clearly standing guard, as Parker left me to talk in one of the offices.

I looked around at the stuffed animal heads that lined the walls. A large fireplace was empty, but I could imagine the crackling fire and warm, toasty goodness of sitting in front of it in the winter.

I turned toward my sentry and smiled. "So this place is great."

He only nodded. "Ma'am."

I smiled again. "I am so rude. My name is Sienna. And you are?"

He shifted uncomfortably, likely knowing he wasn't supposed to be talking to me. After a beat, he cleared his throat. "Daniel, ma'am."

"Oh stop." I tucked my legs under me and settled into the supple brown leather chair. "Call me Sienna." I swept a hand across the open space of the living room. "This place is . . . wow. I mean, talk about rustic chic."

Daniel looked at me as I continued, totally unfazed. "I've never been to Montana. You seem like a salt-of-the-earth kind of guy. Are you from here?" I probed. One of the secret tricks in my arsenal of getting people to open up was to get them to talk about themselves. People *loved* to talk about themselves. They couldn't help it.

I sat, patiently smiling at Daniel and waiting for him to give in. It took about five seconds for him to crumble. "Texas."

Daniel and I chatted. I prattled on and on about everything and nothing and ignored the shouts and muffled grunts that filtered through the thin walls of the lodge. At one point, the angry shouts subsided.

Parker came storming out into the hallway, a split in his lip as though he'd taken a hit. He didn't pause for me, so I jumped up, squeezing Daniel's forearm as I rushed passed. "Thanks for the chat, Dan! I can't wait to try those snickerdoodles!"

A light blush tinged his nose pink as I scurried after Parker.

"What was that about?" I asked as we exited the lodge and walked toward Parker's car.

"Found my brother. We're staying here for a while. Until we can get it all sorted out."

I ignored the commotion behind us as I walk-jogged toward the car. After a short drive up a dirt path, Parker stopped the car in front of a small, tidy cottage.

So much better than the motel.

Things were already looking up. A few large trees dotted what I considered the yard, which bled into a rambling pasture with a five-strand barbed-wire fence meant to keep cattle contained. I peered out over the grass and tamped down the disappointment when I could hear them but couldn't see any real live cows up close.

The cottage was white board-and-batten with simple cedar shutters and a black door. The small front porch was just wide enough for two rocking chairs and a small table between them.

I love it already.

Parker exited the car, and instead of walking toward the cottage, he rounded the hood to open the door for me. I felt a twinge at the simple, kind gesture.

"Thank you." As I unfolded myself from the car, I breathed in the cool mountain air. It smelled unlike anything I had ever experienced—fresh and invigorating.

My eyes tracked Parker as he moved toward the back seat. Looking out over the car, I could see a man across the road and up a ways. His large arms were crossed over his chest as he glared at us from outside another cottage.

"Parker? Who is that?"

He stood. "My brother. Evan."

I squinted, trying to get a better look at the man. His hair was dark, like Parker's, and he was built as strong, though maybe just a bit leaner.

"Why is he staring at us?"

I thought I heard a sigh, and I eyed Parker, trying to figure him out.

"I'm fucked."

It was the first time I'd noticed the weariness that had crept into Parker's eyes, the tension pinching his shoulders. Whether it was the shitty night's sleep on the lumpy motel bed or the car ride or the events of the past few days, it was catching up with him.

Unease rolled through me. Parker was supposed to be the strong one. "You said we'd be safe here. Are we not?"

Parker dragged a hand through his thick hair. "We're safe for now. As long as we can stay. If anyone finds out what happened in Chicago—"

"I won't tell." I cut him off, fierceness making my voice hard. This had to work. I'd left everything behind. There was nothing and no one left to go back to. Parker and I were the only two alive who knew what happened that night in the restaurant. No one could force me to tell his secret.

Our secret.

Resigned, Parker went back to unloading the car. "I'll grab your stuff."

I steeled my back. No one tells me what to do without hearing something about it, and certainly no one gives up hope if I have a say in the matter.

The thought was there, and my feet were moving before

I could think it all the way through. I stomped over the grass and across the gravel toward Parker's brother as I fought the tears that burned my eyes and clogged my throat.

Evan's eyes widened as I approached. I straightened my shoulders and lifted my chin.

"Hi! You must be Evan. I'm Sienna. Parker's wife."

I LEFT a dumbstruck Evan to find Parker roaming the cottage. He looked unsure of where to put my bag as he stalked around the small space. I followed him into the tiny bedroom at the back of the house and stared down at the bed.

The one bed.

I blinked at him and back at the bed.

"I put your bag on the less rapey side of the bed." He gestured to my duffel tucked between the wall and the bed frame.

I paused, a smile stretched across my face. "Did you just make a joke, Parker Marino?" I bumped his arm, and he shifted away from me.

I gently cleared my throat.

How the hell was I going to tell him this?

"Um . . . so . . . I did a thing."

His eyebrow tipped up in surprise.

My hands were twitchy and I rubbed them together. "We can't take our chances. This ranch is our only option, right?"

He nodded.

"Then it's settled. We're getting married."

He only stared at me until his scowl deepened. "No."

"Parker, listen to me. It's the only way. A wife can't

testify against her husband, right?" My shoulders bounced. "That's a thing. And we need to lie low here. It's less complicated than having to make up a lie or have them use us against each other."

"You think telling everyone we're married will bring *fewer* questions?"

I shrugged. "Sure. Married people are weird. No one's going to go poking around and asking questions about a marriage, right? That would just be rude."

"I'm not sure federal agents give a shit about being rude."

"Maybe not. But I also doubt they'd think I would turn against my own husband."

I knew by the flicker in his eye that I had him. My logic was flawless. By marrying Parker, I could keep my promise. Only a small wave of nausea bubbled in my belly as I thought about how long I'd have to pretend to be married to this brute of a man who could barely stand me. Sure, he wasn't bad to look at, but unless his vocabulary expanded to more than grunts and one-word answers, it was going to be a long few years.

Holy shit. A few years. I may have to keep this up for who knows how long? What the hell have I done?

THREE
PARKER

I agreed to marry Sienna.

Not just fake married, pretending to have a wife, but truly, *legally* married. It was probably the first legal thing I'd done in a while.

What a selfish prick.

I knew as well as anyone that keeping our sham marriage a secret would be easier if we really went through with it and had the legal documents to back our story up. An uncomfortable sensation moved through my chest when I thought about what that marriage meant for Sienna. I had nothing left in Chicago to go back to, but what about her? Why would she ever agree to this?

My mind flipped back to the night at the restaurant. My biggest fuckup was being chased and making a left instead of a right, heading straight into the darkened business. I had no idea she would be there, the last person closing up for the night. I had rained upon her every horrible thing from a past that had finally caught up with me.

"I need an outfit." Sienna's soft voice called to me from the bedroom of our cottage. I sat up from where I'd slept as she walked into the living room with a rumpled pile of clothes. "All I have are baggy T-shirts, leggings, and one pair of jeans."

"That's not a problem." Two of the duffel bags I'd brought were stuffed with cash. I'd buy her a goddamn closet full of clothes if it took away the scared look she'd been carrying around and replaced it with the sunny smile that tingled my skin.

For the past week, everyone at the ranch had given us our space. Unknown to us, an old business associate, Michael, had followed us out here, looking for trouble, but apparently my sister, Gemma, and Evan's girl were more than he bargained for. I would have loved to have seen the smug look on his face wiped clean when he was stuffed into a cell. I needed to talk to Evan. And Gemma. But until Sienna and I could get our story straight—and sneak a wedding in—we were holed up in our tiny cottage.

Today's the day. The day you tie a noose around the neck of the woman who's trying to save your ass.

Sienna's eyes were rimmed in red, and I hated that I had no fucking clue why she had been crying. Probably because she knew by the end of the day, I would be her husband.

She held her chin high as she walked past me and out the door. She was a spitfire—I'd give her that.

Over the past week, I'd tried to talk with her, but what could I say? Everything was totally fucked, and I was still trying to figure out what to do about it. So far, her plan of getting married to get the heat off our backs was still the best solution.

Ma Brown—or rather Agent Dorthea Brown, the woman in charge at the ranch—was explicit in that we were having a meeting on Sunday. Our time was up.

We drove off the ranch and toward town. Sienna's soft

voice filled the car with her observations of the landscape, questions she didn't wait for me to answer, and endless small talk. It was mind-boggling how she never ran out of something to say, and despite my silence, she pressed on.

Her voice became a comfort. It helped me gauge her mood and know when she was comfortable or when the fear started to creep back in.

As I drove down the long strip of Main Street, Sienna visibly relaxed. It seemed as though the bustle of the small town energized her. She kept a keen eye on people walking down the sidewalk or popping into the coffee shop.

By the time I'd found a parking space, her smile had returned, and my shoulders relaxed. Without hesitation, she hopped out of the car and started walking down the sidewalk. I kept in step beside her, careful to keep her close without crowding her.

"Good morning!" Sienna beamed a gorgeous smile at a man walking toward us.

He scowled in her direction and brushed past her. A muscle in my jaw clenched. It was one thing for her to have to put up with my shitty moods, but the guy didn't so much as acknowledge her greeting.

Sienna's voice dropped, and I didn't miss how she moved a fraction closer to me. I had to stop myself from wrapping an arm around her shoulder. Instead, I straightened my back. "Fuck that guy."

I liked the small smile that teased the corner of her mouth. "I thought small towns were supposed to be warm and welcoming," she said.

I shrugged. My entire life had been lived in a city. I never knew warm and welcoming.

She stopped in front of a small boutique, Rebellious Rose. Sienna shielded her eyes as she looked up at the sign.

"I'm going to try here." I had taken a small step toward the door when she cut me off. "Alone."

I paused, considered, and nodded once. I pointed down the road. "I'll try there."

She gave me a soft smile and swung the door open as the gentle, tinkling bell welcomed her inside.

As I crossed the street toward a men's clothing store, I couldn't help but notice the wary glances of everyone I'd passed. When we'd first arrived in Tipp, I'd spent a few days quietly looking for my brother. Cautious at first, the town did seem to warm up. I was no stranger to using my size and a few well-timed compliments to get what I needed from people. I visited the local bar, diner, library. Everyone was tight-lipped, but their frosty demeanor thawed eventually.

I wasn't always such an asshole.

For some reason, Sienna's sunny personality got under my skin. It made my muscles tight and uncomfortable. There was an unmistakable draw to her. A need to protect her and keep her safe.

Months ago, in Chicago, I had been randomly seated in her section of the restaurant, and that was all it took. One look and I was speechless. When I realized she didn't know who I was, I was even more entranced. She had no concept of my money or power or what I could do for her because of my connections to the Mafia. By the time I'd dislodged the coal in my throat, she'd moved on and accepted that I was a broody recluse who ordered the same meal every time he came in. I forced myself to limit my lunches to a few times a week. Like a drug, I could get my fix of her bubbly laughter and the way she'd always ask "The usual, hun?" with a wink.

I was a criminal. Once I chose that path, I'd known

where I was headed, and I would have cut down anything—
or anyone—who stood in my way. A man who froze out his
own brother and disowned his half sister just to keep them
from the fray. It was a life of subtle chaos. Sienna didn't
deserve to be stuck with someone like me.

And now I was marrying her. Condemning her to a life
of lies. Doling out a prison sentence to keep me from
my own.

"Can I help you, sir?" The store clerk sized me up as I
walked in.

I looked around at the selection in the small shop.
Denim, cowboy hats, and leather boots lined the walls. "I
don't suppose you have a suit?"

PACING the hallway of the Cedar County courthouse, I
couldn't stand still. I tugged at the cuff of the black button-
down shirt I wore. It covered the tattoos on my forearms,
but others peeked out over the backs of my hands. I kept my
left hand tucked into my pocket—a habit I couldn't seem to
shake.

Sienna had stepped into the bathroom, choosing to
change and freshen up at the courthouse. After what felt
like forever, she stepped back into the hallway.

She wore a short-sleeved lemon-yellow dress that
nipped in at her waist with a bow. The sunny color matched
her personality, and it made her green eyes pop against her
lashes. The fitted top was high necked, but a deep V
revealed the sexiest hint of skin. The full skirt stopped
midcalf and swung freely with her movements.

For a moment, I let time fade away, and I just stared.

She's perfect.

When she spotted me at the end of the hall, she turned on her heels and clipped down the corridor. Her strides were long and confident. Well, as long as they could be for someone who barely topped five feet. My eyes tracked down her slim legs to the heels she wore. I swallowed a groan before tearing my eyes away.

"Hey."

"Hi." Her smile was bright, but it didn't reach her eyes. Sienna's cheeks were flushed, and she'd put on makeup that made her already gorgeous features stand out. My eyes dipped to her matte-red lips. I wanted to devour her.

"You look handsome."

"Thank you. So do you," I said, faltering. "Look . . . nice," I stammered.

Fucking moron.

"Thanks! It has pockets." She dipped her hands into the skirt and swished it back and forth.

I cleared my throat and held out my elbow. "Are you ready?"

Sienna stiffened slightly and closed her eyes. "Not really."

I huffed out a breath. "Me neither."

Beside me, she took three deep breaths before setting her shoulders and walking toward the door. "Stop." Her small arm shot out in front of me, halting our forward progress. "Before we do this, I have to know something."

I looked at her as she continued: "Why do you only have nine fingers?"

I took my left hand out of my pocket and flexed it by my side. At the bottom knuckle, my pinkie was gone, a smooth scar in its place. "A debt was owed."

Her eyes didn't leave my hand, and she looked a bit queasy. "Someone cut it off?"

Behind her a door opened, and a paunchy man with a wide smile and a clipboard walked into the hallway. "Y'all getting married today?"

Sienna turned, and it was a wonder the man didn't hear her gulp. Her expression was filled with dread.

I knew the feeling.

She sucked in a breath, fighting against the threat of tears. "One minute, please." She smiled at the clerk and turned from me.

Was she backing out?

Sienna's voice was soft as she closed her eyes. "Uncle Davis. I'm sorry you can't be here. Thank you for all that you were for me. I hope I make you proud."

I stared as she squeezed her eyes tight before opening them again. It was agony to think she was mourning her uncle and still selfless enough to marry me. I studied her. She was grieving and I had missed it. Everyone I had cared about had either left me a long time ago or been pushed away by me. I had embraced the safety of my isolation.

I placed a steadying hand on her shoulder, and instead of pulling away, she turned into me. I held her, allowing myself to breathe in her faint scent—like salt water and summer breezes. I pulled it to the bottom of my lungs and savored it. Over her head, the clerk looked at me and smiled. I offered him a tight-lipped grimace in return.

Sienna released her breath. "Okay. Let's do this."

She breezed past the man who held the door for us. I greeted the clerk at the desk, answering the preliminary questions as Sienna stood frozen at my side. I filled out the marriage application with the information I knew and slid the paper across the wooden counter toward her. She gripped the pen in her left hand, a slight tremble in it as she wrote.

The clerk looked it over and shot us a bland look. "Take a seat. We'll call you when it's time."

I gestured toward the small wooden chairs against the wall. Sienna sat, gripping the arms of the chair. I sneaked a glance at her face to find her eyes staring straight ahead. Her chest lifted with deep, steady breaths. I tapped a rhythm on my knee with my finger.

Today is a big deal. Women usually gush about white dresses and flowers and walking down the aisle—not outdated courthouses that smelled faintly of wood cleaner and stale coffee.

How does she take her coffee? Probably heaps of sugar and a fuck ton of creamer. That's the only way she's got so much energy.

I quietly chuckled at my own assessment of her.

"What's so funny?" she whispered.

I shifted in my seat. "Nothing."

"Nerves?"

When my eyes met hers, she looked almost hopeful. I didn't have the heart to tell her that besides knowing that marrying her was the ultimate dick move, this day meant nothing to me.

"Yeah. Something like that."

Sienna's small hand gripped my forearm and squeezed. For a moment, I stared. Despite the fabric of my suit between us, the contact was searing. My heart pumped in my chest. When she dropped her hand into her lap, I was overcome by the ice racing through my veins at the absence of her touch.

I tried to ignore the nagging feeling that this was wrong, but it replayed in my mind on an endless loop. I angled my body toward hers. "Maybe we shouldn't . . ."

"Shut up." Her hushed, clipped tone caught me off guard, but then softened. "It's the only way."

She was tough. If Sienna could survive that night in the restaurant and watch her uncle die right in front of her, then she could survive a sham marriage. A few years, hopefully less, and she'd have her life back. After this was through, I'd make sure she was set up and never need or want for anything again. It was the least I could do.

"Sienna, I . . ." My voice was gravelly as I searched for the words. She lifted her chin to look at me.

Was it me or did her stormy eyes soften when I used her name?

"Parker and Sienna. You're up." The clerk held a piece of paper. "Take this and go see the judge. Right through there."

We followed her directions, silently entering the judge's chambers. The lighting was low, adding to the stormy unease that rolled through me. Sienna slipped her hand into mine and squeezed as the judge looked at us.

I looked down on her. Sienna's smile was tight as she stared at me as if to say, *Act happy, you fucking idiot.*

I followed her lead and wrapped an arm around her slim shoulders, letting her perfume wash over me. I hoped my smile didn't look like a scowl as I held her tight against me.

The judge rounded his desk and stood in front of us.

"Rings?"

Panic licked at the base of my skull. When Sienna came up with this scheme, it hadn't even occurred to me that we needed wedding rings. As I looked at Sienna, I could see her pulse hammer beneath the thin skin at the base of her neck.

I cleared my throat. "No, sir. Custom made. We're picking them up next week." The lie rolled off my tongue with the practiced ease of a scumbag.

The judge nodded. "Please join hands and face one another."

We did as we were told. Sienna's eyes were a riot of blues and greens, but for the first time I noticed a ring of yellow nestled against the pupil. Her eyes didn't hold mine but slowly moved across the features of my face and neck.

"As we proceed, with your hands joined, you are willingly entering into this marriage. You are promising to love and honor each other."

She held my left hand in her own. If my missing finger made her squeamish, she didn't let it show, but rather stroked her thumb over my knuckle. The tenderness of that gesture stuck a hot poker under my rib cage. The judge looked between us. "Do you, Parker, take Sienna to be your lawfully wedded wife?"

Our eyes met. *I'm sorry.*

"I do."

"Do you, Sienna, take Parker to be your lawfully wedded husband?"

"I do."

"By the authority vested in me by the state of Montana, I pronounce you husband and wife."

We simultaneously let out a breath, and the humor in it wasn't lost on her. Sienna started giggling, tears pooling in her eyes. From the outside, she looked happy, but I knew the truth.

Panic. Hysteria.

"Parker, you may now kiss your bride."

Sienna's laughter was cut off with a strangled cough.

Less than five minutes and we were married. Sienna was my wife.

I was already a colossal asshole, so without hesitation, I stepped forward, wrapping my arms around her slim waist, and lowered my mouth to hers.

FOUR

SIENNA

PARKER'S MOUTH was on mine. *My husband's* mouth.

I was overwhelmed by the scent of Parker's skin as he moved into my space—spicy and expensive. The seconds that dragged on as he lowered his mouth to mine were unbearable. The pull to him was undeniable as his palm cupped the side of my face and his fingers threaded into my hair. My heart throbbed in my ears as his lips met mine. They were soft and full.

Before I could react, Parker broke the connection and stepped back. I was far too worked up for such a quick, chaste kiss. My face flamed with a mixture of desire and embarrassment. Everything about this was wrong.

I stepped back, forcing a smile for the judge. "Thank you."

Parker stared at me, his light eyes intense below the furrow of his brow. I grabbed his hand and swiveled toward the door. Once I had rushed past the clerk, grabbing the marriage license as I passed her, I pushed open the door to the hallway. Finally I could breathe. The pressure of Parker's lips still tingled on mine.

"Okay, well . . ." I rubbed my damp palms down the full skirt of my yellow dress.

"Yeah." He cleared his throat and shifted his stance.

What the hell do we do now?

I was at a loss for words and just stared at him. Despite his huge frame and the tattoos that snaked around his arms, his eyes were soft. Kind.

Parker had saved me and I'd made a promise. It was done.

"We should get back."

He nodded.

On the drive toward the ranch, silence stretched, long and aching, between us. A finger tapped my lower lip, where it still buzzed from our kiss as I looked out the passenger-side window. No matter how many times I told myself it meant nothing, there was something hot and burning behind the way Parker held me.

My wedding may have been in a county courthouse with no ring and no wedding dress, but at least our first kiss had been wedding-worthy, even if the marriage itself was total bullshit. A tingle settled between my legs, and I shifted to conceal my discomfort.

When we finally pulled up to our cottage, the tiny home seemed to shrink. It was stifling. I rushed inside and headed straight for the bedroom to change. I needed to get away—escape the last week of my life and settle the nerves that rattled below my skin.

When I came back out, dressed in jeans and a soft tee, the cottage was quiet. I pulled on a pair of canvas sneakers and went outside. With his hands braced on the fence, Parker had his back to me. He still wore his slacks and dress shirt, and the fabric strained against the expanse of his shoulders. He didn't look out onto the pasture but rather hung his head. Tension rippled through the muscles in his back as his breaths sawed in and out.

Times like those, when Parker let his stoic expression slip just enough to look almost *human*, my heart ached for him. His soul was as lost as mine. He needed space as much as I did.

"I'm going for a hike up the ridge," I called out to him. He only turned his head and nodded.

My husband. The man of few words.

Trudging up the gravel, I headed toward a path that wound into the base of a large butte, and I followed the well-worn hiking path through the grassy fields and into the woods.

Oh god, how my life had changed. The warm fall sun heated my skin as I pushed myself harder and faster. My legs burned as I continued up the sloping hills. I glanced back, high enough to see the small cottages dotting the property below. Parker was no longer at the fence. Quiet nature sounds surrounded me as I breathed in the mountain air and tipped my face toward the sun.

So different from Chicago.

I thought about my hometown, and my stomach knotted. There was nothing left.

Was this my home now?

No matter where I ended up, I would be fine. Just like always. I would repay Parker by being an honest and loyal wife. Fake marriage or not, he deserved as much. At least he was nice to look at. I pressed a hand to the small flutter low in my belly. *Nice* was an understatement. I'd known since our first encounter at the restaurant that Parker was hot as hell. At first I'd openly flirted, hoping he might ask me out. When he never offered more than a grunt or *thank you*, I took the hint and stopped trying so hard.

Now that delicious, salty man was my husband.

"Hey! Hello?" a voice called from behind me.

My eyes flew open and struggled to adjust to the sunlight.

"Hi." A young woman with cropped blonde hair and a smile waved as she walked up the path. "Sorry. I didn't want to scare you by creeping up on you."

I had seen her before, but we hadn't met. I offered a small smile as she approached. She was dressed for a hike in tight leggings and boots. Despite the warm weather, her tight shirt rode high on her collar, and the long sleeves covered the length of her arms.

"I'm Gemma. I'm, um, Parker's sister."

Oh shit. Showtime.

"Oh, hi! Sorry, I'm a little out of it today." I did my best to brush the hair from my sweaty face. "I'm Sienna. Parker's wife."

If she was shocked by my proclamation, she didn't show it. She only tipped her bottom lip up and shrugged. "Sisters, I guess."

Holy fuck. I have a sister-in-law.

A lump swelled in my throat, and I swallowed down the emotions that clawed at my chest.

"Mind if I walk with you?" she asked, carefully watching my movements.

"Course not. I have no idea where I'm going."

She looked at their feet, and we shared a small laugh. "If you're here long enough, you'll figure it out. Stay close to the main path. It loops back around."

We started walking in awkward silence. The warm, early fall breeze cooled my hot skin. The smell of pine and earth swirled around me. I tried to sneak a glance at Gemma. Her hair was a pale blonde and cut in a blunt bob.

As the moments stretched on, Gemma began to hum and sing to herself. It was a warm, raspy melody.

"Wow. You have a beautiful voice."

Her eyes went wide as if she'd forgotten I was even there. "Oh, Um. Sorry, I didn't realize I was singing out loud."

"Are you kidding? It's gorgeous. I wish I could sing. Unfortunately I'm pretty sure they'd pay me to shut up at any open-mic night."

We shared a laugh, and when I saw my opening, I took it. "This ranch is something else, huh?"

Gemma looked at our surroundings, the light slanting through the trees as we got closer to the ridge. Her eyes went glassy as she looked into the forest. "I hated it when I first came here. Now it feels more like home than Chicago ever did."

"Do you miss it?"

"Chicago?" She shrugged. "Sometimes. I miss the food. The noise of the city. Always having something to do." A clearing opened in front of us, and the path continued up the butte. "I don't miss feeling afraid."

Her mood shifted as she walked. Tension wedged itself between us. Something was up with Gemma, like she wanted to talk with me but she was also pissed off. Her steps became faster and harder as she trudged up the path, and I struggled to keep up.

I was breathless. "Did I say something wrong?"

"I just can't figure it out. What are you doing here?"

I stopped on the path, stunned by the sudden flash of anger. "Parker and I came here to find Evan. We had run into some trouble and—"

"And you brought the trouble with you. Val and I were almost killed."

My mouth dropped open. I had caught only bits and pieces of what had happened to the women, and she wasn't wrong. Michael, a hateful man looking for revenge, had followed us out here in hopes of finding Evan.

It had worked.

Because of us, Val and Gemma had been put in grave danger.

My eyes dropped to my shoes. "You're right." Gemma's anger wavered for a fraction of a second, just long enough for me to keep going. "We were in danger when we left. Parker had gotten some information that Evan might be here, and we took a chance. He didn't mean to put you in danger."

A barking laugh tore from Gemma's throat as she tilted her head back. "That's rich. Sounds like you don't know Parker at all."

Gemma continued the hike and I stomped after her. I started to protest after I realized that I *didn't* know him at all. Certainly not enough to convince his sister.

She looked at me and shook her head. "You seem nice enough. Normal. Certainly not dumb enough to be with a skank like Parker." Was that pity laced in her voice? For some reason, the thought of Parker with someone else shot a pang into my side. Gemma stepped into my space. "Married? Parker? I'm calling bullshit."

My pulse raced through my veins, panic rioting through me. We'd been fake married less than a day, and I was already fucking it up.

I lifted my chin and spoke the only truths I had. "He makes me feel safe. Parker saved my life, and he has kind eyes. He is my husband."

Gemma squinted at me as if she was trying to figure out

what I was hiding. Somehow this became more of an interrogation and less of a friendly hike between sisters.

True to her word, the path wound around and pointed back toward the ranch.

"What about your family?" she asked.

Relief washed over me. At least she didn't want to talk about Parker and my relationship any longer. I shook my head. "No, I don't . . ." Reality dawned on me, drowning me below the surface of the water. "There's only Parker."

Gemma stopped where the forest exited toward the grassy fields. She pinched the bridge of her nose. "Well, it looks like you're in luck. Ma loves her misfit toys." Gemma took an exaggerated bow before leaving me staring after her. "Welcome to Redemption Ranch."

FIVE

PARKER

THE STRESS of the past week wedged an ice pick through my skull, and pain radiated down my arm. If I was having a stroke, I wished it would just fucking do the job already. I leaned my head back against the couch and sighed.

Sienna had told people we were married. Now that it was true, we needed to figure out the rest of our story. Tomorrow afternoon, Ma Brown would be deciding whether we could stay at the ranch awhile or if she would send us packing. If we stayed, Sienna and I would have to get our stories straight.

Everything had changed the night at the restaurant. For Sienna's sake, I hoped that we could stay at the ranch until I knew no one else was coming after us. With the protection of federal agents, I could at least breathe easy knowing she would be safe. She deserved that much.

Though I had plenty of money for us, I needed a job. Even in the city, I kept busy. Not a single day of my life had been spent not working. After a week in Montana, hiding out in the tiny cottage, I was crawling out of my skin. I jumped off the couch to pace the floor. I needed to move.

What the hell kind of job are you going to have on a cattle ranch?

The absurdity of it had a laugh nearly erupting from my chest. I may be a city boy at heart, but I knew hard work. I could learn fast. Whatever job Ma could throw at me, I'd learn, if that meant we had a place here. For a little while, at least.

My eyes landed on the small bookshelf by the fireplace in the corner of the living room. I scanned the titles—an eclectic mix of Westerns, romance, and nonfiction bird-watching. The knock at the cabin door was swift and firm. I hated there was no peephole, so I swung the door open, cautiously positioning my body to absorb the blow if whoever came by unexpectedly tried to push open the door. As I peered around the doorframe, my little brother's face came into view.

"Open up, dickweed."

Despite the tension between us, I couldn't help but crack a smile. I let the door fall open and stepped away, welcoming him into the cottage. He was almost as tall as me, a bit leaner but built like a fighter. Life hadn't been kind to either of us, despite my best efforts to keep him away from the darkest aspects of life connected to the Mafia. It was a lifetime ago that we were taken from our mother, shuffled from home to home, each placement worse than the last.

"Evan." I nodded at my brother. I could still see traces of the scared thirteen-year-old whose eyes went wide when I told him my plan. We would run away, and I would get a job and take care of us. His eyes were full of hope and pride then. Now he looked indifferent, and I swallowed the bitterness on my tongue.

"It's been one hell of a week." Evan dragged his hand

through his dark hair. It was longer than mine and poked out like it always had when he raked his fingers through it.

"You got that fucking right."

For a moment we stood there, each staring at the other, unable to bridge the chasm that formed between us.

"Lip's healing up."

I touched a finger to the spot on my face that had caught the brunt of Evan's fist when I first arrived at the ranch. "Don't even feel it," I lied. Evan's fist had come down like a hammer, and it had hurt like a bitch.

Evan scoffed, calling me on my bullshit.

"What do you need, Ev?" I crossed my arms over my chest as he looked around.

"Where's your old lady?"

For some reason I didn't like Evan calling her that. I tipped up my chin. "Sienna's out exploring. Where's the *cop?*" I lifted an eyebrow in his direction, and his nostrils flared.

Now that *is interesting.*

"She's gone." His voice was gravel, barely getting the words out.

"Probably better." Men like us are better off alone.

Evan's jaw clenched. "I'm not here to talk about Val. You've been here a week, and I need to know what your plan is."

"I have a meeting with Agent Brown tomorrow. It'll be decided if what testimony I can provide will be of use to them. If it is, we'll stay until things calm down."

"You're gonna turn?"

"If that means Sienna can stay here for a while, then yes. There's nothing left in Chicago. The Family is rotting from the inside. Everyone is out for themselves." I dragged my hand down my hair and squeezed my neck. "I'm done."

"Hmph."

"Look, man. I've been helping the cops with low-level shit for a while now. That's how I found out you were here."

"You were an informant?"

I nodded. "Just piddly shit. Feed the cops information to get them distracted enough that we could run the business. I meant it when I said I had nothing to do with Michael taking Gemma and everything that happened with you two. When it all went south, I said *fuck it*." I looked at my brother for the first time in what felt like an eternity. I stepped forward and held out my hand. "I was relieved to hear you were alive."

Evan stepped forward and gripped my hand in his. Silence filled the cottage.

"Well, since you're here, you should know a few things."

We walked toward the kitchen table and settled into the stiff wooden chairs.

"Agent Brown—we call her *Ma*—is no-nonsense, but if you follow the rules, you won't get kicked out. Don't give her a reason. Round here they call it *Redemption Ranch*. Agents, protected witnesses, we're all equals, and we're all expected to pull our weight. If you stay, you'll get assigned a job. Family dinner is on Sundays, and if you want to get on Ma's good side, you'll go."

I nodded, soaking in the information. A question gnawed at me. "Why tell me this? After everything that went down . . . why help?"

Evan stood and walked toward the door, my question hanging in the air. Finally he turned to me. "If anyone around here needs redemption, brother, it's you."

～

EVAN'S WORDS soaked through me for the rest of the afternoon. I couldn't help but peek out the curtains, looking for Sienna. She'd been gone for the better part of the day, and the sun was sinking lower behind the mountains.

Irritation rolled through me.

It's getting late and she's not home.

I caught myself and laughed. Pining for my new wife to come home.

As I continued to pace through the house, I heard her delicate footsteps climb the stairs of the porch. Her hesitation was palpable as a minute ticked by without her entering the cottage. I stared at the closed door, wishing I could know what she was thinking.

Finally she opened the door and walked into the cottage. Sienna stepped inside and paused. I didn't miss the slightest flinch as her eyes met mine.

"Hey."

"Hi." She shut the door and walked into the kitchen. Though I thought she was stunning in her lemon-yellow dress, Sienna in jeans and a T-shirt stole my breath. Her golden hair was piled on top of her head in a messy bun, revealing the slim column of her neck. One sliver of skin and my heart was galloping. I flexed my hand to keep from wrapping my fingers around her delicate throat to feel her thin skin as I stroked my thumb across it. I imagined the thrum of her pulse as she reacted to my touch.

I forced my spine upright. Clearly, the kiss we'd shared earlier in the day had rattled loose something primal and hungry inside me. I needed to know my place and keep my thoughts in check. I would learn to share a space with her without itching to claim her as my own.

Sienna moved in the kitchen with careful consideration,

like she was learning the layout as she hunted for something. After pulling a glass from the cabinet, she filled it with tap water. Her throat bobbed as she took a drink, and I forced myself to tear my eyes away.

"Oh fuck!" Sienna spit the water into the sink and dumped the glass.

I hid my chuckle. "Well water."

She scowled at the glass as though it were personally responsible for her displeasure. "Yuck."

"You'll get used to it." My voice came out harsher than I'd intended, and I cursed myself after she placed the cup into the sink with a snap.

Before she could escape to the bedroom, I moved forward. "Sienna." She turned, but I didn't know what else to say.

She sighed, resigned to the fact that she was standing in a small cottage with the man she had agreed to marry. "We need to figure a few things out," she said.

I nodded.

"For one, the story of how we met." Her eyes were the prettiest shade of sea glass.

"That's easy. The truth."

She chewed her bottom lip, and my own mouth tingled as I remembered the way Sienna had melted against me as I'd kissed her in the courthouse.

"Okay," she continued. "So you came into my restaurant and, what, sparks flew?"

My frown deepened. "Your restaurant?"

"Oh, well . . ." Sienna tucked a loose strand of hair behind her ear as she leaned back against the kitchen counter. "My uncle's. He owned it. I'm actually not sure now that he . . ." She trailed off, not needing to finish.

I hated that I'd brought up such a painful memory again. "We say that I came in for lunch and was seated in your section. I was immediately drawn to you but not sure how to strike up a conversation. You didn't realize who I was, and I liked that. I could be myself. You didn't force me to talk, and I liked that too. I came to the restaurant more and more, just to see you, and we fell in love. We married in secret. Then I was attacked, and together we left."

She shot me a bland look, not realizing I had just been more honest with her than I had in the past year. At least, it was how I wished that particular story would have ended. When she didn't react, I started panicking, worried she could see right through me.

I cleared my throat. "It's important that the lie is close to the truth so that it's easier to remember. Easier to fake."

"You're the expert." Her words were a knife to my chest, and I couldn't figure out why. I knew our relationship was fake. It meant nothing to her. A debt she felt she owed.

"What happens if someone asks to see the marriage license? They'll see we didn't actually get married until we got to Montana."

I frowned, considering the hole in my plan. "It won't matter. We're married. It's legal."

The same awkward silence that had filled the cottage all week settled over us. Earlier in the week, I had endured it as she unpacked her duffel bag and unloaded groceries into the fridge, but now there were no menial tasks to keep us busy.

"So, um . . ." The silence stretched between us as Sienna crossed her arms over her chest, jutting her tits up. A better man would have looked away. "People need to think we're in love, right? So when we're together, we need to act like it."

I stuffed my hands into the pockets of my jeans.

Sienna tipped her stubborn chin as she continued: "You may put your arm around me, hug me, hold my hand. Pet names are agreeable."

I nodded. I wasn't sure about the pet name thing, but if she was giving me a reason to touch her again, I'd take it.

"If the situation calls for it, we can kiss."

My heart thumped, and my eyes flew to her ripe bottom lip. I wanted to scoop her up. Take her mouth and call it *practice*. I needed to keep my dick in check. Sienna wasn't the kind of woman I was used to. Everything about her screamed commitment. Long term.

I huffed a humorless laugh. I was concerned about the fact that *my wife* was the commitment type.

"Is something funny?" Sienna's small hands were planted on the swell of her hips, fire in her eyes. For a beat, I stared. "Look, if you don't want to kiss me again, then just say it. But I think someone's going to notice that the newlyweds can't stand each other if we don't at least *pretend* to be in love."

There it was. Sienna couldn't stand me.

My nostrils flared as I tamped down the raging temper that threatened to erupt. In two strides, I was crowding her space, soaking up her ocean scent. Our breath mingled in the inches between us. "I won't touch you without your permission. But if the situation calls for it"—my eyes tracked to her mouth as her tongue darted out to wet her bottom lip —"I'll kiss my wife."

Her breathing was shallow, and tension wound down my spine. My cock thickened as I imagined not only kissing her, but claiming her. In another lifetime, Sienna was my wife and it was our wedding night. I would take her to bed and lay claim to every sinful curve. Every inch.

Instead, she gathered her resolve with a breath and pushed past me into the bedroom, leaving me hard and aching for a woman I was tethered to but could never have.

SIX
SIENNA

I could kill someone for a vibrator.

Through the thin walls of the cottage, I could hear Parker shuffling around. The television clicked on, and the muffled sounds drowned out his sighs and grunts that were making me insane.

I banished all thoughts of Parker Marino.

But my nipples pricked to life when I recalled the heat that rolled off him whenever he stepped into my space. My thoughts slipped back to the grumpy, stoic man sleeping on a couch twenty feet from me, but my fingers were a poor substitute. So on my wedding night, I buried my whimpers into the pillow.

In my fantasies, Parker's strong silence gave way to a man who opened up to me. A man who used his muscular body to claim me completely. But that was not my life, and Parker was not that man. Unfulfilled, I let myself drift to sleep with his name on my lips.

In the morning, I rolled over as the early sunlight filtered through the gauzy bedroom curtains.

The ranch was quiet on a Sunday—no trucks crunching

across the gravel, no shouts of ranch hands across the field. The low moos from the nearby field had me perking up. I peeked out the window to find the cows had ventured toward our cottage and were close to the fence line. I instantly fell in love with their rusty hides and the way their long hair swooped low across their wide, flat noses.

Weariness washed over me as I thought about the day ahead. Parker and I had a meeting with Agent Brown, the woman who ran the ranch. Our fate was in her hands. If she allowed it, we could stay at the ranch, protected from the men who'd upturned my entire life. Though I had to remain married to Parker to keep him from a life in prison, or worse, we would be safe.

Hot tears burned in my sleep-deprived eyes.

Would I ever see the South Side of Chicago again?

My quiet, unassuming life would cease to exist. I drew in a steadying breath.

Focus on the positive.

You're in a wild and interesting place.

Your new husband may despise you, but he's not bad to look at.

You're alive.

Parker's dominating form standing over me as I trembled on the floor of the restaurant flooded my mind. When he held out his hand, I didn't hesitate. Now I owed it to him to hold up my end of the bargain. Our safety was in maintaining the lie.

The shower groaned to life through the thin cottage walls. Heat crept up my neck, but I pushed away the image of Parker's strong, muscular chest under the spray of the shower, bubbles dripping across the solid planes of his stomach. I moved toward the dresser, tossing my pajamas in a heap on the floor before pulling the first set of clothes I found over my head. While Parker was occupied in the shower, his large hands moving across his—nope. Not thinking about that.

While he was *busy*, I could quietly leave the cottage and explore more of the ranch. I could tell he needed his space. Craved the silence. If I could help make things less awkward for the both of us, that was exactly what I would do.

After tiptoeing into the kitchen, I scribbled a quick note to Parker, letting him know I was staying on the ranch but would meet him at Agent Brown's office for our meeting. Behind me, the old wooden floor groaned. Bent over the kitchen table, I whipped up my head.

I was eye level with Parker's insane body. The small white towel did nothing to hide his trim hips. A light trail of hair dipped beneath the low V of the towel, right to a very distracting bulge in the front. I couldn't *not* stare. My mouth went dry as my eyes moved across his tattooed body. The designs snaked up both arms, moving across his chest and winding around his torso. I wanted to trace the lines with my fingertips. My tongue. As my eyes assaulted his skin, they snagged on a small bar of metal.

Holy fuck, is that a nipple ring?

My eyes whipped to his. A smug smirk tugged at his lips as one hand gripped the front of the towel.

My throat was thick. "I'm leaving. The cottage! Not, you know, *you* or anything. I'm just . . ." I wiped the wisps of hair away from my face. "You know what I mean. I'll meet you at the lodge. Bye." Smug humor danced in his eyes as I swiveled on my heels, cursing myself for being a blubbering mess of a woman in front of the half-naked god of a man.

The front door snapped closed behind me, and I leaned

against it. As I gulped the fresh mountain air, my pulse began to steady. When I'd finally composed myself, I looked down.

"Goddamn it." I rolled my eyes at myself. Pushing open the door as quietly as I could manage, I peeked around the corner. Standing in the spot where I had left him was my husband, thick arms crossed over his broad chest, a rare smirk teasing his full lips.

I shot him a glare as I leaned down and scooped up the canvas sneakers just inside the door.

"Have a good day, darling wife." Unexpected humor laced through Parker's voice, and my heart thumped against my ribs. I grumbled a goodbye and held my sneakers to my chest along with the last shreds of my dignity.

EVEN ON A SUNDAY, the ranch hands were quietly bustling in and out of the outbuildings, tending to fence posts and animals and backbreaking chores. As people passed, I smiled and waved, and no one seemed to notice or mind that I was a new face. It was completely different from my first experience in Tipp. In town, everyone seemed wary of us. Maybe it was because Parker was scary as hell, but there was something more—a skepticism that kept the towns-people at a distance.

On the ranch, men and women worked together to keep things running smoothly. When a cowboy tipped his hat in greeting, a fluttery bubble of laughter tickled my belly. I was energized by the people, the animals, and the dust.

I followed a dirt path that circled a small pond near the main lodge. Trees dotted the path, filtering out the morning sun. I wrapped my arms around my middle to ward off the cool morning breeze. The old wooden dock creaked beneath my feet as I walked along it. Peering over the edge into the water, I sighed. It seemed like the perfect place to sit with someone, drink a glass of wine, and fall in love. I kicked a small pebble from the dock and watched it sink, disappearing into the water before I turned to continue my walk through the ranch.

Looking into a barn, the smell of animals drew me closer. As my eyes adjusted to the low light, I recognized the shape of horses silhouetted against the bright Montana sky beyond the large stall openings that led to the paddock. I eased closer, slowing my movements and quieting my steps. With a gentle click of my tongue, a chestnut horse moved toward me in its stall.

"Hey, buddy." I kept my voice just above a whisper. He took a tentative step toward me, peeking out from long, black lashes. "Hi."

I reached out, slowly lifting my hand into the air. In one step, the horse's velvet nose tucked under my palm. "Well aren't you sweet?" I stroked up his nose, keeping my touch light. "What's your name?"

"Jeremiah Johnson."

My head swiveled at the deep voice behind me. My eyes went wide as I took in the striking man in boots and denim. He seemed about my age, though probably a little younger. I smiled back at the horse. "That's a very strong name."

"From an old Western my dad loved."

"Ah," I conceded, stroking between Jeremiah's eyes. "Maybe he'll let me call him JJ." Jeremiah huffed a breath through his nose, and I laughed. "Okay, maybe not."

The man stepped up and leaned on the gate separating the stall from the barn. He eyed me, but not in an obnoxious way. Simply curious. Objectively, he was handsome. His tight cowboy jeans fit him well. He was lean from what I assumed was hard work on the ranch. "You're new here."

I turned to him and smiled. "I am." I offered my hand. "Sienna."

The man took my hand in his gently, and I couldn't help my mind contrasting his light touch with Parker's rough palms, which I couldn't seem to get out of my mind.

"I'm Josh. I work with Chet, taking care of the animals. Make the rounds, muck stalls, routine health care, that kind of thing."

"A veterinarian? On site?"

"Nah. We're just stockmen, but we might as well be." He laughed. "The health and well-being of the herds is our main job. We've got quite the operation here. Everything from mechanics to ranch managers to rotating vets. It's easier to keep things quiet the closer we keep the staff."

My eyes went wide. "Oh. So you're a . . . you know . . ."

"A criminal?" he offered with a laugh. "No. My dad was a federal agent with Ma and Robbie Brown for a long time. My family moved out here to be closer to his assignment, and when he died, my mom and siblings moved on. I never left. Ma lets me stay on and work while I go to school over in Chikalu Falls. They have a decent ag program. Guess this place has a way of sticking with you."

I lowered my stare. "I'm sorry to hear about your dad."

Josh draped his forearms across the gate. "Yeah, me too. It really doesn't get any easier as the time passes though."

The tender, bruising ache that lived in my ribs twinged. "No. It doesn't."

Josh turned at the sadness that crept in my voice.

"I lost my parents too. A long time ago. I still miss

them." I offered him a small smile, then glanced down at his shirt.

"Go Army." I smiled, trying to lighten the mood.

He dragged a hand across his chest. "Uh, yeah. After high school, college didn't really seem like my thing. The Army though." He tsked his tongue against his teeth and smiled. I bet that smile got him a lot of attention down at the local bar on ladies' night.

"Stop sniffing around the new girl." A scratchy, impatient voice cut through the dusty air in the barn. Walking toward us, an old man carried buckets of feed to each stall.

"Oh, no, it's not—I'm a married woman," I said, suddenly horrified that anyone would think there was anything going on between us.

Josh tipped an eyebrow at my admission but didn't otherwise acknowledge it.

The old man shuffled past us, elbowing his way through the gate. "Goddamn lazy kids," he grumbled.

Josh leaned down. "Don't mind Ray. He's the resident grouch."

Parker's face flipped through my mind, and I couldn't help but smile. Ray wasn't the only grump on the ranch anymore. "He's fine. But I should get going. Thanks for chatting. You were my first official warm welcome."

Josh nodded and touched his fingers to the bill of his baseball cap in a gesture that was gentlemanly and completely endearing. "I'll be seeing you, Sienna."

I lifted a hand in goodbye as I walked out of the barn and back into the sunlight. I spent the rest of the day moving in and out of the outbuildings that dotted the property. Some were unremarkable—storage sheds and farm equipment. The barns were my favorite. Between the cattle and horses, I laughed at their personalities and varying levels of indifference to my presence. I wondered if I might be allowed to ride a horse during my stay here.

If we stay here.

Dread pooled in my stomach. A single day and I already felt safe. Secure. Much of it had to do with my new husband, but there was more. The ranch itself was protected. Everyone around seemed to be in on the ruse and on the lookout for danger. After the last few weeks of constantly looking over my shoulder, not sleeping, and the unfamiliar nausea of anxiety, I felt like I could breathe.

I glanced at my watch, realizing I'd spent the better part of the day wandering. Time was up and my future— whether Parker and I could remain under the safety of witness protection—was completely up to Agent Brown.

SEVEN

PARKER

"The main purpose of Redemption Ranch is to be a safe haven for those who deserve a second chance. I'm not entirely convinced that's you." Agent Brown was a hard-ass. The glint in her eye was pure fire.

"I understand." My jaw clenched but I remained silent.

Sienna stood by my side, her head barely reaching my shoulder. A protectiveness surged through me and clogged in my throat. My knuckle brushed the outside edge of her arm, and heat poured into me.

"I do not tolerate deceit. If I find out any of this"—Agent Brown waved a hand between us—"is bullshit, you're gone. I don't care that I love your brother like one of my own. He asked for a very large favor for you to stay here, but don't forget—you're no one to me."

"Yes, ma'am." Evan had pulled a solid, and it meant Sienna was safe.

Jesus, I owe him. Big.

"We live by a certain set of rules," she continued. "You will fully integrate into your new identities. You are to have no connections to your former life. Ever. You will be assigned a job at the ranch until you secure other employment. Housing is available to you if you need it. When called upon, you will provide testimony in federal court. Can you both agree to those rules?"

I gripped Sienna's trembling hand in mine, speaking for us both and hoping Agent Brown didn't notice. "Yes, ma'am."

Sienna's pale eyes stared at my hand as it covered her own. Our marriage may be fake, but the way her body reacted to mine was very, very real.

Addicting.

Sienna shifted beside me, her back straightening. "In terms of the work we do here, if I have any say in the matter . . ." She trailed off before taking a breath and finding her nerve. "Before I came here, I was in school to be a nurse."

Oh. This is news.

I had assumed Sienna was a server at the restaurant and nothing more. But she had other plans. Dreams. And I'd fucked them all up by trying to hide in the restaurant. Sienna's chin tipped up, and a ripple of pride tightened my chest at her resolve. "If there is an opportunity to assist the stockmen on staff or work in a medical capacity, I would prefer that," Sienna said.

Agent Brown narrowed her eyes only a fraction as she considered Sienna. When Sienna didn't wilt under her careful assessment, Agent Brown's green eyes softened. "Consider it done."

Agent Brown turned her attention to me. "And you, Mr. Marino? Any special requests for work?"

"Whatever you need from me, I'll do it."

She considered me for a moment, then nodded. "Fine. Any special skills?" A few strokes of her pen and she looked up. "Preferably legal ones."

A cynical laugh pushed through my nose. She may be a hard-ass, but she was kind of funny too. "I'm good with numbers. Bookkeeping."

Her eyes assessed me as she searched for any hint of a lie. "You'll start tomorrow. I'll give you a schedule and a list of work to get you started." Sienna squeezed my hand once, and the jolt it passed had me pulling away. She tucked her arms around her body, and I hated myself for being so cold to her.

"Finally there is the issue of your names." Agent Brown peered over her glasses at us. "Typically those in witness protection keep their first names for sake of ease, but you'll need a new last name."

Sienna's mouth dropped open slightly before snapping shut.

Tension crackled in the air as she looked at me.

Was I supposed to just . . . pick one?

I racked my brain, searching through dozens of possibilities. Finally one came pushing forward. "Davis. Our last name will be Davis." I looked down at my wife for the briefest moment. I was sure the name had caught her by surprise—hell, it had caught me off guard too—but it felt right.

"Fine," Agent Brown said, like she couldn't care less that we'd just changed our entire identities in a snap decision. With a final sweep of her hand, we were dismissed.

As we exited her office, I paused. Meeting Agent Brown's eyes, I fought against the anger her judgment tugged out of me. "Evan extended an invitation to family dinner tonight." I stepped toward Sienna and wrapped one arm around her tiny shoulders, leaning into her warmth, continuing the show for the special agent. "We'd love to join. If that's okay with you, of course."

"Every resident is welcomed to family dinner. It starts at six o'clock. Mr. and Mrs. Davis."

"Ma." I nodded.

She paused at my use of her nickname, but the faintest hint of a smile flickered across her face. I'd call that a win and take it.

As soon as I closed the office door behind me, Sienna shifted from beneath the arm still draped over her shoulders. There was no one to perform for. The show was over.

"Why did you pick that name?" Sienna's whisper was insistent as we moved through the lodge and out the back door.

I shrugged. "Just popped in my head." I cooled my eyes, deadening them to the thump that pounded beneath my breastbone.

"That's my uncle's name—was," she corrected. "That was his name."

I knew that, of course. She'd cried over his body, sobbing his name before I pulled her away. She'd also mentioned it in the car during our trip out here. She had prattled on and on, and while she likely thought I had ignored most of it, I recalled every word. He was gone, but I could tell how much she had loved him.

If she couldn't have my last name, this was one thing I could give to her. The tightness in my chest gave way to panic. Sienna's open affection and sunny personality were getting under my skin. It was making me soft and forcing me to make decisions because I thought it would make her happy.

That was the quickest way to get us killed. I couldn't be catching feelings for my *wife*, so I did what any other asshole would do. I lied. "Just a coincidence."

Hurt flickered over her small features, and my self-loathing grew. But it was safer that way. If she had any clue what she was doing to my insides, there was no way she'd stick around. At the first indication that I was some creep who imagined what it would be like to kiss her—really kiss her and worship that little body of hers in the privacy of our cottage—the lie would fall apart. She'd see I was just another asshole who was sniffing around her.

No. We had an agreement. I'd saved her in the restaurant, and she'd made a deluded promise to try to save me. She'd given up everything for a man she barely knew. The least I could do was keep my hands, and my thoughts, to my goddamn self.

A FEW HOURS LATER, it was time to show our faces at family dinner.

Sienna stepped out of the bedroom and my heart nearly stopped. She was dressed in a new pair of jeans that hugged her slim curves. A simple black shirt molded to her torso before flaring out at the bottom. At my obvious assessment of her, her long lashes dipped lower, and she tucked a honey-blonde strand of hair behind her ear. "I had some leftover money after buying the dress. I used it to get a few things. I hope that was okay."

The words clogged in my throat. "Yeah." I had plenty of money. If it meant that she could feel good *and* look like that? I would make sure she'd be heading back to town as soon as possible with a purse full of cash.

I had no words.

"What do you think? Will it be okay for dinner?"

"It's fine." I grabbed my coat and opened the door.

The night was warm, and the lodge was close enough to

walk, so we set out on foot. Up ahead, a few cars pulled into spaces, and one or two others seemed to have walked from various cottages, as we had.

I held out my elbow, and she looped her arm through. A strange thrill jolted me. Was it pride? Nerves? I couldn't name it, but I never minded having a beautiful woman on my arm, and Sienna was no exception. She was stunning.

When Sienna slipped her hand down my forearm and into my hand, I looked down at her. "You ready for this?"

"Showtime." The smile she planted seemed almost genuine. Elegance sparkled out of her as she greeted and smiled at everyone we passed. Normally my smile looked a lot like a grimace, so I didn't bother. Though, for her sake, I did offer a few silent nods when I was acknowledged.

The air was full of friendly and familiar conversation. It was clear we were the outsiders as most everyone else milled around, hugging or shaking hands. It was also evident that some people were federal agents, while others appeared not to be. It was a confusing, eclectic mix of people, and no one seemed the least bit bothered by it.

Food was arranged on a huge kitchen island. Two large pots of chili, boiled macaroni noodles, and any topping you could imagine putting on chili sat in small bowls. Family dinner was served family style—everyone grabbing a bowl and loading up their supper. Sienna stayed close—I never let her get so far that I couldn't feel the warmth of her back against my chest.

She carried the weight of conversation. People were enamored with her, and I completely understood. She was a light.

As I frowned into my chili, her voice pulled me from dark thoughts of her trapped in our marriage. "All this needs is some corn chips. That's how my mom used to make it."

When I looked up, she was beaming at me. No hint of despair.

Showtime, remember? Such a fucking idiot.

I cleared my throat and shifted in my seat. "I've never tried it that way. Sounds good."

The crunch of a chip bag caught our attention. My half sister, Gemma, tossed an individual-size bag of Fritos in Sienna's direction. She scooped it up and looked at my sister.

"It's how I like it too." Gemma's frostiness toward us was completely my fault, but I liked that she seemed to thaw a bit for Sienna.

Sienna beamed at her before tearing into the bag and dumping the corn chips on top of her chili. "Thanks!"

Something warm and liquid spread across my chest—a strange tug toward some other life. A life where Sienna was my wife—my *real* wife—and she and Gemma got along like sisters. My eyes found Gemma's. A hint of fear was still there.

At one point in Chicago, Gemma thought I had her kidnapped. Quite the opposite was true. When she'd been taken, I risked everything to try to find her. Shit hit the fan, and when I thought Evan was dead, I sicced my men on the case to find who had caused it all. My contact at the police department eventually led me here. Back to the only real family I had left.

I needed to find a way to have a real conversation with Gemma.

The large oak dining table was full of people, elbow to elbow as I allowed the conversation to flow around me. I glanced at their faces. I was used to this—my entire life I'd managed to be an island, even when I was surrounded by people. My job meant I was rarely alone, but I never allowed myself any type of meaningful connection.

No. I learned early on that connections to people meant they could hurt you. Betray you. In my line of work that also meant they'd kill you and take your place.

Evan was noticeably absent. It seemed pretty clear he was torn up about Val leaving the ranch. Suffering in silence was a family trait, apparently.

I eased into my chair, feeling too big and out of place among this eclectic group. I draped my arm across the back of Sienna's chair to give myself a bit more room. My hand trailed to the small hairs on the back of her neck. My fingertips brushed absently against the thin skin there. Her pulse hammered beneath my finger as I stroked.

I leaned down to whisper to Sienna. My breath trailed over the shell of her ear, and I reveled in how the skin of her neck prickled. "I'm sorry I didn't say this earlier, but you look stunning."

Sienna turned her face toward mine, leaving mere inches between us. Her eyes dipped to my lips and back up again.

Was this still a show?

"Thank you." The breathy quality of her voice sent a signal straight to my cock, which thickened inside my pants. Sienna placed a casual hand on my thigh, and I nearly groaned aloud at the table. If she moved it a fraction of an inch inward, she'd find out real quick how real she felt to me.

Dirty thoughts of her stroking me beneath the table coursed through my mind.

Suddenly Gemma's voice cut through the haze. "So what's the deal with you two?"

EIGHT

SIENNA

"So what's the deal with you two?" Gemma's voice rose above the dinner table chatter, and her bland stare held me in place.

Parker's long fingers stroking the skin on my neck didn't help my frazzled brain.

Oh, you know. He killed someone for me, and I thought it would be a great idea to get married to keep him from rotting in a prison cell. Now I wonder all day what he looks like naked. No big deal.

"Sienna is my wife." Parker's too-formal statement had me slowly cutting my eyes toward him and offering a tight smile.

Let me handle this, big guy.

I forced a laugh and slapped his knee as if we had shared some hilarious inside joke. "Oh stop. You're being so silly." I turned to Gemma. "He likes to tease."

Gemma's brows furrowed. She knew as well as I did that Parker wasn't the teasing type. I turned to him. "I'm sure Gemma was just curious about how we met. Our love story."

When he blanked, I continued. "It's very romantic, actually. I was working in my uncle's restaurant—Solitario, have you ever been there? Anyway"—I swatted the air with my hand and plowed through the rest of the story—"one day Park was seated in my section. All by himself. He was broody and mysterious and quiet. He never really talked to me!" I glanced at Parker to find him watching me, entranced as I told the rehearsed story to Gemma and those around us. It was as close to the truth as I could make it. "Finally we struck up a conversation, and the rest was history."

"So you, what, talked once and decided to get married? You know he's a criminal, right?"

"Gemma." Ma Brown's single-word warning had Gemma casting her eyes to her lap. "You know as well as everyone sitting at this table, if you are a part of Redemption, your past is left in the past."

"Yes, ma'am," she grumbled.

I swallowed as heat rose in my cheeks. I hated that Gemma had called Parker out like that. He was stone-still beside me. Honesty was going to be the only way I could get us out of this. "From the first day I saw him, I saw kindness in his eyes. There's always been more to Parker than meets the eye. I'm surprised you didn't know that."

I stood, flipping my napkin into my bowl and gathering my dishes. I wasn't going to sit there and let her, or anyone else, judge Parker. I turned to him. "I'm ready. Are you?"

In a swift movement, he was at my side, taking the dishes from me and moving toward the kitchen. Silence fell over the dinner table as we made our exit.

I stomped behind Parker as he emptied the bowls and rinsed them in the sink. My feet carried me back and forth across the kitchen floor. Keeping my voice low, I fumed: "Look, I know she's your sister, but what the fuck?"

Parker stood in front of me, his huge hands gripping my shoulders. I looked up at him. "Thank you."

He pulled me into the mass of his chest, and I melted. Encircled by his spicy, masculine scent, I breathed him in and allowed myself the briefest moment to enjoy the warmth of his arms.

"No one has ever done that before."

I stepped back to look at him. "Done what? Yelled at your sister?"

His hand came around to the back of my neck. I wanted to close my eyes, to moan and lean into his touch. Instead, my eyes stayed locked on his. "Defended me."

A ripple of heat pooled in my lower belly. "Oh."

My eyes fell to Parker's mouth. Did he want to kiss me? Did I want him to?

Just once. Yes.

My eyelids drooped, and I was lost in the idea of Parker's mouth on mine. The small sample I'd had at the courthouse wasn't nearly enough.

A clatter from the dining room had me jumping back. A nervous laugh tore through me as the jitters radiated down my back. The lust and threadbare restraint I'd seen in Parker's eyes were gone.

The moment had passed.

"Let's get you back home." Parker's hands ran down my bare arms and back up again, warming them under his touch.

Home. Alone with Parker.

My skin was on fire.

∾

BACK AT THE COTTAGE, the uncomfortable silence hung over us once again. Somehow we just couldn't seem to find our stride in the confines of the small space. I walked through the house, opening up windows and letting the autumn air float through.

It helped, but barely.

I finally sighed. "This is silly. We can't just keep trying to move around each other and not acknowledge how awkward this is."

He laughed a bit at that. "Yeah. It's a little hard to avoid each other in here. I'm sorry."

"So let's stop. No more avoiding each other. And no apologizing. We need to stick together and just . . . exist."

He considered my words for a beat and then nodded. "Okay."

I breathed easy for the first time in what felt like weeks. We could do this. There was more to Parker than the strong, silent, hulking man—that part was easy to see. What wasn't as clear was who exactly that man was who was hiding beneath the hard exterior. My gut was telling me it was someone intriguing. Someone I would love to get to know.

"I'm going to get into something more comfortable. Then maybe we just, I don't know . . . hang out?" I hurried back into the bedroom, closed the door, and leaned against it.

Hang out? Why was I so freaking awkward around him? Why do I care?

I slipped off my jeans and black top and tugged on a pair of dark leggings. Over my camisole, I layered a cropped sweater that hung off one shoulder. It was insanely comfy and felt like pajamas without looking frumpy.

When I stepped back into the main living space, Parker was sitting on the arm of the couch. As soon as he saw me, he stood. His eyes raked up my body, appreciation for the tight material evident in the way his gaze snagged on my thighs before he coughed and looked away.

"It's still early." The rough edge of his voice sent a tingle down my back. "How about a walk? There's a firepit out back too. We could do that."

Why does it feel like it's ten thousand degrees in here?

"A walk would be great."

Under the vast Montana sky, I no longer felt stifled. The inky sky held a broad, full moon, and as we ambled up the path away from our cottage and toward the walking paths I'd traveled earlier in the week, a billion stars started winking to life.

The autumn air was cool but welcome.

Parker and I walked in comfortable silence until he finally spoke. "Are you okay?"

I looked up to the sky. A thousand emotions tumbled through me. "Ugh." I sighed. "I don't know. I think so."

He paused with me, looking around at the way the entire ranch was silhouetted in the growing darkness. Like a beautiful oil painting, it was too perfect to be real.

His voice was low. "We don't have to do this."

"You heard Ma. If she finds out this is fake, she won't tolerate it. And you said this is the safest place for us, right?"

With a resigned nod, he tucked his hands into his pockets. "It is. At least until we're certain no one from Chicago knows where we're at."

"The restaurant. It was on the news. I didn't say anything, but on the way out here, I saw it on the television. People are talking about it. If anyone finds out that you were there . . ." Panic rose in my voice. I couldn't imagine him in jail. He'd saved me, but with his past, it was doubtful anyone would believe us.

"Stop. It's all right. We've got a plan. For now, we stick with it."

I steadied my breath and gulped in the night air. "Okay."

We continued down the path, winding around the property, stopping to look out over the pastures. "I want to try to make amends with Gemma. I hate that your sister doesn't like me."

"Not used to not being everyone's favorite person in the room?"

I squinted in his direction. I wasn't used to Parker's playful teasing, but I didn't hate it. Parker kept in step with me, staying close but never allowing his hand or arm to brush mine. "No. Gemma has been through a lot. Evan brought her around. We only found out she existed after our mother died. I knew it was a mistake, but there was no talking him out of it."

"Why was it a mistake? Didn't you want to get to know your sister?"

He blew out a breath and seemed to be considering how much to tell me. Whether or not he was willing to let me in.

"Life with Mom was . . . hard. She wasn't the best parent. Gemma looks just like her."

I considered him for a moment. "But you can't blame her for that. She can't help who she looks like."

"I know that. But a part of me wanted to keep her away from it all. I don't know. I guess I thought if I could push her away, she'd find a new life. An existence better than hanging around lowlifes."

"You should tell her that."

He grumbled something beside me.

"I'm serious, Park. I'm telling you—she doesn't know."

"What else did she say?" he asked, shifting the topic and effectively stopping any further probing into his past.

Not wanting to push him too far, I decided on a lighter approach.

"Well, she also called you a skank."

He huffed in disbelief and his brows snapped together.

I bumped into the hardness of his biceps. "You are, aren't you!" I laughed and wrapped my arms around my middle, protecting myself from the chill that lingered on the fall evening.

Parker paused, and when I stopped beside him, he turned toward me. I tried to read his face in the growing darkness as he shucked off the button-up shirt he wore. My eyes snagged on the tight tee beneath it. His muscles strained against the soft cotton, and the bump of his nipple ring caught my attention.

So. Freaking. Hot.

In one move, he pulled the button-up around me.

"No, I'm fine, I . . ."

Parker paused, and even in the dim light I could see the warning in his eyes. "Just shut up."

I tried my best to hide the smile that wanted to erupt across my face. Instead, I slipped my arms into the sleeves of his shirt. His warmth was captured in it, and I let it seep into me. Parker made quick work of buttoning the shirt, moving down my torso as his earthly, masculine scent mingled with the fresh Montana air.

One wide palm cupped my shoulder before moving down my arm to my wrist. The shirt was huge on me, the sleeves hanging several inches below my fingertips. Parker gently folded the material, cuffing the sleeves to my wrist.

My heartbeat hammered as I did whatever I could to steady my breathing. Parker was towering, strong, and *all male.* My body reacted to him in ways I knew were completely inappropriate.

But he is your husband.

My traitorous mind danced around thoughts of leaning into him, stealing more of his warmth as he wrapped those solid arms around me. My eyes drifted closed as he worked on the other sleeve. The enveloping darkness protected me from embarrassment as I reveled in the lightness in Parker's touch. I never knew how intensely erotic a man sharing his shirt could be.

When he finished, for the briefest moment, his body stilled.

Why could I not stop thinking about him kissing me again?

I lifted my chin and looked at him. Desire was obvious in my eyes. Yes, I wanted this man to grab me and kiss the fuck out of me. My nipples puckered, and a hot ball of lust warmed in my belly. I wanted to forget all about death and fear and running and lies. I wanted to forget myself and get lost in his touch. I wished everything could melt away. Everything but us.

He leveled me with a steely gaze as my breath hitched in my throat. "Fake marriage or not, I will always be faithful to you."

NINE
PARKER

I should have kissed her. I was so fucking close. Instead, I opened my stupid mouth and reminded her that everything between us was total bullshit.

I'd meant what I said. Despite my past, I would always, *always*, be faithful to Sienna. I owed her at least that much. But at the mention of our forced arrangement, the heat in her eyes cooled, and she stepped back. The sunny smile she planted on her face was strained. Though she tried to appear casual, I saw the shift.

I knew better than to touch her for too long. Something deep inside me was drawn to her. I had a need to protect her, but something else inside me wanted to scoop her up and lay myself bare at her feet. I'd never wanted to expose my darkest memories, my fears, and my secrets to anyone, but there was something about Sienna that felt safe. And I was the one who was supposed to be protecting *her*. I was only going to make it more uncomfortable if I walked around mooning after her and wishing things were different.

The tension between us was already unbearable.

Rather than push her, I led the way back down the path toward our cottage. We walked in silence. I wondered what she was thinking. I thought of nothing but her.

"It's getting kind of windy for a fire."

Sienna rubbed the outsides of her arms. "Yeah, maybe next time."

I unlocked and pushed open the door of the cottage and was immediately hit with a mixture of the autumn breeze and Sienna's fresh scent. Her bright perfume that hung in the air breathed life into the cottage.

Our home.

"I'm kinda jazzed up still." Sienna slipped her feet out of her canvas sneakers. I noticed she didn't remove my shirt, and something akin to pride swelled in my chest.

"Not too late. Movie?"

Her face twisted in a cute look of disgust, like she wasn't thrilled with that suggestion. "How about brownies?"

"Brownies." It wasn't a question but I was curious. How the hell did she think we were going to make brownies?

"If you don't love brownies, then I'm out. I want a divorce."

Her playful tone and laughter should have had me playing along, but her words sliced at me. Immediately the thought *fuck that* shot through my mind. I needed to watch myself. The airy way about her made it easy to forget that she may be bound to me by law, but really it was an obligation. She had no true desire to be mine, and it was best if I remembered that.

Sienna's hopeful eyes danced with humor. Despite the cloud that hung over me, I did my best to not dampen the mood. "I'd kill for some brownies."

Her eyes widened. When her lips tucked in, I thought I'd fucked up. But a burst of laughter erupted from her chest. It breathed more life into the cottage, and I exhaled in relief. The bubble of her laugh was the most incredible sound I'd ever heard. As she swiped tears from her eyes, I couldn't help but chuckle along.

"Holy shit, Park. That's so wrong."

I smiled again, this time at her calling me *Park*. No one had ever thought to use a nickname for me, and it was surprisingly cute coming from her lips.

We moved toward the kitchen. Sienna pulled the ingredients from the pantry with ease, and I stood around like an idiot. She piled bowls and flour and sugar and spoons onto the small kitchen table.

I looked down at the pile, pushing things around as I dug through it. "I'm out of my depth here."

Sienna sidled up next to me and bumped me aside playfully with her hip. "I got this. You can just hang out. Moral support."

"Resident taste tester."

She caught my eye and smiled. "Exactly. These brownies are going to rock your world."

I sat at the table, leaning into the wooden chair, my legs propped up on another as I watched her cook. She was a fucking mess.

Flour dumped everywhere.

Batter dripped from the bowl after she'd poured it haphazardly into the small square pan.

I swear she used ten thousand fucking spoons to make one pan of brownies.

But goddamn did they smell delicious as they cooked. I stared at the perfect curve of her ass as she bent to slide the pan into the oven. She glanced over her shoulder and caught me staring.

"Sorry," I mumbled before standing up and dumping the dishes into the sink.

Sienna didn't call me out but simply started stacking the bowls and spoons as I filled the sink with hot, soapy water.

"I got this." I tried to block her from the sink, but she pushed her way next to me.

"No way. I know I'm a messy cook. It wouldn't be fair to leave it all up to you."

I moved my head toward the table. "Sit down."

She eyed me carefully before wiping her hands on a kitchen towel. She whipped it over me, balancing it across my shoulder and giving it one last pat. "Have a drink with me?"

I watched Sienna move in our kitchen as she pulled down two small glasses. My gruff tone didn't seem to faze her anymore. My button-up shirt hung below her ass, and I almost wished she'd taken it off so I could have a better view of her backside in those leggings.

Almost.

I grumbled in assent and focused my attention on the mountain of dishes that needed to be cleaned. I scrubbed as she poured. To my surprise, rather than take a seat at the table, Sienna hopped up on the counter next to the sink. Her short legs dangled, and my eyes traveled the length of them down to the white socks that were scrunched at her ankles.

Sienna poured red wine into the two small juice glasses. "No real wineglasses, but these will do." She lifted the cups.

"I don't need fancy."

Placing my glass next to the sink, Sienna pulled hers to her mouth. I stared as the wine washed across her lips, staining them ever so slightly. Her sip was tiny, but I imagined it slicked over her tongue. I glanced up and found her eyes on me, watching me watch her.

"It's good," she said. Her voice low and sultry.

My cock surged to life, and I shifted toward the sink, trying to hide the way it pushed against the zipper of my jeans. Deep and raw, I ground out, "Looks like it."

Sienna lifted her small cup. "Want a taste?"

I raised my soapy hands to show her I couldn't. She leaned forward, her eyes never leaving mine. The glass came to my lips, and she tilted it toward me. The dark burgundy wine hit my lips, and I parted them, allowing the smallest sip to enter my mouth.

Sienna licked her swollen bottom lip as she watched me and lowered the glass.

A sound of pleasure echoed through my chest. "That is good."

Setting the cup down, she lifted a thumb to my lower lip. As it dragged across the bottom, I fought the groan that threatened to tear from me.

"Missed a drop." Rather than wiping it away, Sienna stole the rogue drop of wine from my lip and brought her thumb to her mouth. Her pink tongue darted out as she sucked the wine from her thumb.

Morals be damned. I wanted to drag her ass off the counter and devour her.

I took one small step toward her. "Sienna." Her name was a warning.

"Yes."

One word.

Oh, how I wish that were an invitation.

My molars ground to dust as I fought the urge to take. Take. Take.

My wet, soapy hands had found the sides of her ass. My

hips nestled between her knees. We were in a staredown. The tiniest movement from either of us would change everything.

A bang at the front door made Sienna jump and yelp. I hung my head as reality took hold, and I moved away. I had been milliseconds from grabbing the back of her neck and hauling that pert little mouth against mine.

The knock came again. "Coming!" Sienna's voice rang out as she hopped off the counter, shoved me out of the way, and hustled toward the door. She shot me one last look before smoothing her hair and peeking out the front door. I plunged my hand back into the soapy, now-cold kitchen sink and scrubbed entirely too harshly at the remainder of the dishes.

"Gemma! Wow, um. Come in."

I turned to see my little sister, her eyes downcast, as she entered the cottage.

"Parker, your sister is here . . ." She turned back to Gemma. "What's up?"

Gemma's cropped blonde hair was a stark contrast to the dyed, dark style she'd worn in Chicago. With her natural color back, she looked even more like my mother, and my chest pinched. I flicked my hands and dried them on the towel at my shoulder.

"Ma said that I was, and I quote, 'acting like a brat' at dinner." Embarrassment or anger, I wasn't sure which, flamed her cheeks red.

"Oh." Sienna moved closer to Gemma. "No. Things are new and unexpected here. It will take some getting used to."

How does she do that? How does she always take the high road?

"Would you like to stay for a little bit? I made brownies."

Gemma's eyes flicked toward me as though she was waiting for me to yell. Kick her out or tell her to get lost. She looked scared of me, and I fucking hated it.

"Stay," I insisted. "I think they're almost done."

Gemma's eyes floated around the small cottage space. "It's almost identical to mine," she said with a soft smile.

"Cozy, right?" Sunshine and joy were back in Sienna's voice. I wanted to rip down the walls of the cottage and go back to having Sienna pliant and tense between my legs, but that was shot to hell.

Gemma continued her assessment of our home as I pulled the brownies from the oven and let them cool on the stove. We both noticed as Gemma's eyes snagged on the neatly folded pile of blankets and the pillow at the end of the couch.

Panic flashed in Sienna's eyes as she looked at me.

Fuck. Fuck. Fuck.

When I'd planned to sleep out on the couch, it hadn't occurred to us that someone might come over. Surely it would seem suspicious that a newlywed couple wasn't sleeping in the same bed.

Sienna moved quickly, gathering up the pile in her arms. "Sorry about that. I was doing laundry," she lied. "I'll just take these back to the bedroom."

Her bedroom.

Sienna scurried out of the living space and disappeared behind the door of her room.

I cleared my throat. Gemma and I had never been close. She and Evan shared a special bond that I never allowed myself to have with her. I knew, from the moment I met her, if she got too close to me, she would be in danger. There was also something else about her that poked the tender parts of my insides, and I didn't like it. When she looked at me with her crystal-blue eyes and the face of my mother, I had a guess as to why.

"So, brownies?" Gemma asked.

"Shit. Yeah." I cut a large corner out of the pan and plated it.

Gemma walked tentatively into the kitchen. "Mind if I have a middle?"

I glanced at her before hacking a square directly out of the center. It earned a small laugh from Gemma, and I softened a little.

"Savage," she said.

A warm trickle of something almost pleasant ran through me. I liked being able to make my little sister laugh. For her to see a side of me that she didn't know yet.

"Milk is in the fridge. Get it yourself if you want it." As soon as the words came out, I shook my head. The gruff tone was my go-to. I needed to work on that.

Sienna came out from the bedroom and made quick work of dumping our wine down the sink. I watched it circle the drain.

Guess that's where we stand with that.

She poured three glasses of cold milk before making her way to the brownies. "What the hell is this?" Sienna asked with mock indignation.

I shrugged. "Gemma insisted on the very middle. She made me do it."

Gemma scoffed beside me, and we shared another laugh.

Sienna pointed her fork between the two of us. "You're both rotten." She moved toward Gemma. "Thanks for coming by, but no apology was necessary." She turned toward me. "I'm beat, so I'll take this in the bedroom. You two catch up. Good night."

Behind Gemma my eyes went wide. What the hell was I supposed to talk to her about?

"Oh, and Gem? I'd love another hike sometime soon."

"Thanks. I'd like that too." With a smile, Sienna closed the bedroom door and disappeared.

I stuffed a mouthful of brownie into my face, hoping it would give me a few more minutes to figure out what the hell to say to my sister.

I'm sorry I never treated you right?

I'm sorry you thought I kidnapped and tried to kill you?

I'm sorry that me being here put you in danger again?

"How's Evan?" He was neutral ground, so I figured I would start there.

Gemma went to speak but then just sighed. "He's a fucking moron."

I nearly choked on my milk. Hearing Gemma, my nine-teen-year-old sister, speak so harshly was actually funny as hell.

"Val left," she continued. "I told him not to lose her, and he did it anyway."

"He gonna get her back?" I asked. I had no clue what was going on between Evan and his woman, only that shit had gone down, and she'd hightailed it out of Montana.

"I hope so. Val is great." Gemma eyed me over her glass. "You'd like her. She doesn't take any shit. But she is a cop, so, you know. You'd have to not be a piece of shit."

I could take a little ball busting, but damn. Gemma was relentless. Hearing those words from a face that looked just like my mother's was a shot to the gut. I set my plate and cup down. Too much history and unspoken truths mucked up our past. Something about this kid wouldn't let me forget about her.

"Look, I don't want to do this."

Gemma's nostrils flared. She was ready for the fight. Trouble was, I wasn't.

"How about we start over?" I asked. I stood and held out my hand. "I'm Parker Marino. Davis," I corrected. "Parker Davis. It's nice to meet you."

Gemma stood to her full height, staring me in the eye.

Could she do it? Could she let the past go?

She moved forward and held out her hand. Her voice was quiet but assertive. "Gemma Walker."

I shook her hand once before letting it drop. "Nice to meet you."

"This is so weird."

Her laugh had me breathing a sigh of relief. "Yeah. All around it's fucking nuts."

She smiled once more, and I had a sneaking feeling that things were going to be okay with Gemma. She was tough as nails beneath those blue eyes.

"I should go. Tell Sienna I said good night?"

My eyes moved toward the bedroom door. "Yeah. Sure. I'll let her know."

Gemma moved to the door and paused before leaving. "Bye, Parker."

"Night, Gemma."

She smiled a sad-looking smile and left. I leaned against the door and let a deep breath move through me.

What a fucking day.

I was weary. Bone tired. I felt like I'd run through the gauntlet and come out the other side a hammered piece of horse shit.

The quiet of the cottage rang in my ears. Under the bedroom door, no light shone through. Sienna had taken all my blankets and pillow with her to cover the fact that I was sleeping on the couch.

Do I knock and go get them? If I end up in the bedroom with her, will I be able to keep my hands off her?

Battle weary from the day, I didn't trust myself. Instead, I stretched across the uncomfortable, too-small couch and folded my arms over my chest.

Tomorrow was a new day. A new life with new jobs. A new opportunity to keep my fucking hands off my wife.

TEN

SIENNA

I LISTENED to the sound of my own breathing for far too long. When I scurried to the bedroom with an armful of Parker's pillow and blankets, I'd be lying if I didn't imagine him knocking on the door once Gemma left.

She hadn't stayed long, and I couldn't hear more than muffled voices, but I was relieved to hear that the conversation didn't sound too heated. Anyone could see they were two broken people who needed each other more than either was willing to admit.

Parker's pillow was beside me, and in the darkness I leaned into it. Taking a hit of his spicy cologne, I held it in my lungs. Warmth spread through me. God, I wanted that man's hands on me. When it was clear he wasn't coming to claim his things, I sneaked out into the living room. His frame was comically large for the couch. Turned at an awkward angle, he'd hung his feet over the edge, and his neck was cramped. I placed the pillow on the floor beside him and draped one blanket over his body. The long, deep breaths that flowed in and out of him were calm. Soothing.

I risked leaning forward. I placed my lips against the shell of his ear. "Good night, husband."

THE NEXT MORNING I rose and dressed for work. Excitement sizzled through me as I thought about the opportunity to work with and learn about the animals. Taking care of people had always been a calling, and living on a ranch, this could be the next best thing.

After a brief debate over what to wear—I settled on simple jeans and a black, long-sleeved T-shirt—I braved walking into the living room.

Parker was already showered and dressed in jeans and a dark Henley shirt. The way the fabric strained over his pecs was sinful. My eyes snagged on the bump at his nipple, and the reminder of the metal bar there made my belly flip.

He barely looked at me as I walked out of the bedroom. "Morning," he grumbled as he finished lacing up his boots.

"Good morning." I smiled at him and waited a beat for him to look my way. He didn't.

Okay. Guess we're acting like we didn't almost go too far last night. Noted.

Parker rose and stalked toward the door. His hand encircled the handle, but he paused before he left. "There's money in that envelope." He gestured toward a thick white envelope on the kitchen table. "Get whatever you need. Let me know if you need more."

I gaped, but before I could protest, he was gone.

Curious, I ripped the envelope open and almost died. Thousands. *Thousands* of dollars in cash was neatly stacked inside the envelope. I looked around as if someone could see what I was holding.

"What the hell?" I said aloud to no one. A small thrill rippled through me. Working at the ranch paid a modest amount, but with this little bit of spending money, I could get a few things I'd been missing since being forced to move to Montana.

Specifically, something small and battery powered.

Did I feel bad about buying a vibrator with Parker's money? Shit no. He was the reason I needed one in the first place.

Feeling lighter than I had in days, I rushed into the bedroom and tucked the envelope in the back of my underwear drawer. After work I could head to town for a little spending spree.

But first I needed to show up and earn my keep. Ma Brown had delivered a small slip of paper to both Parker and me sometime in the early-morning hours. Mine simply said a time and location, along with the name Chet Williams.

I found my way toward the main barn, stopping twice to ask someone to clarify the directions. Each person was friendly and helpful, welcoming me to Redemption Ranch and wishing me good luck on my first day. By the time I'd reached the barn, I was feeling ten feet tall.

Life bustled all around me. Everyone seemed to have a purpose, determination etched on their faces. Brushing horses, cleaning out stalls, moving animals from one space to another. Toward the back, I found a small office. After knocking twice, I waited.

"Come in!" A rough voice bellowed.

I turned the handle and opened the door to find Josh and an older man shaking hands. Josh moved past me, tipping the brim of his ball cap in my direction. "Ma'am."

I smiled back. "Hi, Josh."

"So you're my new recruit." The older man leaned against the desk and crossed his arms. His face was weathered, like an old map that had been wrinkled and faded with time. A faded tattoo of a pinup girl peeked out from beneath the roll of his shirtsleeve. His deep-brown eyes held mine, but instead of feeling scrutinized, I felt welcomed. Accepted.

I raised my palms. "I'm here to help. Back home I was in school to be a nurse."

He nodded. "That'll come in handy. Being you're helping out, we'll start you with the easy stuff. Mostly animal care, postprocedural and the like."

"Yes, sir."

"Please, call me Chet. Let's get you started."

The slim man swiveled in his chair, opened a small safe behind his desk, and deposited a little black notebook before spinning back toward me and standing. He placed a hat on his head and walked past me and out the door without another word. I followed him into the bright Montana morning and started the first day of my new life.

〜

I smelled like horse shit.

Horse shit, but happy horse shit. I laughed at myself as I tried to scrub the dirt and smell from my nails. The morning hours flew by, and my head was still spinning. Chet often jotted things into a small leather pad, and I wished I had a notebook or something to write down everything he had taught me.

Chet was kind and accommodating. He didn't seem to mind when I stopped him a thousand times to ask a question or for him to clarify something. In fact, he seemed to like my eager absorption of the information he gave me. A time or two he would go off on a tangent regarding an animal, where they came from, or an old case he found interesting. I listened with rapt attention, his drawl only adding to the fascinating stories he told.

By 4:00 p.m., my mind and muscles ached, and Chet agreed it was time to call it quits. I had the rest of the afternoon to myself. I wondered how Parker's day was going. Did he like his new job? Was everyone as friendly to him as they were to me? I doubted it. Parker's gruff appearance and general lack of friendliness were enough to scare off most people. It was a shame too. If only he'd let people in, they'd see the softness that he hid underneath the armor.

A battle for another day.

Parker must have still been working because the cottage looked just as we'd left it this morning. I left a quick note, letting him know I took the car to town and would bring home something to eat for dinner. I'm not sure why that mattered, but I hoped he liked the idea of me taking care of dinner. We still hadn't worked out all the details of if and when we'd eat together or who would be responsible for that, but I could handle it for today. It made me feel . . . wifely.

I flipped through the bills Parker had left me, tucking several into my purse and grabbing the keys to his car. Phone service was horrible around the ranch, but once I got closer to town, the GPS would pick up and help me find exactly where I was going.

I parked directly in front of the same little shop where I'd purchased my wedding dress, Rebellious Rose. There were other shops, but I was drawn to the eclectic and inviting storefront. As I pushed open the door, the store owner called out a greeting as he helped someone at the counter.

I worked my way through the store, weaving around the tables of neatly folded clothing. I sniffed a few candles, lamenting the fact that there wasn't a way to bottle up Parker's fragrance.

"I know you." The store owner's friendly voice floated over my shoulder. When I turned to look at him, he leaned over a display, his head resting on top of his hands. His amiable smile was broad but questioning.

"Hi, yes. I was in here before."

"I remember. You bought a sexy little yellow dress. Did he like it?" He wiggled his eyebrows once.

I felt a small blush heat my cheeks as I recalled the fire in Parker's eyes when he first saw me in the dress. "Yes, I think he did. Thank you."

"Think? Friend, we need to do better than that."

I laughed with him and stuck out my hand. "I don't think we were properly introduced. Sienna. Davis. I'm Sienna Davis." I cleared my throat. It was still unfamiliar and tender to use my new name.

The store owner pinched his lips together and nodded. "Johnny Porter." He leaned in closer. "It'll get easier once you get used to it." With a wink he moved to a different display.

This is what Gemma was talking about. They know.

"So what can I help you find?" Johnny worked to rearrange and organize candles and bottles along the neat shelves.

"A few more outfits," I said. Gathering my bravery, I continued: "I'm also wondering if you sell anything . . ." *Oh god, how do I put this?* "Um. Intimate."

A hint of elation sparked in his eye, and he looked

around his empty store. "This way."

I obeyed, following him to the back of the store. On the left, a table of simply stunning women's lingerie was tastefully displayed. The items ranged from simple, silky undergarments to barely there strings and something with far too many hook-and-eye closures. Desire pooled in my core as I thought of the stunned look on Parker's face if I walked out of the bedroom in something like that.

"Also," Johnny continued, "if you peek over there, there are some more intimate items. The selection is small, but if there's something specific you're looking for, I can always order it." With a wink he left me to explore.

I moved farther toward the back of the store and stopped. Behind a tall black partition was a subtle arrangement of items. My eyes moved over the display—nipple clamps, flavored lube, numbing gel, dildos of varying size and shape, and, as if the heavens opened up and I could hear the song of the angels, vibrators.

I swallowed thickly as my suppressed desires came bubbling to the surface. Sharing the same living space with someone as deeply masculine and sexy as Parker was driving me up a wall. I'd tried touching myself in the shower, but I couldn't manage to get the release I needed. Eyeing the display, I debated between a small, discreet pocket vibrator or the long, thick pink one with the nub that jutted out in front. Thinking of the hum buzzing against my clit had sweat prickling at the back of my skull.

You know a man built like Parker is huge. If you want to pretend it's him, you know which one to go for.

Glancing around to be sure no one could actually hear the debate raging in my head, I grabbed the box and added a few pieces of sexy underwear to the pile.

Discreetly, Johnny moved toward me, scooping the

items into a black bag and moving it behind the counter. "I'll just keep these things back here until you're ready for checkout."

The man was truly masterful. I was humming with excitement, and I felt at ease that I could spend the next hour not worrying about the vibrator but could instead concentrate on finding clothes that made me feel human again.

Time passed quickly, and I sent up a quiet thank-you to Parker for the money he'd given me. Maybe I should have felt wrong or guilty for spending it, but I didn't. As I always did, I saw the silver lining. I was thrilled to have a few new outfits that would make me feel confident and comfortable —even if I really didn't have anywhere to wear them.

Reminding myself how dirty and stinky my new job was, I also made a stop at the tack-and-feed store. I snagged a few pairs of jeans and shirts that would protect my arms and legs while I learned to care for the animals on the ranch. Finally I stepped into a bar—the Tabula Rasa—on Main Street after seeing the sign CARRY OUT DINNER. Conversation died at my entrance. A sea of eyeballs tracked my movement toward the counter. Awareness puckered my skin and I started to sweat.

Why was everyone staring at me? What the actual fuck?

I tried to get the attention of the bartender behind the counter, but he actively ignored me. I scanned a plastic menu and waited. And waited.

"Here, this'll help." Chet's rugged voice caught my attention. "Hey, Al. How about you help Ms. Sienna here. She's new."

Immediately the bartender swiveled, and a smile bloomed on his face. His rough exterior and gangly limbs covered in tattoos morphed into a welcoming, friendly stance. "My apologies, Ms. Sienna. I didn't realize you were with Chet here."

I looked between the two men.

"Sienna just started working at Redemption. Today was her first day. She's helping me with the animals." He shot Al a wink. "She's a quick study. I think it'll work out."

"Well that's great to hear. What can I do for ya, darlin'?"

Still a bit shell-shocked, I stumbled through my dinner order. "To go, please," I added at the end before he walked away to punch the order into his machine.

"That'll do ya." Chet smiled before moving back to where he sat alone at his table, but not before asking Al to switch the football game to the Giants.

"Thank you!" I called out to Chet. He tipped his hat and hunched over a black notebook, scribbling notes as he caught glimpses of the football game. I sat on the barstool and smiled. This weird little town was a mystery, but there was something intriguing about it. I wanted to learn more about who knew what and why it seemed so cold and unfriendly at first blush.

Minutes later, Al returned with a stack of Styrofoam piled into two plastic bags. It seemed like a lot more food than I'd ordered.

Reading my expression, Al added, "I threw in some of Irma's peach pie—only second to her apple. She makes the best pie in Cedar County."

A wide smile pinched my cheeks. "Amazing, thanks!" I couldn't wait to get it home and share it with Parker.

My keys rattled against the door as I fumbled with the bags and boxes while I pushed through the entrance. Parker stopped in his tracks, looking thoroughly annoyed, and panic pulsed through my veins.

"There you are." He stepped toward me, his blue eyes turned dark and intense.

"Hi. I brought dinner." I hefted the bags up, and he immediately grabbed them from me. My eyes raced to the striped bag from Rebellious Rose, and I moved to grab the handles before he could peek inside. "I'll just put this away, and then we can eat."

Shoving the entire bag at the base of my closet, I breathed a sigh of relief. Smoothing my hair back, I walked out of the bedroom and found Parker plating the food.

"This looks good."

I relaxed a bit. The prospect of food seemed to quiet the irritation I'd sensed in him when I got home. I shrugged. "I sure hope so. There was a sign that said takeout, so I gave it a shot." I pointed to the two smaller boxes still on the counter. "The bartender says that's the best peach pie in Cedar County."

An appreciative grumble rattled in his chest. "I love peach."

My eyes whipped to him.

Did he mean that like I think he meant that?

When he looked away, I realized the sexual comment was completely unintentional, but not totally lost on him. It still rattled something hot and loose inside me. I pulled a glass down from the cabinet and stared at the sink. I craved a cool drink of water, but the thought of well water gave me pause.

"In the fridge."

I turned and shot him a questioning look.

"Bottled water. There's some in the fridge."

"When did you . . . ?"

A shrug was all the answer I was getting. I couldn't help but smile at the simple, kind gesture.

ELEVEN
PARKER

CLEARLY, Sienna was shocked that I'd gotten her bottled water.

Was I that big of an asshole that something as simple as bottled water would leave her speechless? Apparently, yes.

"Thanks." Sienna grabbed a bottle of water, twisted off the top, and slugged down half of it in a matter of seconds. Watching her move in the cottage eased the tension between my shoulders. I'd seen her note but couldn't help but stress about her being alone in town. Inside these walls, I could keep her safe.

She grabbed another bottle of water and placed it next to my plate before sitting across from me. "So, darling husband, how was your day?"

A smile teased at my mouth. "It was fine. Different. I found out that not everyone here is a witness or agent. Some are just people working, but they're in on it. They know what this place is and don't seem to mind."

"Weird, right? Same with people in town. They *know*. The weirdest part is they're kind of standoffish at first, but once they know you're here at Redemption, they open up quite a bit."

I considered her words. "Hmm. Makes sense. If they don't know you, they don't trust you. If you're here, it means at least Ma knows you."

"That's a lot of faith for an entire town to have in one woman."

I shrugged. "Must be a hell of a woman."

A comfortable silence fell between us as we ate our supper.

Finally Sienna cut in. "So work was okay?"

I only nodded, but when she looked at me expectantly, I sat back in my chair. "Ma has me helping with the books. Mostly sifting through receipts and organizing it. It was boring."

"I was surprised you said you wanted to work on the financial side." Her eyes raked down my chest. "You, um, just seem like more of a manual labor kind of guy."

"Like I said, I would do whatever she asks of me. But if she wants my help, it's with the books. It's what I did . . . before." I stumbled on my words. I knew she was aware of my past, but something inside me didn't want it right out in the open. I wasn't proud of what I'd done with my time in Chicago.

"So you're a closet nerd."

I met Sienna's blank stare. "Call it what you want. Knowing numbers comes in handy when you're cooking the books." It was a weird flex, but whatever. Something primal in me wanted to impress her, even if that meant highlighting some less-than-legal talents.

Sienna burst out laughing and covered her ears. "Oh, I don't want to know! Isn't willful ignorance a thing?"

"I think you mean 'plausible deniability,' but yeah. It's a

thing." How this woman could laugh and find levity when talking about fraud was beyond me. We'd each cleared our plates, and I grabbed the small containers of pie, sliding one in her direction. "How about you, wife? How was your day?"

Her stormy green eyes lit up. "It was amazing. I'm working with this really cool old guy named Chet. He knows something about *everything*. When I went to town, I even bought a notebook so I could start writing some of it down. He's so interesting. I don't think he's originally from here, but he's a cowboy through and through."

I liked her voice, the melodic way it flowed over her words. I wanted her to keep talking so I could stay quiet and listen. "It's good you like him. Did you find anything else you liked in town?"

A slow stain of pink started at the base of her neck and wound its way up to her cheeks.

"Sure. A few things. Outfits mostly. Thanks again for the money." Her words tumbled together and I almost laughed. Any idiot could see the silky scraps of fabric in the bag she'd tried so hard to hide after she came home.

Whatever, my wife was hot as fuck, and she secretly wore sexy underwear. I loved knowing I was privy to that knowledge, even if, at the same time, it made me die a slow and torturous death.

"Like I said before, let me know when you need more."

She peeked out from under her lashes. "Is the money . . . legal?"

I couldn't help but laugh at her shyness. "It is. Mostly." When her eyes went wide, I added, "What? You don't spend your adult life cooking the books and not let it work out in your favor. But relax. The cash can't be traced.

There's more than we can spend, and it's yours when you need it."

I hoped she wasn't too proud to spend my money. Sure, it wasn't always earned honestly, but it was taken from people worse than me. For that, I didn't give a shit. I'd happily spend the money from lowlife pricks.

The Tipp bartender was right—Irma's pie was delicious. I thought of making another vaguely sexual remark about the taste of peaches, but didn't. Sienna needed to feel comfortable in her own home, and despite the dirty paths my mind wandered, she deserved better.

For a moment, we let the quiet fill the cottage.

"Would you want to—"

"What do you say we—"

We shared an uncomfortable laugh after we talked over one another.

"Go ahead," I commanded. Inside I was dying to know where she was going with her sentence.

Her eyes flicked downward and she smiled. "Would you want to go into town? Maybe get a drink at the bar? They had pool tables."

My blood warmed. I liked the idea of taking her out on a date.

"It would be a great chance for people to see us out. You know, together."

And there it was.

The reminder that whatever was between us wasn't real. Could never be. We needed to put on a show for everyone to accept, and believe, we were happily married. All because she felt she owed me some sort of debt.

My mood darkened. "Get your coat."

～

I WAS quiet on the drive to town.

"Is something wrong?" Sienna's voice cut through the quiet, but I didn't look at her.

"Nope."

When we approached the soft glow of town, much like the first night we arrived, most of the mom-and-pop shops were closed for the night. Windows darkened, doors locked up tight. Save for the lights and music coming from the Tabula Rasa, it was nearly a ghost town.

Inside, the bar was an entirely different story. Music flowed from the jukebox, and tables were littered with families, groups of people dancing or watching football, and solo drinkers at the bar.

Suspicious eyes followed up to the thick oak slab of the main bar, where Sienna made a beeline toward two empty stools. Before I could pull one out for her, she hopped up on one. I slid in next to her, meeting the eyes of several men who didn't seem too happy to see us in their bar.

I lowered my voice and leaned into her. "I don't think this is a great idea." I straightened my back and clenched a fist.

She beamed back at me. "Trust me."

The bartender turned, his hard eyes landing on me. He was tall and lean, built like a fighter. His white beard was long but taken care of. The tattoos that snaked around his arms were old, and most were representations of MC membership. He wasn't wearing a cut, so I doubted he was still active, but no moron tangled with a motorcycle club without backup.

I was about to stand my ground, pull Sienna from the stool, and drag her tiny little ass back to our cottage if I had to. She never gave me the chance.

"Back so soon?" The bartender seemed entranced by Sienna as she beamed back at him.

"Guess I just missed you!" she teased. "Actually, I needed to thank you in person for that ridiculous pie. It was incredible. Best I've ever had."

The surly bartender's face split open with a smile, and he fucking *winked* at her. When his weary eyes slicked to me, Sienna jumped in. "Al, please let me introduce you to Parker. My husband."

As she introduced me as her husband, I slipped my arm around her shoulders. Realization dawned on him and his posture softened.

"Welcome, man." He wiped his hands on a green towel and shoved one in my direction. "Name's Al. The Rasa is my place. Nice to meet you."

I held his hand in a firm grip. Sienna was right—this town was fucking weird.

"Thank you for the pie."

Sienna nodded once as if she was satisfied with our interaction. We each ordered a drink, an IPA for me and a porter for her. I glanced at her in question.

She shrugged. "I like dark beer."

I sipped the hoppy beer in front of me. "Good to know, wife."

God, why did I keep doing that? Calling her wife *like it was its own nickname. And why did I like it so much?*

"Okay, husband. Let's play some pool."

That was why. Sienna did it too—called me *husband* in a way that was playful and made something shift around in my chest. I followed her around like a hulking shadow as she cut through the crowd. The pool tables were busy, so we settled at a high-top table near the dartboards.

"Wanna give it a go?" she asked.

"Sienna, I thought that was you." We both turned, and I instinctively stepped forward, taking a half step in front of her, blocking her with my body.

"Josh!" My head whipped to Sienna as excitement bubbled out of her. The guy was only in his midtwenties or so, sure, but he was cocky. And fit. The way he smiled a slow, easy grin at her had my blood simmering. The unfamiliar roll of jealousy nearly knocked me on my ass. I stood, hands at my side, tension vibrating through me.

"Parker, this is Josh. He works under Chet. Josh, this is Parker."

He reached to shake my hand, and I gripped it just a fraction harder than necessary. "Her husband."

I could practically feel Sienna rolling her eyes, but Josh didn't miss a beat. "Welcome to Tipp. I hope Redemption's been treating you well."

We moved apart, and I pulled Sienna under my arm, tucking her into my side. Her small hand grazed the front of my shirt, grazing the bar through my nipple as her hand moved down my abs. I flexed for her, and she pressed her hand into me.

That's right.

The truth was, I liked having Sienna's hands on me. I liked nestling her under my arm and being rewarded with a hint of the summery smell of her hair. I knew it was temporary. All for show. Part of me didn't care.

The smarter, self-preserving part of me knew I was playing with fire. I knew that when all this was done, I could set Sienna up. She'd never have to worry about money or protection again. She would move on with her life.

Gone.

It didn't matter that she was my wife. When this was done, like everyone else in my life, she'd be free of me.

"What do you think?" Sienna's hopeful voice shone a light on my dark thoughts, and her forehead crinkled.

"Hmm?" I had missed half the conversation, tied up in thoughts of Sienna.

"Do you want to? Go over and sit?" She angled her head toward the small table where Josh looked on.

"If that's what you want to do."

We joined the small group and exchanged greetings. A few were general ranch hands, one a federal agent, and the last was a waitress from the café in town. The agent's eyes took in every interaction, every nuance as we moved chairs around to make room.

If Sienna and I were going to sell this thing, we needed to sell it. Her eyes went wide with surprise as I pulled out her chair and let my fingertips graze her back. As she lowered into the seat, I leaned down and kissed the top of her head.

If spending time outside of our cottage home was supposed to ease the tension between us, we were failing pretty spectacularly. My fingers itched to brush across her knee.

I let the conversation flow around me. Everyone was far too entranced by Sienna to give a shit whether or not I contributed to the conversation.

"That's a hell of an injury." Clearly speaking to me, the agent—Chris, I think—pointed toward my missing pinkie.

I held his eyes and nodded.

"Looks like a table saw or . . . something."

I looked down and flexed my hand. Normally I kept my hand hidden away in my pocket. Most days I forgot the pinkie was missing at all, but the way Sienna stiffened at my side had me on edge.

"Or something." Fuck this guy. He didn't need to know the truth behind what happened.

The agent stared for a long, tense moment. "In some cultures, a finger is penance."

Silence stretched across the table.

"Hey, let's dance!" Sienna stood and tried to pull me out of my seat. I rose with her, following her movements toward the dance floor, but I kept my eyes locked on the agent.

Dick.

A low, unfamiliar country song rattled out of the speakers of the jukebox. Some people were line dancing around us, and a few couples did a two-step. Sienna and I stood awkwardly on the edge until she stepped into my space. Too short to wrap her arms around my neck, she looped her arms under mine and held on to my back.

I swayed with her in my arms but eyed her carefully. "What was that about?"

She chewed her lower lip, and I wanted to dip down, suck that lip into my mouth, and feel her press against me. "It's none of their business."

I shrugged. "People are curious."

"It was rude." When I stayed quiet, she asked, "Would you have told them?"

"The truth? No."

She thought about that as the upbeat song shifted to a sad, bluesy tune as we continued to sway. "Maybe one day you'll tell me the truth."

My throat felt thick, so a noncommittal grunt was all I could manage. The day we married, Sienna found out I'd lost my pinkie to pay a debt. What she didn't need to know was that I had cut it off myself.

TWELVE
SIENNA

PARKER WAS ALWAYS GORGEOUS, but he was downright irresistible when he opened up. Little by little, I was seeing cracks in his carefully constructed armor. One of these days, I was going to find a way to wedge inside one of those cracks and break him wide open.

We continued to sway on the dance floor. More and more people filtered in, pushing us closer together until my front was pressed flush with his.

"Do you like country music?" I asked. A wife should know at least that much about her husband.

Parker thought for a moment before answering with a small shrug. "I like the sad ones."

Moved by his simple statement, I pressed my cheek into his firm chest. His heart clunked beneath my ear, and I focused on the steady rhythm of it.

As we stayed silent and swayed and watched others dance around us, an elderly woman leaned into our space. "I just have to say, y'all are the cutest couple."

"Oh! Thank you," I replied.

The dark, crepey skin around the woman's eyes crinkled as she smiled between us. "Have you been together long?"

A fizzing bubble of laughter nearly erupted from me, and Parker squeezed me tightly to keep me from losing it. "Actually, um . . ." I started.

"Newlyweds." The rumble of Parker's voice vibrated from his chest into me.

"Oh, Donald, did you hear that?" She patted the collar of her husband's shirt and smiled at him. "Young love."

Donald looked just as enamored with us as his wife. "That is somethin'. You hold on to her." He winked up at Parker. "Be a shame to let that one walk away."

I looked at Parker, ready to share a smile, only to find his stare hard and cold.

"Yes, sir," was his only reply.

I thanked the couple again, and they shifted to continue their dance, lost in each other. It was sweet and encouraging to see a couple so in love after what I assumed was many years together. I looked up at Parker, his lips set in a firm line.

When I opened my mouth to speak, he cut me off. "We should go." Despite the fact that we were midsong, he strode off the dance floor and sauntered toward the table. "Nice to meet you, everyone. We're headed out."

"All right." Josh stood to shake Parker's hand. "You two have a good night. See you at work, Sienna."

I grabbed my coat and purse. I plastered a fake smile across my face. "Thanks, Josh. See you then."

We said our goodbyes to the rest of the small group, left some money for our drinks and a tip, and walked into the cool autumn evening. Parker stalked to his car in silence. Chilled by his mood more so than the nip in the air, I pulled my jacket tight.

Once we got to the car, Parker pulled open my door, and I barely got inside before he slammed it shut.

"What the hell?" I mumbled to myself as I watched him round the hood.

The ride home was tense and silent. Darkness had fallen and enveloped the entire ranch in a blanket of indigo as we pulled up. The stars guided us toward the tiny cottage we called home.

Weary and drained from how quickly the evening had turned sour, I walked behind Parker as we made our way to the front door. Rather than unlocking it, he swiveled on his heels to face me.

Parker took two slow, measured steps and placed his hands on my hips. His fingers dug into me as he turned us and backed me up against the door. With his head hung low, he crowded my space. Our breaths mingled as mine grew shallower. Parker grabbed the lapels of my jacket and hauled me up against his broad chest.

His mouth crashed down on mine, melting away any thoughts I had. The soft, surprised noise that came from me was swallowed whole by him. His warm, masculine scent had my brain swimming in endorphins. My hands found his waist, and I dug my fingertips into the muscle and skin. Parker's hands moved from my jacket to my neck and hair as he tilted my head and deepened the kiss.

This was not the restrained, tentative kiss from the courthouse. This was hot, messy, and demanding. My back arched, pressing me farther into him. His thick thigh found its way between my legs, putting a dull pressure right where I needed it. I wanted to grind against him, feel the bite of my jeans against my clit as his hands roamed over my body and I came apart.

The long, hard length of him pressed against me, and I

nearly moaned at the size of it as the hard ridge pressed into my hip. Rules be damned, I wanted to climb that man like a tree, wind myself around him until we both dissolved.

Too soon, Parker broke the kiss. He pulled his hands from my face and hair.

Torture washed over his face as he looked down at me. I was sure I looked pliant. As willing and ready as I felt. He could have stripped me bare with one word.

Instead, he moved to unlock and open the door. With a push, he swung it open. "I'm going for a walk," he announced, and strode away from me.

Dumbfounded, hot, and horny as hell, I stared after him as he disappeared into the darkness. My body still tingled where his hands had pressed into me. We had talked about displays of affection and kissing for the sake of the ruse, but this was something different. It crossed a line. Parker had kissed me tonight without an audience.

And then he'd run.

Frustrated, I stormed into the cottage, flipping lights on as I went. The whiplash from that guy was getting really fucking annoying. I threw down my purse and determined the only way to calm the hell down would be a shower.

Even the cold spray couldn't cool my burning skin. It was flushed. Hot. I was completely turned on. In my rush to take over the bathroom, I'd forgotten to grab my robe or pajamas. In only the towel, I peeked around the bathroom door and looked into the living room.

Empty.

Parker was still out blowing off steam or whatever the hell "going for a walk" meant.

Why had he kissed me?

I tiptoed back to my bedroom. Embarrassment and arousal flamed my cheeks. The last thing I wanted was to be caught by Parker in a towel when he'd just kissed the fuck out of me and then run off.

I dried my body, hanging the towel in the small closet, and slipped into sleep shorts and a tee. I sat in the bed, pillows propped behind me, and gathered the blankets to my chin.

Parker was infuriating.

He was stupid.

God, he's so fucking hot.

My eyes snagged on the small, crumpled Rebellious Rose bag that I'd shoved into my closet. Knowing exactly what was inside, my body hummed to life. My pussy throbbed once, and I couldn't take it. I needed relief.

One real kiss from Parker and I was wound so tightly I knew I'd come within seconds. I listened carefully, no noise filtered through the thin walls of the cottage. Walking as quietly as I could, I removed the small box and opened it. The long pink vibrator was heavy in my hands, and my heart pounded against my chest. It was big and thick, with a soft protrusion at the base meant to rub against my clit.

A thrill danced through me as I thought of finally getting relief. I slipped back into bed and burrowed under the covers. Closing my eyes, I trailed a hand down from my collarbone, across the stiff peak of my nipple, and over my belly. Dipping below the waistband of my shorts, I found the valley between my thighs. I closed my eyes and imagined my hand was Parker's.

I dipped a finger through my slit.

Fucking soaked.

Damn, how I wanted it to be Parker's hands on me. I swirled a fingertip through the wetness and circled my clit. My hips jutted up, seeking more. I wanted release. I wanted to be full.

Quietly fumbling with the vibrator, I pressed the top button, and it hummed to life. I pressed it once again, and it buzzed harder and louder.

"Fuck." I pressed it again, twice more, until it went back to the lowest, quietest setting. I listened again and, hearing nothing, dragged the thick tip of the toy across my clit and over my pussy.

Envisioning Parker holding his thick cock, I teased my opening. Swirling the blunt silicone head around. Pushing in, just an inch, and pulling out again.

Warm me up, Parker. I'm so ready. Take me.

I slipped the vibrator inside, picturing Parker being the one to split me open and fill me up. The soft, buzzing appendage on the top of the vibrator glanced against my clit, and I nearly yelled out loud. Clamping my mouth shut, I reveled in how it felt to be full while the toy shook against my greedy clit.

I started pumping in and out, allowing the vibrations to radiate through me. Barely minutes and I was so fucking close.

A knock at the bedroom door had a scream lodging in my throat.

"Sienna." The deep, gruff tone in Parker's voice only added to the intensity. I kept the vibrator firmly planted inside me as I clenched around it, my clit screaming for release.

I swallowed hard and tried to sound as normal as I could. "Yeah?"

"I just wanted to apologize for—wait. Are you all right? Talk to me." Concern filled his voice.

I squeezed my eyes shut. If he said one more word in that deep, authoritative tone, I was going to come with him standing just beyond the door. "Fine."

"What's that noise?"

Jesus, fuck.

I fumbled with the buttons, trying to turn the toy off, but only managed to increase the vibrations, making it louder.

"Sienna."

That was all it took. My name from his lips in his stern voice, and my orgasm crashed over me. Pulsing around the vibrator, wishing it was his cock, I came.

"I'm fine!" My voice was pinched and not at all normal.

"What are you—oh. Fuck. I'm, uh, forget it."

As I came with a pillow shoved over my face, his heavy footsteps receded into the living room. My body came down from the high, and my panting breaths filled the silence. I was still reeling from Parker's voice pushing me over the edge. It was so, so wrong.

The first time my husband made me come, he was six feet away and never even touched me.

I pinched my eyes closed and hoped Parker didn't know exactly what I was doing. It was going to be hard enough to look him in the eye after that soul-searing kiss, but if he knew I immediately made myself come because of it?

I. Would. Die.

THE NEXT MORNING, I tried to pretend that I didn't go to bed only to have a restless night of sex dreams about my husband. It felt so good to come, but I was still left wanting. My body knew exactly what—or rather *who*—it wanted, and nothing battery powered was going to give it to me.

Dressed for another day of work on the ranch, I

attempted to look as casual as I could. Parker was lacing up his boots as I walked out of the bedroom.

"Good morning."

His eyes raked over me, a knowing smirk planted on his stupid face.

Oh yeah. He knows.

"Morning, wife. Sleep well?"

I turned away and lied, "Great!" before grabbing my jacket and hurrying out the door.

THIRTEEN
PARKER

I can't be certain, but I'm about ninety-nine percent positive Sienna has a vibrator and made herself come last night. After stomping around in the dark and berating myself for kissing her, I wanted to talk with her. I owed her an apology for storming out of the bar and then kissing the fuck out of her. Or if not an apology—because in reality I wasn't at all sorry it happened—I at least owed her an explanation.

My plan had been to explain that I would hold fast to the thread of self-restraint I had left and that it wouldn't happen again. That was, until I knocked on her door and heard her breathy pants. The soft hum in the background made me painfully hard as I put together what was happening just beyond her bedroom door.

In my office, I palmed my cock under the desk just thinking about it.

"Settling in?" My brother's deep voice had me turning toward the open doorway. Evan stood, his broad shoulders slumped. He looked miserable.

I stood to shake his hand. Our relationship was still

strained, and he'd been a ghost around the ranch, so when he settled into the chair in my office, I simply stared at him.

After a long silence stretched between us, I tried to keep the conversation neutral. "Not working today?"

"Morning chores are mostly done. I'm just taking a break before getting back to it." He looked around the small office. It had a dented gray filing cabinet, two chairs, and the old wooden desk I sat behind. The small window allowed fresh air and light, but the walls were otherwise plain. "Jesus, dude. It's depressing as fuck in here."

I laughed a bit at that. Evan always hated offices, and the idea of him being a businessman was almost comical. Too stifling for his free, roaming spirit. "Not all of us *speak for the trees*."

He flinched at the phrase. A battered copy of *The Lorax* was the only children's book we had in the house as kids. When he was really young, on nights Mom didn't come home and I'd put him to bed, I would read it to him. I still knew every word by heart.

The tension was unbearable, and I cleared my throat. It was enough to pull Evan from his thoughts. "So you're married."

I looked at my little brother, assessing how much he knew and how much I should share. Sienna and I had a secret, and I'd pledged my word that I would keep it. Though entirely selfish, we were deep in it now, so there was no turning back. "I am."

Evan let out a little *hmph* noise. "What happened to the man who used to say relationships should only last as long as it takes you to pump and dump?"

I flinched at the memory. I really was an asshole. I gave my little brother a hard look. "Things changed."

He scoffed. "Clearly."

I flipped a hand in his direction. "What about you? Where'd your girl run off to?"

Evan stiffened, and I knew I'd hit a tender spot. "Back to Chicago." His voice was hollow. In all the years I'd worked to keep him from becoming bitter and jaded by our lifestyle, taking jobs so he didn't have to, I'd never seen him like this.

Broken.

I thought about myself and how, after things quieted down, in a few years when people finally forgot that Parker Marino ever existed, Sienna would finally be rid of me. She could leave.

A piercing ache lanced through me.

"You gonna be a pussy or are you getting her back?" I asked.

Evan's blue eyes sliced back to me. "I'm working on it."

I relaxed in my chair, content to no longer think about my wife, the prospect of her leaving, and why that bugged the fuck out of me.

Evan reached to my desk to snag a pencil and flip it through his fingers. "So what's Ma got you working on?"

"Right now, just bullshit record-keeping and some filing. Going through receipts and some of the books."

He lifted an eyebrow. "Back to business running the numbers?"

I smirked. In Chicago much of my job was handling the money that came in and out from various jobs. The Mafia ran several legitimate businesses, but when bigger jobs rolled through, that money needed to be accounted for, and someone had to cook the books. It was a challenge—to move things enough and cover your tracks. I was fucking great at it.

I shook my head. "Mostly just cleaning up the mess.

Redemption Ranch is doing good business, but the organization is shit. It's chaos."

Evan slapped his hands onto his knees before pushing up to stand. "Better you than me. I'm heading back out there."

I stood with him, unsure what to say. Do we shake hands? Hug? I settled on a tip of my chin and my best attempt at a smile. "See ya around, little brother."

Evan left, taking his slumped shoulders with him. He was proof a woman could ruin a man. Take someone larger than life and whittle him down to the husk of the man he used to be. One look at him and anyone could see he was lost over that woman.

My thoughts drifted to Sienna and how often her face or body or laugh popped into my mind. Women like her were the most dangerous kind.

I DOVE INTO WORK. I needed the distraction and a little distance from the tiny cottage that seemed to always smell just like Sienna. In the cramped office, I could keep my head down and work the numbers. My door was open, and a surprising number of people walked past and offered a mild greeting. Ma had come to check in on me, give me a little direction, and introduce me to Steve. He was my main contact and up to now had managed all the ranch's finances. He didn't seem thrilled to be working with me, but his lack of organization made it clear he needed some help. Steve didn't try to micromanage me but rather gave me a stack of receipts and handwritten notes and told me to get to work.

So far, Ma and everyone else working on the ranch had given me a long leash, and I appreciated it. I wasn't sure what I expected, but a day that felt typical, even boring, was a welcomed surprise. From the outside, I doubted many would be able to tell that Redemption Ranch was anything other than a working cattle ranch.

I spent the rest of my day in silence, hammering through the work I was given. I sorted and organized, created spreadsheets, and wrote down questions. Every free moment was filled with numbers so I wouldn't think about Chicago, or my siblings, or Sienna.

"I'm out of here." Steve rapped his hand on the door-frame to catch my attention. "You should call it quits too."

I looked up from the stack of papers. I was nearly done sorting through the first mess, but my shoulders ached, and my back was tight. "Yeah. Right behind you."

I stretched in my chair as Steve walked away. A day's work felt good, especially when it seemed like the most honest day of work I'd had in a very long time. I made my way through the lodge. Nearly everyone I passed said good evening or hello. Everyone was so damn friendly. It made my clothes feel a size too small.

The cottage was a short walk from the lodge, so I took my time to stretch the muscles that had tightened from sitting all day. To my right, the path looped around a small pond, and I decided to take the long way and walk the path before heading home. I thought I would miss the noise and the buzz of the city, but there was something about the quiet that was surprisingly enjoyable.

A short distance across the adjacent pasture, two figures on horseback trotted in my direction. I recognized the whip of Sienna's flaxen hair as it trailed behind her. On the warm fall breeze, her laughter floated toward me. With her head tipped up, she laughed at something the man beside her had said. As they came into view, I recognized him instantly.

Josh was young and friendly. The way his eyes tracked her told me exactly how captivated he was by her.

Possessiveness filled my chest. The duo trotted up to me and halted the horses before reaching the fence line.

"Park!" Sienna's smile was radiant, and I was relieved the awkwardness of the morning had dissipated.

I lifted a hand in greeting, and the man's eyes snagged on my mangled hand. I tucked it into the pocket of my jeans.

"Parker, you remember Josh."

Annoyance danced through me at the fact she'd be spending her days with *Josh*. "That's great, babe."

If the pet name caught her by surprise, it didn't show. Her smile only widened as she continued to prattle on. "Josh was asking how we met, and I was just telling him about the restaurant."

Josh watched her as she leaned on the horn of the saddle. "I was telling Sienna how I met my girlfriend at the diner in town too. Apparently picking up servers is the way to go."

Girlfriend? Oh.

I warmed to him slightly, still not loving the way he looked at her in an all-too-familiar way. I offered a tight smile. "I'm headed home. You coming?"

Sienna smiled brightly. "We're going to finish our ride. I'll be home soon, husband."

I hid my smirk as I turned and offered an open-handed salute over my shoulder. I knew it was all a scheme—offering up bits of banter to play into our facade, but there was something about Sienna calling me *husband* that tugged a smile from me every damn time.

On the short walk to the cottage I thought about how free Sienna looked on top of that tan horse—her hair blowing back, a wide smile across her face. I wanted her to feel that freedom every day. She deserved to ride across the prairie with a man she would be free with. A man she could stand beside not out of obligation, but out of *love* and devotion. A man who could look other men in the eye and not fight back the demons of his past or want to rip his fucking head from his shoulders for looking in her direction. A man who had goodness inside of him.

I looked down at my hands. I had scrubbed blood from them so many times I'd lost count. I absently rubbed the smooth, scarred skin across my knuckle.

You will never be that man.

FOURTEEN
SIENNA

A SMALL GROUP gathered by the fire on Sunday after family dinner. It had been over two weeks since Parker had kissed me and I'd gotten off to the gruff sound of his voice. He hadn't mentioned it, and I hadn't dared to bring it up either. The days passed in a steady rhythm of early mornings and learning everything I could with Chet and Josh. Evenings were spent around the ranch or exploring our new town. Gemma and I had gone hiking twice, and slowly things were getting less and less awkward between the two of us. With the eclectic variety of people who worked in and around the ranch, I met someone new nearly every day.

But being alone in the cottage was hard for Parker and me, so I enjoyed the time we spent with our makeshift family.

It was barely evening, but the warmth of the fire helped chase away the chill in the autumn air. Ma and her husband, Robbie, were fascinating as they told the story of how Redemption Ranch came to be. Both federal agents, they'd fallen madly in love. Moving around the country on separate assignments and keeping secrets wasn't working for them, so she'd come up with the idea for the ranch. They could do their work but be settled. Put down roots. Robbie had found the land and helped make it happen for them. Instead of either giving up their career or forcing one to change, they'd simply changed the plan altogether.

There was beauty in that.

Parker and I dutifully played the part of a happily newlywed couple. Around the fire, he held my hand tenderly in his own. His thumb stroked the skin on the back of my hand. I leaned into his warmth or laid my head on his broad shoulder. Every so often, I caught him smelling my hair or gently brushing his lips over the top of my head.

But as soon as no one was looking, Parker's hand would drop, and he'd add an additional few inches of distance between us.

It was a farce.

Trouble was, I found I was reminding myself of that fact more and more often.

I shifted in my chair, attempting to ease the ache in my back, and Parker frowned at me.

"Hey." Gemma leaned over to whisper in our direction. "I need your help."

Parker stiffened. "Anything."

Gemma only glanced at him. "Relax, Cujo. It's nothing serious."

I barked a laugh at the nickname, and my smile softened for Gemma. "What's up?"

She rolled her eyes in the way only a nineteen-year-old with years of practice can. "Evan is the *worst*. He is so miserable."

Collectively our eyes moved to Evan as he stacked wood for the fire. The stack was meticulous, but he continued to adjust and add more logs.

"I can't take it. Can you guys invite him over sometime so he stops trying to hang out with me?"

I laughed at her predicament. Everyone around the ranch had been talking about Evan and Val's relationship and how she'd returned to her job in Chicago and Evan was pining for her. *Hard.*

It was terribly romantic.

I shared a look with Parker, and when he just shrugged, I spoke up. "Of course. Do you think he wants to go to town? We could go bowling or something."

"I doubt it. He hasn't wanted to do much of anything lately except for talk about Val and rehash every fucking moment of their relationship. He's worse than any girlfriend I ever had."

I chuckled a little at the thought of Evan being so distraught that he was driving his little sister up a wall talking about his relationship. "Park, why don't you go talk to him," I urged. "Maybe we do a dinner at our place sometime."

Gemma breathed a sigh of relief. "Yes. Thank you! I need a break. He's not the only one around here who wants something they can't have."

When I shot her a curious look, she cut herself off and sank back into her chair. I looked at Parker, who, resigned, unfolded himself from the small chair and stalked toward Evan.

When was the last time the three of them relaxed and enjoyed each other's company?

It was an awkward family reunion, but each had so much to offer. Somehow they just couldn't see it. Tension crackled along with the fledgling fire as I listened to the conversations flow around me. Evan followed Parker and sat in a chair, staring at the fire and not speaking. Parker poked the fire with a stick. Gemma's eyes met mine and went wide, silently communicating, *Do something.*

I cleared my throat. "Josh has been teaching me to ride." Parker stared at me blankly, clearly not helping me out any. I gritted through my teeth, "Doesn't a ride sound fun?"

Finally getting the hint, he straightened. "Uh, yeah. We should do that. Evan. Gem. Come take a ride with us."

Evan tore his far-off gaze from the flames and looked between us.

"Great!" chirped Gemma.

Evan nodded solemnly and followed our group as we said our goodbyes.

Ma squeezed Evan's forearm as he passed her. "Be careful now."

"Yes, ma'am."

The short walk to the paddock was quiet. Gemma and I attempted small talk with the men but ended up talking to each other as they walked in near silence. The sun sagged in the sky as the nightfall was getting earlier and earlier.

"It'll have to be a short ride," I guessed. "It's getting a little late."

I swallowed past another knot in my throat. I felt *off* but tried to brush it aside. Gemma needed help handling her brother Evan, and I was an expert at dealing with people.

"Evan, do you know how to saddle up the horses? Josh said you would."

"I do." Evan got to work with four of the horses in the main barn. Though they were workhorses, they were rested, and Josh had said an evening ride would be good exercise for them.

Once they were ready, I pointed to the large stallion by Evan. "I am not taking that one. He's pure hellfire."

"He's scary as fuck," Gemma agreed.

"Gem." Evan's quiet voice was harsh as he reprimanded his sister for her language.

"I'll take him." Parker's deep voice sent a tingle down my back.

"I want the cute one with spots," Gemma interjected.

Evan tipped his head toward the second horse. I nodded. "I can take that one."

With practiced ease, Gemma and Evan swung themselves onto the back of the horses. I was still learning, so I centered myself next to the mare. I placed one hand on the saddle horn and the other on the back of the saddle. Putting my left foot into the stirrup, I took a long, deep breath. As I hoisted myself up, strong hands wrapped around my hips, effortlessly lifting me into the saddle. I stared down at Parker's blue eyes as he looked at me.

"Thank you." My voice squeaked out breathier than I'd intended.

"Quit mooning over her and let's go." Gemma's youthful impatience forced a laugh from me, and I gently urged the horse forward, leaving Parker to mount his and catch up.

It was a warmer night. A riot of tangerine and crimson sliced through the darkening sky. Across the wide-open plains, it was stunning. Breathtaking. In the not-so-far-off distance, the mountains cut into the sky, their black silhouette only enhancing the colors of the autumn sunset.

We all stared at the sky, and I wondered what everyone was thinking. Evan seemed to relax, his tight shoulders lowering just a fraction of an inch. Gemma's horse found its pace beside Parker, and their low voices soothed the tension in my back. Aches rolled through me, and I cleared my throat again. I never liked people being at odds, and the fact that three siblings could be so close but so disconnected saddened me.

Growing up an only child, I'd longed for siblings. When my parents died, those hopes had too. I continued my silent observation of the trio, just as Gemma shifted in her saddle. She unbuttoned the front of her long-sleeve shirt and lowered it down her arms, settling it at her waist. In the fading sunlight, a flash of shiny pink skin caught my eye. Under her tank top, scars ripped across her collarbone and down one arm. I tried not to stare, but my position slightly behind her kept me hidden from her view. Parker's eyes flicked to her, and I didn't miss the way he stared straight ahead and the muscle in his jaw clenched.

Something terrible had happened to that young woman.

I trotted my horse closer, and Gemma whipped her shirt back into place. "We should head back," she said. Her voice had a slight tremble, but she clicked her tongue and increased the speed of her horse as we approached the barn.

Evan smiled at her as she trotted ahead.

"He seems like he's in a better mood. Guess we did our job."

Parker only nodded. I hated it when I couldn't figure out what my surly husband was thinking. Our horses were side by side, walking at a lazy pace back to the barn. My fingers itched to reach out, stroke the tattoos that peeked from under the sleeves he'd pushed to his elbows. More and more the tenderness and affection I thought had been blooming between us was wilting. Instead of getting more comfortable with each other, the tension seemed to stretch thin, a rubber band ready to snap.

Resigned, I lifted my chin and determined I would find a way for us to survive this marriage.

FIFTEEN

SIENNA

"You KNOW, stitching up my husband was not how I envisioned learning about wound care."

Parker flinched as I pulled the final stitch tight and cut the thread.

"Sorry." I focused on the small gash that moved across his left shoulder blade.

"It's fine." His deep voice filled the space in our cottage.

"I'd really feel better if you had this looked at by someone who actually knew what she was doing."

"I would have done it myself, but I can't reach it."

"You don't always have to be so tough, you know."

He grumbled. "You should talk."

Not fully understanding what he was implying, I stared at the broad expanse of his shoulders. The rolling hills of muscle tempted me. My hand itched to sweep across them and dip into those hills and valleys. I cleared my throat. "So what happened? The real story."

"I had a minor disagreement with a fence." Parker's discarded shirt was in a heap on the floor, and the tear across the back indicated that his story seemed true.

"I thought you were working at the office today?"

Parker tilted his head in my direction. "I was. I found something odd when I was going through receipts, and I needed to find one of the managers. Ask a few questions. I took a shortcut—slipped through a fence and snagged my shoulder."

I pulled my hand from his back. A sick feeling churned in my belly. The truth was, there were times when I had my doubts about my husband. Parker tended to be quiet, almost secretive. On a few occasions, he'd accompany me in town and tell me he needed to use the computers at the library while I shopped or got coffee at the local diner. If I offered to go with him, he'd make up an excuse or find a reason to go alone. Experience had taught me that when Parker was done talking, the conversation was over.

Sensing the mounting tension between us, Parker stood and stalked toward the bathroom. He looked at the black stitches on his back. "Not bad. Thanks."

"It's terrible. The scar is going to be pretty ugly."

Parker moved away from the bathroom and into the bedroom, where he kept his clothes. I tried to look away from the way his abs rippled as he walked. Parker pulled on a fresh T-shirt, and I swallowed disappointment as his nipple ring disappeared beneath the cotton.

"So, on Sunday, when we went for the horseback ride with Evan and Gemma . . . were those scars across her chest?"

Parker's eyes hardened. "Yes."

I blew out a breath. "Jesus. They looked terrible."

Parker started to clean up the small suture kit and didn't look me in the eyes.

"They didn't really seem that old. They were still kind of pink and angry looking, even in the low light."

He paused. "That's because they aren't old."

I toyed with my lip. I was so curious as to what had happened to her, but he seemed reluctant to say anything. The guilt painted across his face led me to believe he had had something to do with them. Had it happened when she had been taken in Chicago?

Clearly not interested in the conversation, Parker dumped the kit into the trash and washed his hands.

With his back to me, I sighed and rolled my shoulders, reaching one hand across to knead the muscles at the base of my neck. I closed my eyes and let my fingers do their work. My entire back ached.

"What's wrong with you?"

Only Parker could make that abrupt statement sound almost caring.

I opened my eyes to see him quietly assessing me. "It's nothing. I'm just tired. I've had an achy back since last week, and I can't seem to get rid of it."

Parker continued to stare at me in silence.

"My *everything* is sore. I think it's more manual labor here than I'm used to. Even being on my feet all day at the restaurant wasn't this hard. I'm just run down is all."

Finally he glanced over his shoulder. "Get some sleep."

Despising the brush-off, I made a face at his stupid muscly back as I stomped toward my bedroom. Typically, his surly demeanor was fun—a challenge—but I was too tired to go round and round with my insufferable husband. After closing my bedroom door a fraction harder than I needed to, I pouted my way under the covers and did my best to ignore the pinching sensation radiating through my back.

~

I HAD BEEN STABBED.

It was the only real way to explain the sudden slashing feeling that radiated across my back. I stifled a cry into my pillow as I gripped my right flank. My breaths came in hot pants as pain consumed me. Sweat pooled beneath me as I shifted and tried to get out of bed.

The darkness wobbled as I tried to orient myself. I was nauseated and dizzy. When I looked down at the hand that had gripped my back and there was no evidence of blood, I had no other way to explain what I was feeling. I reached for the water bottle on my bedside table. My hands shook as I brought it to my parched lips. Even the cool water didn't help the searing pain that ripped through me.

You are going to die.

Panic overtook me. I was going to die in a remote cottage in Montana, and I had no idea why. Parker's strong arms flashed through my mind. I steadied myself at the edge of the bed as reality tipped sideways.

I needed help.

I needed *him.*

Carefully I lifted to my feet and walked toward the door as I gripped my back. I steadied my breath, gripped the handle, and turned it.

The living room was dark save for a small table lamp next to the couch. Parker was looking down, reading a book, and his gorgeous face was illuminated by the light. Through the pain, it struck me that he wore black glasses I had never seen before. As my movements caught his eye, his head whipped up, his brows snapping together as he focused on me.

I could barely speak as another wave of pain ripped through me. "Park," I managed, breathing through the pain.

"I need help." Unable to steady myself, my knees rapped against the wood floor as I tumbled forward.

SIXTEEN

PARKER

I FLIPPED the pages of the paperback just as the couple in the story was finally about to fuck. I stared at the new chapter heading. I flipped back. I flipped again.

Fade to black? What the fuck is that shit?

Unable to sleep after how I'd treated Sienna, I had pulled a paperback off the shelf. The choices were limited, and though a book on bird-watching probably would have put me to sleep faster, the romance novel won out in the end.

In the quiet of the cottage, a creak and movement to my left caught me off guard. My head whipped up, and in the dim lighting, something resembling my wife lurched through the bedroom door. Sienna was hunched over, a sheen of sweat across her features.

I shot to my feet just as her face twisted.

"Park." Her voice was barely audible, and blood rang in my ears. "I need help." She crumbled, her knees slamming to the ground before I could reach her.

"Sienna!" My voice boomed through the small cottage

as I fell to her side. She continued to grip her flank. "What happened? What's wrong?" I demanded.

"I don't know. My back. It hurts so bad."

I moved beside her and pushed the thin material of her sleep shirt up her back. No bruises, no blood. I covered her again and pulled her into me. Shivers racked her small body. I sat with her curled in my lap, helpless.

I don't know what to do. I don't know what to do.

Anger pushed my fear aside as Sienna howled in pain. Tears stained her face as she sobbed. I moved to one knee, shifting my weight so one arm could loop under her legs and the other behind her back. In one swift movement, I lifted her into my arms.

"It's fine. You're fine." I wasn't sure if I was reassuring Sienna or myself, but I knew something was terribly wrong, and I had to get help. I moved to the front door and slipped my feet into shoes as I kept forward momentum.

The vast darkness of Montana swallowed me whole as I stepped into the cool night air. Pitch black covered me. I had no idea where to go. What to do. A small porch light across the way caught my eye as I adjusted a sobbing Sienna in my arms.

"Evan!" I bellowed. I didn't give a fuck if I woke the entire state of Montana. "Evan! I need you!"

In seconds a small light in the cottage across from mine flicked on.

Moments later, Evan ripped open the door to his home, the light behind him illuminating his silhouette. "Parker!" he called.

"It's Sienna. Something's wrong. We need a hospital."

"Two minutes!" he shouted across the dirt path and grass that separated our cottages. Two minutes felt like an eternity as I attempted to reassure Sienna as we moved toward my car.

I pressed my lips to her temple. She was on fire, but I kept my lips against her as I spoke. "I've got you. I'm here."

Sienna writhed and a vise gripped my chest. I faced Evan's cottage and shouted, "Evan, hurry the fuck up!"

Before I could finish, he ran out of his cottage and raced toward us. I set Sienna in the back seat and started to pull away, but she gripped my shirt.

"No!" she cried. "Please don't go."

I looked at Evan and thrust my keys at him as I slid in next to her. Evan sat in the driver's seat, cranked the engine, and tore out of the ranch without a second thought. At the entrance to the ranch, he slowed only to salute the guard on duty.

"Evan, I think she needs a hospital."

His eyes shot to me through the rearview mirror. Sienna lay next to me, clutching her back and trying to get comfortable.

"How did she get hurt?" Evan asked.

"I have no idea. She was asleep in her bedroom, and when she came out, she was crying and grabbing at her back." I turned toward her. "Sienna, baby, what happened?"

She was still crying and panting, but she attempted to talk. "I don't know. It's been sore for a few days. I just woke up, and the pain is so bad. Parker, I feel like I'm dying."

I didn't have a clue, but I placed my hand across her legs and pulled her into me. "Hurry up," I ground out as Evan flew down the country road.

~

The Tipp Medical Center was small by big-city standards, but for a town in Nowhere, Montana, it was surprisingly busy. The car slammed to a halt in front of the building, and I was pulling Sienna from the back seat before Evan had even parked.

"I'll meet you inside," he called over the roof of the car, but I didn't even acknowledge him as I scooped her up and moved through the doorway. I pushed past what looked like an EMT and a giggling nurse and thundered toward the desk.

"She needs help. A doctor."

Sienna cried out, and I tightened my grip on her.

The nurse at the station stood and hurried around the large desk. "Follow me, son." She moved past a small triage room and directly into the emergency care center. Over her shoulder she called, "Doctor Bob! I have a live one for ya."

When we entered the room, the nurse gestured toward the hospital bed, and I gingerly placed Sienna down. She writhed and crawled up the bed like a caged animal. "It hurts, Park. My back hurts so bad. I think I'm going to be sick."

Two other nurses rushed in and began examining her. "What's her name?" one asked.

"Sienna," I ground out a bit too loudly for the crowded room.

The first nurse moved toward me, pulling my arm toward the exit. I hesitated, looking back at Sienna.

"I need you to come here and answer a few questions so we can help her."

I stalled, my eyes still pinned on Sienna.

"What happened?"

Finally rational thought took over, and I rattled off the

facts that I knew. Sienna had been sleeping when she came out of the room in pain. She stated it was her back. She felt nauseated and dizzy.

The nurse nodded and began peppering me with questions I didn't have a clue how to answer—*Did she have any allergies? Has she ever had surgery? Did she take a tumble?*

"No. She didn't fall or anything. Not that I know of." I hated that I couldn't answer any of the other questions. I should know those things.

"Did you two get into a fight?"

My head whipped to meet the cold eyes of the woman in front of me. She dared let hers flick down, then up once. I towered over her, but she didn't seem the least bit intimidated.

Enraged by her insinuation that I would ever lay a hand on Sienna, it took four measured breaths to get myself under control.

"No." My voice was barely above a whisper.

She softened. "And who are you to her, dear?"

"Her husband." The answer rushed out of me without hesitation as anger filled my gut. My fists clenched at my sides after Sienna cried out again.

"Is there any chance she could be pregnant?"

My mind went blank. A hard *no* was on my lips when I faltered. I didn't think Sienna would sleep with anyone, given our arrangement. That hadn't been a part of our agreement, but we hadn't talked about it either. The bitter taste of anger and jealousy at the thought of another man's hands on my wife sent wild and violent thoughts through my brain.

"Sir?" The woman placed her hand on my tense arm, and my mind stilled.

"No. No, I don't think so."

A second nurse conferred with the one in charge of babysitting me and, with a terse nod, went back in to care for Sienna. The elderly woman's dark-brown eyes roamed my face. "We're going to take care of her. First we need to get her pain under control, and then we'll figure out exactly what's going on. I know this is difficult, but you need to give us space to figure this out."

My chest rose. There was no fucking way I was leaving her, but the sturdy woman stood her ground. Through the window, I saw Evan talking with someone who had taken over the front desk. Our eyes met and he gestured toward me.

I looked down at the old nurse. "That's my brother."

She gave me a soft, understanding smile. "We're taking care of your wife. Go."

My eyes sliced to the glass doorway separating me from Sienna's low moans. My stomach pitched and rolled, but I forced myself to move toward Evan. We met in the middle of the room with a handshake.

"Thank you."

Evan nodded and dragged a hand through his hair. "Is she okay?"

I pinched the bridge of my nose. "She better be. They're looking at her now."

"What the fuck?"

A nurse walking by scoffed at his language, but when I glowered in her direction, she turned and walked away.

"I'm sorry for waking you up like that, man. I didn't know what to do."

Evan stepped toward me, his hand clamping down on my shoulder. "I'm glad I could be here for you."

The cries from Sienna's room quieted, and I felt like I

could breathe for the first time in nearly an hour. The older nurse who'd questioned me walked toward us. I laced my fingers behind my back.

"Her pain seems to be under control right now, but the medication we gave her is quite strong. She's asleep, and you're welcome to sit with her while you wait for the doctor."

I nodded once, and Evan silently followed me toward her room. Inside, Sienna was quiet as she lay on the hospital bed. She'd been stripped of her clothing, and a gown loosely covered her. An IV and wires trailed up her arm and connected to a machine that monitored everything from her blood oxygen levels to her heartbeat and blood pressure. Evan and I settled into two small chairs at her bedside.

I stared at her beautiful face, memorizing the angles of her cheekbones and the swoop of her light lashes.

Evan's voice was barely above a whisper when he spoke. "She's not your wife, is she?" My head whipped in his direction. "In the car. You said she came out of *her* bedroom. And the other day, Gemma made a comment about how it was odd that there were blankets and a pillow on the couch, like someone was sleeping there."

Fuck. Fuck. Fuck.

I did not need this right now. I was wound tight and emotionally drained, and I did not need my little brother unraveling everything Sienna and I had tried to cover.

I ground my teeth together. "We are married."

Evan eyed me again. "But she's not your *wife*, is she? There's more to it."

I sank my elbows to my knees and pushed the heels of my hands into my eye sockets and sighed. I was so fucking tired.

"Don't lie, man. Not to me."

When I looked at him again, Evan wasn't the muscled tough guy he'd grown into. He was a scared twelve-year-old kid I had promised to protect.

SEVENTEEN

SIENNA

I STARED at the gauzy curtains of my bedroom window as an autumn breeze lifted them. With a low groan, I slowly pushed myself to a sitting position. The light beyond the mountains was a soft petal pink. I had come home from the hospital yesterday, still hopped up on pain medications, and now I wasn't sure if it was evening or morning.

"I told you to stay in bed." Parker's rough voice danced over my skin, making goose bumps erupt on the surface.

I glanced over my shoulder. "I'm getting stiff. I can't stay in bed again all day." His brows were drawn down low over his blue eyes. He looked pale. Tired.

"Just a minute on the couch, maybe," I pleaded.

Without a word, Parker moved toward me, barely touching my elbow as he guided me around the bed and into the living room. We walked slowly through the cottage. My back was sore, and my body ached in places I didn't know existed before this week. As I glanced around, I noticed the cottage was pristine. Parker was very tidy, but the entire house looked like it had been scrubbed and polished.

"Wow. It's so clean in here."

He harrumphed but didn't respond.

Every surface was glossy and free of clutter. The counters were wiped clean, every dish put away. The green knit throw blanket was artfully draped across the sitting chair, and a small vase of wildflowers was on the table. "Did you do all this?"

He appeared exasperated at my questioning. "The flowers are from Gemma, but . . ." He looked around the small space before lifting one chiseled shoulder. "Sometimes I stress-clean."

I arched an eyebrow, and he turned away, swatting the small pillow out of my way and onto the floor. Parker helped me settle into the worn-in couch, and I sighed.

"Are you in pain?"

I shook my head. "No, I'm feeling pretty good today. Just stiff, like I said." Tension wound around him. I grabbed his left hand and tightened my grip when he tried to pull away. "Sit with me, Park."

He hesitated, looking around the cottage for anywhere else he'd rather be. Finally he folded his large frame into the couch, his weight pulling me closer to him.

Parker grabbed a glass of water from the side table and pushed it toward me. "Drink this."

The growly command had a small smile teasing the corner of my mouth, but I took a small sip to hide it. "You're so grouchy."

"I'm not grouchy. The doctor said after kidney stones, you need to up your fluid intake. Do you want to get sick again?"

Knowing he was right, I let the ice water cool my dry mouth. It had been two days since Parker and Evan had rushed me to the medical center. After a series of tests, they'd discovered my flank pain was caused by a rather large kidney stone. Two, in fact.

It was the most intense pain I'd ever experienced.

Parker had stayed by my side as the doctor explained the procedure to remove the stones, and the pain medication had helped to keep me comfortable. By the next day, I had been released to go home and rest while I recovered. The procedure had left me feeling wiped and more than a little sheepish around my new husband.

Since we'd returned to the cottage, he was short and bristly, but also doting and attentive.

My stomach growled loudly, and I pressed a hand into it.

"You're hungry." Parker shot to his feet and stalked into the kitchen. I was healthy enough to appreciate his ass and the way it moved in his jeans as he walked, and I smiled a little to myself. When he pulled open the refrigerator door, I couldn't believe my eyes.

"Where did all that come from?"

Parker stepped to the side, allowing me a full view of the stocked fridge. Take-out containers and ceramic dishes lined the shelves, one stacked on top of another.

"You slept all day yesterday and most of today. It has been nonstop." Parker rubbed a finger and thumb over his eyes. "Everyone has been stopping by to check in on you."

I shook my head in disbelief. A prickly and uncomfortable feeling washed over me. I wasn't used to someone taking care of me. I was always the one checking in on people, bringing food, volunteering to help. Being on the receiving end of it was an odd sensation.

"Who's everyone?" I asked.

Parker selected a container from the fridge and started piling the food onto a plate. "Literally everyone. Ma, the young agent, Daniel, who gives you puppy eyes all the time, Evan and Gemma, Chet and Josh, of course." He thought some more. "That guy who runs the clothing store. Even Al, the bartender at the Rasa, stopped by."

My tummy rumbled again. "Did he bring pie?"

Parker shot me a bland look. "You'll get pie when you eat real food."

I glared at his back and shot him my best pout.

After hearing the beep of the microwave, I pushed to my feet and padded toward the kitchen table. "I think I'm okay. Just worn down, mostly."

"The doctor said you'll live."

I smiled at my gruff and crabby man. Part of me was beginning to understand and appreciate his rough facade. I suspected that underneath the stony exterior was a worrier.

"I'm sorry if I was a bother." My voice was barely a whisper, but he'd caught it.

Parker stepped toward me, placing both of his large palms on my shoulders. "You aren't a bother. I didn't know how to help you. I..." Parker paused, cleared his throat, and turned. "Eat."

I settled into the chair and ate for the first time in three days. The warm food was comforting and eased the chill that felt nestled into my bones. A small fire burned in the fireplace, and I smiled at Parker.

"You got it working."

He nodded. "It's getting colder at night. Evan and I cleaned it out, and it heats the place up pretty quickly."

"It's cozy."

Parker continued to roam the cottage like a caged animal while I picked at the spaghetti and meatballs on my plate, trying to figure out how to talk to him. "These meatballs are pretty good," I tried.

"Mmph," he muttered, then disappeared into the bedroom for a moment before returning bare chested and holding a fresh T-shirt. My mouth hung open, and my eyes snagged on his nipple ring again.

"They're not as good as the ones at Solitario."

That caught my attention, and my chest swelled like a balloon. "Those were my meatballs! I'm glad you liked them." I felt a renewed sense of happiness at his unintentional compliment as I scooped up a heaping forkful of spaghetti.

He paused before pulling the black cotton shirt over his head. "Why do you think I got the meatball sandwich every damn time?"

I smiled around a mouthful of food and shrugged. As Parker turned to pull his shirt on, I noticed the fresh bandage covering the wonky stitches I'd done on him. I swallowed the food and noted, "Hey! You got a new bandage."

He glanced over his shoulder as though I hadn't stitched him up like Frankenstein's monster only a few days earlier. "Uh, yeah. I popped a stitch. A nurse at the hospital noticed."

My brows came together. "What do you mean?"

"I think one came loose when I was carrying you. One of the nurses noticed blood on my shirt and offered to clean me up."

I groaned and laid my head in my hands. "Oh god. I'm sorry. I'm sure they saw how horrible the stitches were. I hope she could fix them."

Parker moved toward the fridge. "She offered but I didn't let her. Told her to slap a new Band-Aid on it and call it good."

"Why? It's so bad. You don't even know because you can't see it."

He straightened as he grabbed a beer from the fridge. "I told her my wife did them and not to touch it."

My cheeks burned as I rose to clear my plate. Behind me, Parker crowded my space to grab the plate and fork from my hands and rinse them in the sink.

"I got it."

I swiped my hands down my pants, suddenly feeling nervous in his presence. "Thanks. For everything."

With a full belly, fatigue threatened to overtake me, and I stifled a yawn.

"You should rest." His deep voice was velvet over gravel, and a tingle raced up my back.

"I know," I agreed. "My body is tired, but my mind is all over the place. I don't think I can sleep."

"Sienna, you need to rest."

I nodded and started toward the bedroom. "Hey, Park?" He looked up from the sink, and I gathered every ounce of courage I could to form the next words. "Keep me company for a little while?"

He braced his hands on the sides of the sink, probably thinking about my ridiculous request. An eternity passed between us. Then he nodded, and my heart leaped to my throat as he walked toward the bedroom.

Still the doting caretaker, Parker pulled back the covers so I could slip underneath them. He smoothed them over me as I wiggled down to get comfortable. I'd hoped he would get under the covers with me, but he sat on top of the comforter, his thick, muscular thighs stretched across the top and his back straight against the headboard. For a long while, we sat in silence, just listening to the country sounds outside my bedroom window.

When I found my voice, it was braver than I'd imagined. "Thank you, again, for what you did for me. When I woke up in the middle of the night, I was alone. In pain. It was terrifying."

My eyes swooped up to him as he stared ahead. His throat bobbed, and he swallowed before answering. "When you came out of the room like that, I didn't know what to do. That's not something I'm used to."

I couldn't help but smirk. I understood. "You're the man with the answers."

He laughed a little at that. "Usually." His deep-blue eyes slid down to me. "But with you, it's always something. Something new or unexpected. To be honest, I was scared shitless."

I turned my body to face him and tucked my hands under my cheek. "You were very brave. You got help, and you got me the help I needed."

His eyes looked at me again, but then I felt their heavy weight move down my body, and I warmed.

"I've been alone my whole life." The words were out before I fully understood why I needed them spoken out loud. To admit to him my truth.

He looked down at me, waiting.

"Uncle Davis was a good man. My parents died in an accident when I was twelve." I swallowed past the thickness in my throat. "House fire while I was at a sleepover."

"Jesus." The word was barely a whisper.

"Davis was my mom's brother," I continued, feeling brave in Parker's presence. "He took me in without question. But he was a bachelor. He owned the restaurant, worked crazy hours. I was alone a lot." I fought the tears of my lonely childhood and missing my parents and my sweet uncle and blinked them away.

When I didn't add more, Parker shifted, getting more comfortable in the bed beside me. "The other night, when I didn't know what to do, the first thought I had was, *Get Evan.*" He shook his head lightly. "I don't even know why, but I knew I had to. That he'd know what to do, because I was frozen."

I placed my hand on Parker's tattooed forearm. It was strong and warm under my hand, and a hot buzz radiated up my fingers and across my chest. "That's okay. It's okay to need people sometimes. Being there for someone—being connected. That's something I've always wanted. And he's your brother. You trust him, right?"

Parker looked at me, his eyes a jumble of dark blues as he considered what I was asking. "I'm not used to trusting anyone." A beat passed between us as my heart broke for him. "I think I want to though."

"I think you two will figure it out. Gemma too."

Parker released a humorless laugh. "Get some sleep."

But he didn't leave. Instead, he settled a little deeper into the bed, and I closed my heavy eyes. I left my hand on his arm, and when he didn't move it from under my hand, I quieted the sigh that threatened to escape.

"Good night, wife."

A grin broke across my face in the darkness as I squeezed my eyes closed tighter and drifted to sleep with the sound of Parker's steady breathing in the air and the smell of him in bed.

"Good night, husband."

EIGHTEEN
SIENNA

Sometime in the middle of the night, Parker had gone from stoically sitting, propped up against my headboard, to stretching his long, muscular body down the length of my bed. It was still dark, but the morning sun was just peeking over the mountain in the distance. Barely opening my eyelids, I squinted in the indigo darkness and tried to make out the angular lines of his disgustingly handsome face.

Parker was still asleep. His heavy breaths rolled in and out of him in deep, soothing waves. I laughed a bit to myself —even in his sleep he sounded irritated. On his back, I had tucked myself under one arm, a nook that fit me perfectly. A quiet thrill danced through me as I took in the warmth of the arm that was clamped around my back, pulling me in tight. I wanted to run my palm down his chest and over the ridges of his abs—and *lower*.

One leg was hitched over his muscular thigh. Heat raced through me as a dull throb had me tipping my hips forward and pressing my thigh into his. My body was screaming for more pressure, and it wasn't nearly satisfied with the brush of Parker's thigh against me. My subtle movement stirred him, and my eyes clamped shut.

God, he smells good.

I willed my breaths to be steady and prayed he couldn't tell that I was already awake. As the fog of sleep lifted, Parker stilled. I felt the weight of his head lift from the pillow. Gently he shifted out from underneath the tangle of my limbs.

Crestfallen, I continued pretending to sleep as Parker slipped out of the bed and into the twilight of the morning. He crossed the room almost silently, and it wasn't until the bedroom door clicked shut that I let out the breath I was holding and opened my weary eyes. I rolled to look at the ceiling as I heard the shower groan to life through the thin cottage walls.

Do not picture him naked. Do. Not.

I bet he looks damn good, though.

Dammit.

I let out a frustrated breath, and for a fraction of a second I considered a quickie with my toy, just to ease the pressure between my legs, but ultimately I just lay there in frustration. I willed myself to get out of bed and get ready for the day. Though I was still going to take it easy, I planned to be back at work to help Chet and Josh with the animals.

I swung my legs off the bed and tested my back and limbs, stretching my arms above my head and bending left and right. A little achy, but I felt better than I had in days. Wrapped up against Parker's muscular body, I'd slept like a rock. Frenetic energy buzzed in my veins every time I thought about how tightly he'd held me as we slept.

A girl could get used to that.

After getting dressed for the day, I practically danced

my way out of the bedroom. Parker's hulking frame was hunched over the coffee maker, and when I'd offered a cheery "Good morning!" his low grumble was the only response I received.

"Poor night's sleep?" I knew damn well he'd slept like a baby.

Dark shadows crossed his face as his eyes moved over me. "I didn't mean to fall asleep in there. It won't happen again."

I tamped down the gush of disappointment. Instead of reacting, I simply grabbed an apple and took a juicy bite. "Huh," I said around the chunk wedged into my cheek. "I didn't even notice."

A muscle ticced in his jaw, and I secretly loved knowing that sleeping next to me left him as rattled as it had me. I slipped on my boots, determined to beat him out the door, and called over my shoulder, "Have a good day, husband!"

Parker bellowed as I clicked the door behind me. "Take it easy today!"

For the entire walk to the barn I had a huge smile plastered to my face. Parker may play a good game, but I saw it plain as day on his face. He was a closet cuddler, and waking up in each other's arms had felt damn good. So good that it pissed him right off. There was no way he could tell me otherwise.

THE HEAT and afternoon sun stung my eyes as I wiped the sweat away with my T-shirt.

"Hanging in there?" Concern wove into Chet's voice as he looked me over.

"Yep," I replied. "All good."

Josh nudged a bottle of water toward me, and I smiled in relief. He winked once, and I twisted the cap off and slugged down half the bottle.

I held on to the reins of my horse as we paused and looked over the rambling herd. The bumps and bounces weren't great for my aching back, but I gritted my teeth and focused on what Chet was trying to teach us.

We paused to look at the expanse of a sprawling pasture. Nothing but sweeping, breath-stealing nature as far as I could see. I tipped my face upward, soaking in the sun. "Do you ever feel like you could just get lost?"

Chet let loose a small chuckle, but his back was to us. "Lotsa things can get lost out here. Sometimes people come lookin'—sometimes they don't."

I shot Josh a questioning glance when he wiggled his fingers and silently mouthed *Wooooo* at Chet's ominous tone. I swatted at him and rolled my eyes.

At my chuckle, Chet called over his shoulder as he looked onto the herd in the distance. "Take a peek at that group over there." His long, wrinkled finger stretched out toward the pasture with cattle lazing in the sun. Josh and I sat for a long while, looking at the cows. With their long horns and floppy bangs, I couldn't help but smile. Some chewed, others rested. One Highland cow bled into another until I wasn't sure at all what we were even looking for.

Chet slowly eased his horse forward, trying not to scare them off, and we followed. "See that one there?" I peered out, trying to see what he was showing us. "Let's get that one out of here."

Josh nodded once, but I asked, "Why?"

"She's not doin' good."

I looked again, trying to see what Chet was seeing. To me, it didn't appear any different from a hundred other nameless cattle. Cute, but nothing remarkable to indicate why Chet had singled her out.

Chet used the moment to help me understand. "Live here long enough and it'll be clear as day. You'll start to see the signs of stress—dilated nostrils, tension in the brow line above the eyes." Chet's arms and hands animated his lesson. "Sometimes you'll see ears pinned backward or a hitch in their gait. Those are all signs that something's off."

"So you separate the cow until you can figure out what's wrong with her."

Chet tipped his hat with a wink. "Exactly. Could be something. Could be nothing."

I smiled, filled with pride that I had figured it out.

Chet wrote something in the small leather pad he kept with him—I assumed notes on the herd—and placed it back in the saddlebag. "Let's round 'er up." He clicked his tongue and trotted his horse toward the group of lazing cattle.

"You're a quick study, city girl." Josh shot me a smile, and a bubble of pride burst in my chest. I was learning that, at Redemption, people were encouraging, understanding. There was no room for false pride or pretenses. If you were eager and willing to learn, there were a thousand lessons willing to be taught. The sense of purpose and community was nearly overwhelming.

I had never felt so *connected* to a place or its people before. Redemption Ranch was special, and a small part of me hoped I'd never have to leave.

～

As THE DAY unfolded into evening, Parker was a ghost, and I found myself annoyed that I didn't know where he was.

Now I'm a nag. Awesome.

I closed the refrigerator, unsatisfied with the unending choices in front of me. A soft knock at the door had me hopeful for some company and conversation. After I pulled it open and found Gemma peeking up from under her blunt bangs, my smile grew wider.

"Gem!"

"Hey, Sienna." Her tentative voice gave me pause.

"Come on in." I moved aside.

"Actually, I was headed into town. I thought you might want to come with me."

Still slightly annoyed that I didn't know where Parker was and excited for some time with Gemma, I decided, *Fuck it.* "I would *love* to."

After slipping on my canvas sneakers, I tossed the strap of my purse over my head and headed toward the beat-up truck parked haphazardly across my lawn.

As Gemma drove, I realized it was a mistake letting her behind the wheel. I braced myself against the door. Holding on to the *oh shit* bar on the ceiling, I tried not to wince as I was bounced around the cab. Gemma's eyes barely met the road, and I rolled my lips together, silently praying we made it to town in one piece.

Finally the long stretch of Main Street came into view. The early evening sun was shining, and shoppers meandered in and out of the buildings. Flowers overflowed from baskets, and flags billowed from the streetlamps. Warm affection for the strange little town filled my chest. If I could stop time, I would take a picture—the flats of Montana flanking the city at the base of a mountain so I would never forget that exact snippet of time.

The truck screeched to a slamming halt, and we pitched forward as Gemma threw the truck in park. "Did you eat?"

"Not yet," I answered as I exited the truck and followed

her toward Brewed Awakening, the small café and coffee shop.

She pointed at the shop. "This okay?"

I smiled at her and nodded.

The smell of coffee and fresh baked treats hit me as we opened the door and walked inside. The shop was busy and curious eyes met ours. I smiled as most returned my greeting with a smile or tip of the hat.

"So different from the first time," I mused.

"What's up?" Gemma asked.

I waved the thought away. "Nothing. Just thinking how different Tipp is from my first impression."

Gemma stepped closer and looped her arm in mine in a surprising but welcome gesture. "It's the best-kept secret in the West."

Together we placed our order, and I insisted on paying —her brother's treat.

"I'm glad you're feeling better." Gemma sipped her latte, the foam decorated with trailing hearts across the top.

"Me too. It was awful." I took a sip of my own coffee, trying to read Gemma's expression. "Parker was great though," I said absently.

"I'm not gonna lie. That was surprising."

I tilted my head in question at her statement.

"I mean, I know you're his 'wife' or whatever, but still." Gemma used air quotes over the word *wife* and prickles danced along my spine.

I raised an eyebrow. "I am his wife." The words came out so naturally, even I almost believed them.

"Look," she said as she put her latte on the table between us. "Parker has always been a lone wolf. He was pretty high up in Chicago and didn't fuck around. People were *afraid* of him."

The Mafia. Parker was well connected and involved with some very scary people. I smiled at the image of a gruff Parker scowling across a table of criminals—he'd fit right in. It wasn't hard to imagine him intimidating plenty of people back in Chicago, but I couldn't bring myself to think too hard about all the bad things he'd likely done. Sure he was still grouchy all the time, but the intimidating image was at odds with the man who wore black reading glasses and cleaned when he felt stressed.

The overwhelming need to defend him bubbled to the surface. "Park is complicated—even I'm learning that."

Gemma shrugged in resignation. "I can see that." For a minute we both looked around the coffee shop, picking at our food and watching the people who filtered in and out. "He asked me to hang out."

My eyes flew to Gemma as a wide smile split my face. "That's great!"

She picked at her nails before dragging the collar of her chambray shirt closer to the center, covering the barely visible scars that peeked out from her collar. I placed my hand over hers. "Give him a chance, Gem. I think he'll surprise you."

Her stark blue eyes met mine, and a resigned smile crossed her lips. "He's lucky he has you. I like you too much to hate you both."

A genuine laugh tore from me as I settled back into my chair. I fluffed the waves in my blonde hair, picking up the ends to check how damaged and frayed they were starting to look. "The dusty air is brutal for my hair. Maybe we need a beauty day soon."

"I would love that!" Gemma lit up. "Since Val left, I have been missing having a girlfriend around here."

"I'm sorry I didn't get to meet her."

Sadness flitted across her face, but she seemed to brush it away. She was hurting from missing her friend. "I'm hopeful Evan can get her back. He has to."

"Well, then, I hope so too. But what about you?" I asked.

"What about me?" Gemma flipped her cropped blonde bob as she looked at me.

"You've been here nearly a year, right? No hot young bull rider caught your eye yet?"

Gemma rolled her ocean eyes, but something dark passed across them. "Hardly." She chewed her lip a bit before continuing. "There was someone I thought might work out, but . . ."

I slowly sipped my coffee, hoping she'd miss my excitement and continue. I *loved* a good love story, and Gemma's story was so sad that I prayed she found a happy ending.

"He was . . . I don't know. It wasn't something that would ever work out. Besides, he's not interested."

"A local?" I could barely contain my squealing interest, so one-word questions were going to have to do.

"Something like that."

A silence stretched between us as realization dawned on me. "An agent?"

Gemma leaned forward, shushing me. "It's nothing. Nothing happened." Hurt was evident on her face, and my heart ached for her. Young love was something that always stung, just a little.

"I'm sorry it didn't work out."

We got lost in the next two hours talking about life in Montana, her college courses, and everything I'd learned about the animals. I could feel us clicking into a fast and easy friendship. Gemma was reserved and had her secrets— I didn't ask any more questions about the mysterious agent who'd broken her heart or her scars and the life she'd left behind in Chicago.

When the fading sun sank behind the mountain and the streetlamps flickered on, we decided it was time to head home.

Gemma bounced toward the driver seat, but I stopped her. "How 'bout I drive home." She grinned before tossing me the keys.

NINETEEN
PARKER

Luc Dubois's chest filled at the sight of Adriana, with her hand running a burning trail across his solid wood desk—the exact spot where he had spent countless hours poring over maps and strategy for the men. He did not miss this invitation. He moved toward her silent siren's song as she hitched a hip onto the solid surface. The billowy layers of her dress gathered at her supple hips as she crossed one leg over the other and sent him a sultry tip of one eyebrow.

"Luc Dubois." Adriana's heady voice was low and thick. "You will make good on your promise."

Luc gripped the sword sheathed at his side and reveled in the warmth of the worn leather as it bit into his palm. Luc had made many sinful promises to Adriana. Promises he intended to keep, if only for tonight.

I lowered the paperback and swiped my glasses off, rubbing my eyes and slightly readjusting myself to accommodate the growing chubby the old paperback had inadvertently given me.

Shit, Luc. Get it, man.

I popped my glasses back on and smoothed the book through my hands. When boredom set in without Sienna home, I'd grabbed it off the shelf. It was one of many romances on the bookshelf and promised a tale of adventure and lust rolled into one. While it looked innocent enough, I discovered the innocuous front cover was hiding a half-naked couple in the throes of passion behind it. I turned to the author's picture at the end. An elderly woman with kind eyes smiled back at me. She looked like she baked cookies and patted your cheek and told you that you were a *sweet boy*. The grandmother I had once wished I had. I thought back to the swashbuckling action and explicit love scenes that I couldn't seem to put down.

Goddamn, Grandma, you're a freak.

As I was about to dive back into *The Conqueror of Desire*, the knob of the cottage turned, and the door pushed open. Panicking, I shoved the book between the cushions of the couch and did my best to look casual. My heart hammered behind my ribs as Sienna waved behind her, then entered.

I cleared my throat and it caught her attention.

She turned, her cheeks pink with excitement or maybe surprise at me sitting in the darkened living room, I couldn't tell.

She took in my simple white T-shirt and jeans, and her pupils stretched, making her eyes nearly black. Her attention snagged on my chest, and I tamped down the urge to stomp toward her, pull her against me, and make Luc Dubois proud. The hand at my hip brushed the corner of the hidden paperback, and I shoved it farther down into the crack between the couch cushions.

Her eyes lasered in on the seat beside me. "What is that?"

Fuck.

"Hmm?"

"That." She pointed at my hand. "What are you hiding?"

I scoffed, trying my best to look annoyed or disinterested. I pulled my glasses from my face and tossed them on the coffee table.

"You shoved something into the couch." Her tone was dangerously accusatory, and my back stiffened. She was a half step from the couch. "Look, if you're hiding something, I want to know."

She could easily reach down and find my lurid little secret. It was completely childish, but I knew the only way to get her off my ass was to distract her.

I hardened my voice. "Where have you been? You didn't tell me you were going out."

"What?" Confusion twisted her beautiful face.

"You heard me." I hated the cold and dismissive tone I had suddenly adopted.

"Excuse me?" Sienna squared herself and planted both hands on her slim hips.

I stood, crossing my arms and staring down at her. I did my best to ignore the tiny part of me that was proud of her for not withering under my glare. "You didn't tell me you were going out. I think I should know."

"You know what?" Sienna's hands flew through the air as anger rattled her tiny body. "This is stupid. I don't need your permission to go out."

"I'm your husband, and I say that you do." Heat flashed in her eyes. If she could murder me on a ranch crawling with federal agents, I would have bet she'd have done it.

I lowered my voice, nailing my coffin shut. "We're *married*. Act like it."

Sienna ground her molars to dust as we stood in a stand-off, me glaring down at her, praying she didn't call my bluff, and her standing with her neck craned, shooting death lasers from her eyes.

"Aren't I?" Sienna's voice had gone frigid as she tipped one eyebrow. I'd been in more tense meetings with violent men than I cared to admit, but in that moment, Sienna was a force to be reckoned with. Fierce. "Married people fight all the time, *husband*." The word dripped with disdain, and a sharp pain lanced through my rib cage.

She glared.

I stared harder.

"Fine." She stormed forward, reaching her hand into the cushions before I could grab her to stop. "What the hell is this?" Sienna yelled as she pulled the paperback from its hiding place. I wrapped my arms around her, trying to tear the book from her hands, but she'd jutted her hips backward, blocking my attempts.

Sienna held *The Conqueror of Desire* over her head like a preacher spreading the gospel to his congregation with his Bible. She paused and stared at the paperback as I straightened and shoved my hands into my front pockets.

She looked at the book, then back to me, then back again. Clearly it was not what she had expected to unearth from the couch. Sienna opened her mouth to speak, then snapped it shut. My nostrils flared, but I refused to look away.

As shock gave way to realization, I could see the bubble of laughter rise from her belly and fizz out of her. Tears filled her eyes as she fought against the giggle. Finally the dam broke free, and Sienna doubled over in howling laughter.

I stormed toward her and ripped the book from her hands. "You know what? Fuck off."

My words made her laugh harder as she bent at the waist and held her sides. I stalked to the bookshelf and shoved the book in the first empty space I could find.

Through her laughter she attempted to speak. "Parker." She wiped a tear from her eye. "Park, I'm sorry. Really. It's fine."

I glared at her again—rooted to the ground. Silence had always been my armor, but her tinkling laughter was peppering dents at an alarming rate.

"You—" Another round of laughter tittered out of her. "You read smutty historical romance. It's totally fine."

I stood as her laughter filled the cottage, breathing life into it, and I did my best to act annoyed. *Unmoved.* To act like I didn't love the sound and was willing to endure her mocking to hear it one more time.

"I just have to know." Sienna steadied her breathing and tried to get ahold of herself. "Please tell me it's a bodice ripper and the wealthy landowner is chasing the virginal heroine." She could barely contain another fit of giggles.

"Actually," I ground out, "Luc is a pirate with a strict moral code, and he's interested in more than Adriana's . . ." I stared at her, steeling my voice with nonchalance. "Delicate flower."

Her eyes went wide as her head tipped back in a cackling laugh. It was my undoing. I couldn't help but let the tug of my smile creep across my face. In the glow of the fading evening light, the column of Sienna's throat taunted me. The thin cords dipped together at the base of her neck and I wanted—needed—my mouth on her.

In long strides I stormed toward her.

Sienna's delicate hands flew up. "Parker, I'm sorry, it's just so—"

I gripped the back of her neck and hauled her against me, crushing her lips to mine. My arm wound around her back, lifting her from the ground as I pressed her into me. My tongue invaded her mouth, and I moaned. I kissed her the way I'd dreamed of kissing her every day since I'd first seen her in the restaurant.

Sienna had become the only thing that truly scared me. It would be brutal when I watched her walk away from this. I shoved those thoughts down as I kissed the fuck out of my wife.

I set her down only long enough to reach behind her and haul her up, wrapping her thighs around my waist. I grabbed her ass and pulled her tight against me. My hard cock ached as she tipped her hips and rode the ridge of it through the denim.

Sienna tasted like lemon cookies and warm summer days. I poured myself into the kiss. She shuddered as my hands raked across her torso. I was rough and demanding. Any second Sienna would pull away, realize what we were doing, and tell me to quit.

She didn't.

A tiny gasp escaped her throat as I savored the skin at her neck. That breathless noise shot into me, and heaviness settled between my legs. Sienna's hands tangled into my hair as I moved my mouth over her. One hand found the hem of her shirt, and I dragged my nails up her back.

Sienna's head whipped up, and I expected to see fear or disgust.

Her eyes were black with lust.

It was a mistake. I'd promised not to touch her and in one move had cracked that promise wide open.

"Tell me to stop," I whispered against her flushed skin.

"Don't you dare fucking stop."

I hitched her up as my mouth took hers again. I carried her toward the bedroom, my tongue slipping into her mouth, and I sampled her again. Sienna was crawling up my body, pressing her heat into me as I made my way across the cottage to her bed.

When I leaned forward, she didn't release me—rather she held tight and brought me down on top of her. When her back hit the mattress, she moaned and her knees tipped open. I pressed her into the mattress with my weight. My heart raced as I felt how perfectly she fit against me.

I fucking knew it.

Sienna looked up at me, her fingers stroking down my face and off the tip of my nose. My cock throbbed as I endured the intensity of her stare. I wanted Sienna more than I'd wanted any woman in my life. But this was fake. She wasn't really my wife. When it was all over, she'd walk away like everyone else and leave me a husk of the man I once was.

Her hands moved under my T-shirt and across my abdomen, branding me with her touch. Her thumb found the metal bar through my nipple and she tipped her hips up as she smoothed her thumb across it. I cupped her breast through her shirt, and she arched into my grip. I thrust my hands upward, pulling the shirt from her and tossing it aside. She clawed at me as our kisses grew frantic and messy. I peeled my shirt above my head and flexed my abs for her. The lusty appreciation that moved across her face had a feral pride filling my chest. Sienna gripped my shoulders and ground her hips into me.

Her nails skated low as she pulled at the button of my jeans. I made quick work of stripping them off, taking my boxer briefs with them. My hard cock bobbed between my thighs, and I gripped it in my fist. One tug—I needed something to ease the tension building at my core.

Sienna had peeled her slim jeans and panties down and leaned back on her elbows across the bed. The gentle curves of her bare tits and hips were a buffet, and I was ravenous.

"Sienna." One word. A warning.

She sank her teeth into her lower lip, and my dick jumped. I needed to be balls deep in that woman or I was going to lose my mind. When she tipped her knees, spreading her glistening pink pussy open for me, I took the invitation.

I covered her body with mine, capturing her lips as I groaned into her mouth. One hand dipped lower, skating across her hip and over the heat between her thighs. I dragged one knuckle up the seam of her pussy.

Soaked.

I pulled the knuckle to my mouth and sucked. "So. Fucking. Wet." Before she could moan again, I smashed my mouth against her, sharing her sweet taste that danced across my tongue. I hoisted her thighs closer, pushing her open as my hips settled in the cradle of her hips. I could feel the heat and pulse of her need as I pressed my hard length against her. She squirmed and lifted her hips, begging for me to split open that sweet, slick cunt.

Her legs were splayed open, her arms wrapped around my torso, pulling me against her. I dipped my tongue into the hollow of her collarbone. Her pulse ticced against my mouth as I sucked the thin skin. We were both panting, lost in each other, our hands grasping and exploring.

I pulled back to look at her. Sienna was gorgeous.

Flushed and naked and pliant. She was offering her body in sacrifice, and I would pay tribute to every inch of her.

I swallowed past the gravel in my throat. "You deserve so much more."

"Parker." Her breathless moan nearly tore me apart.

I captured her mouth in a kiss, gripped my aching cock, and centered myself at her entrance. In one rough thrust, I was buried deep in my wife. We both groaned. Sienna was tight, gripping every solid inch of me. I stilled as she adjusted, her inner walls squeezing me, drawing my balls up, desire forming into a hot needy orb at the base of my spine.

I held the bulk of my weight above her, and when her greedy hips pushed upward, I started dragging my dick out and filling her back up. My cock was soaked as I pumped my hips into her. Sienna took my face into her hands, and we kissed again, her breath pushing out with the rhythm of my thrusts. I grunted into her, willing to be buried deeper as I fucked her hard.

She wrapped her legs around me as my hand slid down to find the diamond peak of her nipple. I rolled it between two fingers and reveled in the squeeze of her pussy. I was hurtling toward my release when I dropped my mouth to her ear. I murmured every dirty and delicious fantasy I'd had about her since Chicago. How tight she was. How hard I got at the mere sight of her. How I planned to fuck her on every surface of that cottage.

Sienna cried out.

"That's it. Soak this cock. Feel me stretch you open as you come all over it." At my rough and dirty words, Sienna fell apart. Her thighs shook as her orgasm tore through her. I was seconds behind her. Pressing my hips forward, I poured my release into her. I groaned her name. After steadying my breath, I dropped to the side, taking her with me. One leg was still hitched over my hip as I stayed planted inside her. I couldn't leave the warmth of her quite yet.

We were both covered in a sheen of sweat, and our ragged breathing filled the cottage. Reality slowly filtered in as the spots behind my eyelids subsided.

"Fuck. We didn't use a condom." I slowly slipped out of her, turning onto my back and staring at the ceiling.

"I'm clean and on the pill. It's been"—her voice dipped low—"a really long time since I've been with anyone."

"Same for me."

Sienna propped herself onto her elbow and looked at me skeptically.

A smile cracked at the corner of my mouth, and I put one hand in the air. "I swear to you. I haven't dated or fucked around in a long time." I thought back to exactly when, and it struck me. "Since I first saw you in Chicago, actually."

A smile bloomed on her face, and my chest tightened. "Is that so?"

I flicked a fingertip across the tip of her nose. "I guess I was all hung up on some waitress."

TWENTY

SIENNA

I LET the bathroom water run hot as I steadied myself against the sink. My legs were still shaking from the intensity of sex with Parker.

Holy shit. We just had sex.

I blew out a slow breath, but my heart still collided with my ribs at an alarming rate. I made quick work of cleaning up. The post-orgasmic glow was wearing off, and fatigue was starting to settle in. Paired with it was a healthy dose of anxiety.

What now? I had just had the most life-altering sex ever. Was this a thing we did now? Was it a one-and-done situation?

Ugh, I hope not.

The tiny spark of hope that something had permanently shifted in our relationship was blooming. Barely there, the little ember had settled into my chest.

I shook my head. I knew that couldn't be what Parker was thinking. There was no way he saw what happened between us as something more than releasing the weeks of tension that had built between us.

I made quick work of cleaning up, expecting to find Parker back on the couch and ready for bed. When I peeked into the living room, it was empty. Listening carefully, I tiptoed toward the bookshelf and found the book Parker had been reading when I got home.

The Conqueror of Desire.

I snickered to myself again and walked back to my bedroom. To my surprise, Parker's large frame was tucked under the covers of my bed. A tingle of excitement danced through me as I took in his impossibly large frame. His broad, tattooed shoulders took up nearly the entire bed, and he lay on his side, propping his head on one hand.

My eyes roamed over him, nerves competing with the hum of desire that pumped through my blood.

As I stood, stuck in the doorway, Parker rolled his gorgeous navy eyes in my direction before pulling the sheet back. "Just get over here."

I smiled. The man did nothing but frown and glower. As I walked toward the bed, I flipped the paperback toward him. It landed directly in front of his naked torso, and he shot me a bland look. I fought against the smile that pulled at the corner of my mouth.

"I'm not making fun." I put both hands up in surrender.

He picked up the book and flipped through the pages. "I got bored."

I nodded. "Mm-hmm."

"But then," he continued, "it got pretty good. Did you know how dirty these things are?"

I laughed as I tucked myself under the sheet and looked up at him. "Is that where you learned to do that thing with your hips?"

A low growl rumbled in his throat as he leaned forward, looming over me. "That was all me, wife."

Parker's use of *wife* again had my core tightening and heat flushing my skin. To my surprise, he leaned down, brushing a gentle kiss against my lips.

"You are very surprising, husband."

Parker moved back into his space, and his lips thinned. I scanned his face, willing to crack his skull open and hear his thoughts, but he went quiet. I was learning that he used silence to keep people at a distance. I was also learning that sometimes, if I waited him out, he opened up anyway.

We sat in silence.

"The cottage is quiet without you," he finally admitted. I shifted my weight, cuddling into him as one long arm wrapped around me and pulled me closer.

"It's quiet without you too," I whispered back. Wanting to keep him talking, I continued. "I had a nice time with your sister, but holy shit. Her driving is kind of scary."

He scoffed, and I peeked up to see a small smile flash across his face. "She's a wild one. A little reckless."

"Eh." I shrugged. "She's also nineteen." It was surprisingly comfortable acting like a real couple coming down from the high of earth-shattering orgasms. "Did you have a busy day today?"

He grumbled and shifted his weight. Parker lifted my hand and started moving his fingers through mine. His massive palm enveloped mine as he stroked my skin and let our fingers tangle and smooth. I wasn't bothered by his missing pinkie—quite the opposite, it enhanced his fierce and dangerous appeal. I closed my eyes, relishing the roughness of his palm against mine. When his fingers caught on my empty ring finger, he paused and I looked at him. The frown on his face deepened, and I held my breath.

"Something's not right." My chest pinched at his words. *Did he know? Did I somehow give it away?*

I had stumbled on the information one day in the library, but until I could be certain, I didn't utter a word. I almost came clean. It was horrible timing, but I almost opened my mouth and told him what I had learned.

But then he continued. "Ma Brown's got me helping with the books, you know?"

My breath whooshed out quietly, and I nodded.

"They're off."

I shifted to look at him again. "Off?"

He nodded. "Just some inconsistencies that seem to be overlooked."

"Do you think someone is messing with the numbers?"

Parker settled deeper into the mattress and stared at the ceiling. "I don't know. I worked the books over long enough to know how to do it well and not get caught. I haven't figured it out yet, but something's off."

A sick and twisty feeling churned in my stomach. That sounded bad. Ma Brown had been a little frosty, given our arrival, but in the time we'd been on the ranch, everyone had been kind and accommodating. Redemption Ranch was truly a place where people who needed to start over could do so. It was a haven. I hated the thought of someone taking advantage of that.

"Was your job very stressful?"

Parker went quiet for a moment. "My apartment was very clean."

A humorless laugh pushed through my nose, and I held him closer.

"I don't know." He sighed. "It's probably nothing." The edge to his voice told me he was done talking about the books and his former job.

I hated the hard line that creased his brow again. I

wanted the lightness back in his voice, the tension melted from his shoulders. My eye caught on his nipple ring, and a bolt of desire shot through me.

I wouldn't mind my mouth on that either.

Determined to lighten the mood and salvage the night, I grabbed the paperback under my hip. "So tell me about your pirate hero and his damsel in distress."

Parker snagged the book from me, flipping through the pages. "Laugh all you want. It's a damn good story."

I nuzzled into his warmth. "Read a little to me."

He paused but flipped to the yellowed, dog-eared page. Parker cleared his throat. *"Luc Dubois did not start his life a brigand . . ."*

FALLING ASLEEP TO THE DEEP, warm sound of Parker's voice gave me the best night's sleep I'd had in months. While Parker was an expert cuddler, I wouldn't call him a teddy bear. More like a raging bull or a stallion who calmed just long enough for you to inch closer. It was still dangerous, but there was something primal that drew you in and fascinated you despite the risks.

I was not surprised when I awoke alone in my bed. Disappointed? Hell yes. Surprised? Absolutely not. I dressed and readied myself for the day, only pausing once or twice to listen through the door for him.

When I emerged from the bedroom and peeked around the doorframe, my heart leaped into my throat at the sight of Parker sitting at the kitchen table eating his breakfast.

"Hey."

Parker's head whipped up. "Hey, yourself." He'd

dressed in a fresh white T-shirt and faded jeans. His feet were bare, and I couldn't place why that made me feel better about the whole thing. There was something easy and casual about him hanging out in our home, not bolting out the door the first chance he got.

I tucked a strand of hair behind my ear and glanced around the small space. The kitchen seemed to have shrunk overnight. I couldn't move past him without brushing against his arm or pushing up against his back. My eyes snagged on the coffeepot.

Coffee. Coffee is good.

I made a beeline for the cabinet, pulling down a simple white mug and filling it to the top with black coffee. It was scalding and bitter on my tongue. I turned to hide my grimace. I needed to get the hell out of there. Work could distract me from the balled-up feelings that were more confusing than anything.

I was married to Parker. Married to him in order to save him from a life in prison because he'd saved my life. Except . . . I stared at my coffee, trying to gather my thoughts. I wasn't a lawyer, but some preliminary information I'd come across at the Tipp library had freaked me out. I needed to do more research before I could talk to him about it. Especially *now* that everything changed between us last night.

"Here." Parker's warmth hit me before I realized he was right behind me, crowding my space. He slid coffee creamer toward me as one hand gripped my hip. The firm pressure of his hand sent warm, melty energy spreading across my hips, and my thighs clenched.

I stilled, unable to move, but as quickly as his hand was on me, it was gone. I turned, attempting to put on my bravest smile and face my husband. He might be growly and impatient and a grump, but he had become my friend. I trusted him. And now that might be shot to hell all because seeing him glowering over a romance novel had short-circuited my brain.

Stupid. Stupid. Stupid.

"So," I started.

Parker finished rinsing his breakfast dishes and didn't look at me again. "It doesn't change anything," he cut in.

His words were an arrow to my chest, deflating me with a slow, sad whistle as I stared at his back.

It doesn't change anything.

"Of course. Right." I swallowed another gulp of coffee, hoping to shove down the coal that lodged in my throat.

Don't cry. Do. Not.

Parker turned, and when he looked at my face, the furrow in his brow deepened. In one long step, he was in front of me. His arms caged me against the countertop as he laid them at either side of me. His dark and masculine smell moved over me, and I willed myself not to close my eyes and sigh. Instead, I stood stock-still and tried not to breathe in the heady, delicious scent of pure, rugged man that rolled off him in waves.

"It doesn't change anything in that we keep our heads down. Keep our secret until we know it's safe."

I quieted my sigh of relief, but it was there. We weren't leaving the ranch. There still an unknown, eventual expiration date on our marriage, but for the time being, nothing had to change.

"Though some things have changed a bit." Parker's deep, gravelly voice had an air of playfulness that was entirely new and exhilarating. He leaned down, nipping the thin skin just under my jaw, and I arched into him. His hips pressed forward, his arms wrapping around me.

Parker kissed the fuck out of me before I left for work,

and I swooned. He may not be a forever husband, but Parker did a damn good job of showing me *exactly* how I want my soul mate to kiss me when I leave.

"How do we feel about teal?" Sienna's warm voice floated over my shoulder as I flipped the page in *Captain of Passion*, only vaguely registering her question.

"It's ugly."

When she stayed silent, I glanced behind me to find her standing in the doorway to the bedroom with a very pretty, very *teal* dress on. For a remarkable woman who had been guilted into marrying a Mafia criminal roughly two months ago, things were going far better than I expected. Except when my inner asshole started showing and my size 13s were shoved into my mouth.

"Sienna."

Her face was stone as she turned. "It's fine."

Damn it.

I flipped the book beside me, but not before carefully marking my page. Captain Leroy was about to go to war for his beloved, and I hated searching for my spot. In a few strides, I reached the bedroom door to find Sienna whipping the dress off her body and tossing it across the room. I moved toward her, melting her tiny frame into me as I pulled her close.

My nose buried in her hair, and I groaned in pleasure against her ear. "Mmm."

Her hands met my forearms and pushed. "Don't." She wanted to be angry, but a laugh was caught in her throat as I hugged her closer.

"Wear the dress. You looked amazing. I'm an idiot."

She rolled her eyes at me but didn't push me away, so I swayed with her in the dim light of the bedroom we now shared every night.

"Or don't." I ran wet kisses up the column of her neck and paused to suck at her pulse point. "We can stay in."

"We promised Gemma."

"Then wear the dress. You're stunning."

"It's ugly." Sienna adopted a gruff and deep voice as she mocked me, and it tore a laugh from my chest.

"It's only ugly because you're so gorgeous. Nothing compares to your grace and beauty."

Sienna smiled up at me as she arched into my embrace. "You've been reading too many smutty romance novels." I watched her green eyes sparkle with happiness and settled her back on her toes. "Well don't stop," she continued.

I captured her mouth in a searing kiss, pouring into her the emotions she'd managed to pull to the surface. "You're a diamond. My diamond." I set her down and smacked her ass. "Now get dressed."

Sienna smirked as I got the rest of our things and warmed up the car.

∿

"So it's like that, huh?" Evan's voice cut above the din of the bar crowd as I watched Sienna on the dance floor with Gemma.

When I looked at him, Evan's curious eyes bore into me. Assessing. I was never one to give much away, but that didn't mean he ever stopped trying to figure me out.

He looked like shit. Val was still gone. He was still miserable.

"Like what?" I took a swig of my beer and shifted on the stool.

"Like maybe it's not all bullshit."

My eyes moved around, seeing if anyone was listening too closely to our conversation. Evan knew the truth about Sienna and me—parts of the truth, at least—but we were still very much trying to keep the circumstances of our marriage a secret.

I rubbed my eyes with my thumb and forefinger and sighed. "If it makes you feel any better, I'm not happy about it. But I like her. Hell, I even trust her."

Evan slowly nodded, his face communicating *wow* even if he stayed morose.

"I ran into her and Gemma at the library last week. She seems happy."

I looked at my wife, her face radiant as she bounced and belted the lyrics into the air. "She's *always* happy. That woman can find the bright side of a dumpster. What the hell were you doing at the library?"

He tipped his chin as though he was offended. "The librarian is helping me with a work-around. She found a way to get in touch with Val." Realization of my comment dawned on him. "Hey, I read."

We shared a rare laugh.

"Sure about that? I thought you were more of the *cute but dumb* type."

"Dick." Evan smiled, and I enjoyed the lightness I felt. Evan and I were finding some common ground. Repairing our relationship. I liked giving him shit sometimes—it felt like something a big brother might do. I knew Evan didn't want to talk about Val, so our attention went back to the dance floor, where more women had joined Sienna's posse. That woman made friends with everyone she ran into.

"I don't know, man." I sighed. "You know how it is. You trust someone, and it only leads to one thing. Betrayal—in one form or another. She'll leave eventually. They all do. I'm just enjoying it while it lasts."

He kept his eyes on me, maybe trying to figure out if I meant the harsh words I was saying. I did. Over and over my life had proven to me that everyone leaves. Even our own mother abandoned us. Being alone meant saving myself the hassle.

And the heartache.

I shoved that particularly unpleasant thought to the back of my mind. All too often feelings of affection and permanency and devotion came bubbling to the surface if I thought too long about Sienna.

As if on cue, the song transitioned, and Sienna flounced back toward us with Gemma in tow. When she got closer, I slid a tall glass of ice water in her direction. Sienna's eyes went wide, like she was surprised I was taking care of her. I wrapped an arm around her middle and tugged her toward me and onto my lap.

"Why does water surprise you?" I asked, low in her ear.

With her face inches from mine, she shrugged and popped a kiss on my cheek. "I guess I've never had someone take care of me like that before."

I studied her face, something akin to happiness settling into my bones. It annoyed the fuck out of me that Sienna had gone her whole life without being properly taken care of. I'd happily step up while I had the chance.

"You do now." I probably shouldn't have sounded so angry about it, but Sienna had gotten used to the shifts in my moods and was beginning to realize that sometimes my rocky voice didn't always match my meaning. The squeeze she gave my shoulder let me know she understood my intention.

Gemma and Sienna chatted while Evan and I watched over them, our eyes always scanning the crowd.

"Did you ever do anything with that application?" Gemma shouted over the music, and my ears perked up.

Application?

Sienna's eyes sliced to me and bore into Gemma. "It wasn't an application. Just information."

"What is?" I cut in.

Gemma turned and smiled at me. "Sienna and I were at the library and saw a flyer advertising a nursing program."

My face stilled. Sienna was planning to become a nurse before I'd ambushed her restaurant and fucked up her life.

Sienna dismissed the comment with a flick of her wrist. "It's nothing."

"Chikalu Falls has a pretty well-respected community college. They might have something," Evan added between slugs of his beer.

"Yes! That's where I go." Gemma's upbeat and hopeful voice bounced between us. "I'm only doing a few online classes, but that's something you could always look into."

Sienna tucked a strand of hair behind her ear, and her bright smile faltered. "That's great, Gem. I'm good, though."

I squeezed her again, a silent question. *Are you okay?*

She looked at me and nodded, but I didn't miss the clear message she shot back: *I don't want to talk about this.*

"So, Gem," I started. "I heard your birthday is coming up. Big plans?" I felt like an asshole for not knowing my own half sister's birthday, but I was trying. As I'd gotten to know Gemma, I realized she was funny and guarded and kind and a little reckless. Though she may look like a carbon copy of our mother and that fact pushed on my heart like a bruise, she was different. There were reasons in Chicago I couldn't let myself care about her—or her me. When we found out our mother had a daughter, keeping her at a distance was the only way to keep her away from the men I worked with and to keep my complicated emotions in check. Here in Montana, we were slowly finding a way to get to know each other for the first time.

"The big two oh!" Sienna shouted. "Of course we'll celebrate!"

Gemma rolled her eyes as only a teenager could, but there was no denying the happiness she was feeling. "A few friends are going to get together. Nothing big."

I swallowed a mouthful of beer and added, "No boys, right?"

Evan laughed, shook his head, and drank his beer. Gemma rolled her eyes, but I was fucking serious.

"Oh." Sienna leaned in close, her breath teasing the shell of my ear. "I like when you play the big, growly older brother."

Gemma laughed. "Who are you kidding? He's always growly."

Sienna's eyes sparkled with mischief.

"Wanna dance?" Gemma asked, and Sienna's teeth sank into her plush lower lip.

I leaned down, letting my voice slide low and husky. "I'm ready to go home too."

Her eyes connected with mine, and a slow smile spread across her face. "Sorry, Gem," she said, but her eyes never left mine. "We're heading out."

Gemma scoffed lightly behind her and mumbled something low about *eye fucking* and being *totally gross* that made Evan laugh. I made a show of pulling Sienna close and kissing her slow and deep. Having Sienna melt in my arms for everyone to see did something to me. Something behind my ribs shifted and clicked into place.

I tossed some bills on the table. "Let's go."

Hours later, I stared at the ceiling as Sienna tucked into my side. We'd barely made it into the cottage before we were tearing at each other's clothes, and I'd hauled her over my shoulder and stalked toward the bedroom.

Her laughter filled the cottage, and she breathed life into my soul. It was almost too much to bear. I enjoyed everything about her—more than I even liked admitting to myself, and I desperately needed to keep my emotions in check.

It was harder to do in the quiet moments when it felt like nothing mattered but making her happy and giving her anything she could ever want. My plan—to go along with this sham of a marriage until I knew Sienna was safe, then let her walk away to live her life—was unraveling at the seams. But it didn't matter that I was falling in love with my wife. When this was over, like everyone else in my life, she'd be free of me. As long as Sienna was taken care of, nothing else mattered. I'd be sure of it.

Sienna's soft, drowsy voice cut through the dark room. "I can *hear* you thinking."

I smirked at her comment but only grunted in response.

"Do you think about it? The restaurant?" she asked.

My gut churned with the memories of that night in the restaurant, and my back went tight. "No," I lied. "I killed a man. There's nothing to think about."

I could feel her nod against my arm. Finally, when I thought she'd fallen asleep, her whisper broke me. "I was so afraid of what he wanted to do to me. I'm glad you did it."

Relief.

The fast and overwhelming flood of relief had my eyes going hot as I clenched my jaw to fight the unexpected wave of emotion. Not since the doctor at the hospital had told me Sienna was totally fine and I had holed myself up in a storage closet to cry my eyes out had I felt such an overpowering sense of relief.

My throat was clogged and I couldn't speak, so I held on to her.

"Let's not talk about it, okay? It makes me sad," she whispered.

I stayed quiet. I hated knowing she was sad. The world was a shitty place, but her laughter was pure light. I needed it.

A playfully evil smile bloomed across my face. "Sienna?"

"Mmm?"

"Remember that first night? After the bar. When I kissed you on the porch? Later, I came to apologize, but you were in your room."

Sienna stilled beside me.

Oh yeah. She remembers.

I stifled a small laugh with a cough, but my voice held

an edge of humor. "When I knocked on the door . . . what was that weird buzzing noise?"

She gently cleared her throat, and I nearly lost it. "Um. I'm not sure. It was probably nothing."

"Hmm. Are you sure? It was pretty loud."

"No. No, I . . ."

Before she could come up with the lie, I tightened my grip around her and started tickling.

"No! Stop!" Sienna bucked and howled and laughed, and I continued digging my fingers into her ribs. "Stop!" She laughed. "A vibrator!" she shouted.

I slowed my assault.

"It was a vibrator," she repeated.

I laughed with her, but Sienna's breathless pants shot heat straight to my cock as it thickened between us.

Her hands flew over her face before she hooked one leg around mine, swiveling on top and mounting me. I gripped her hips as she slapped my shoulder. "You're an asshole."

I pressed my erection into her, feeling the heat of her pussy through her thin pajama shorts. "Yeah," I agreed.

Sienna ground down on me, and I groaned.

"Well, let's see it." My fingertips dug into the fleshy curve of her hips as I stilled her. I reached to flick on the small bedside lamp. Sienna was bathed in soft yellow light.

She toyed with her lip as her eyes shot to the table next to us. She hesitated only a moment before reaching into the drawer and digging the toy out from the bottom. Sienna held the vibrator up between us in all its pink, veiny glory.

TWENTY-TWO

SIENNA

I HELD my vibrator between us, my cheeks burning.

What. The actual. Fuck.

Parker looked at it but only jutted his lower lip out and nodded. "Impressive."

I tossed it on the bed next to us. "Stop. It's your fault I needed it anyway—walking around with all this manness." I gestured to all of him as he rolled his hips into my aching core. For a fleeting moment I worried Parker would see the vibrator as a threat. In my experience, men's egos could be fragile little things. "But I've got you now," I crooned.

Parker breathed out a humorless laugh. "Oh, baby. I'm not intimidated." He shifted our weight, toppling me over until his heavy body was pressing my back into the mattress. His eyes were dangerously black, and my entire body hummed with anticipation. "See . . . it's not a threat." He licked his lower lip, and I tracked the movement, wishing it was my tongue dragging across it. "It's a teammate."

Parker gripped the headboard with one hand as his hips ground into me.

Oh my god, yes.

My body screamed, heat pooled between my legs, and I knew my sleep shorts were already soaked through. The hard line of his cock combined with the thought of Parker wielding a vibrator? Shit. The thought alone could nearly make me come.

Parker palmed my throat and chest as he kissed my face and neck. "So can we? Can we play?"

A moan tore through me, and my thighs shook. Parker shifted, sitting back on his heels and looking down on me. He was gloriously naked, a perk of the huge man claiming he was too hot at night to sleep with any clothes on.

Parker peeled my top from me and sucked the hard nub of my nipple into his mouth. My voice was ragged. "What did you have in mind?"

He let his wide, rough palms spread over my ribs before pushing my shorts down my thighs. I lifted my legs to allow him to remove them.

"You like to hear the dirty words, don't you?" My pulse ratcheted higher. "You want to hear how much I want to watch your pussy stretched around that vibrator."

"Yes. More." I tried to scissor my legs, but he was planted between them. My hands rubbed up the thick expanse of his muscular thighs, and I couldn't look away from the blunt tip of his cock jutting toward me.

"When I fuck you with your pretty pink toy, I'll be stroking my cock and thinking about all your tight little holes."

"Jesus, Parker." My entire body was flushed with anticipation. I wanted Parker to do all the nasty, devious things he said and *more*. I wanted him to explore my boundaries and push me past them.

My pussy throbbed as I arched forward to capture his nipple between my lips. I ran my tongue around the cool metal bar, and we both groaned in pleasure. Parker's hand reached between my legs, and I widened them as I settled back onto the pillows. "You like that. Look at this mess." He dragged two thick fingers through my folds and held them up before sucking my arousal off them. When he groaned in pleasure, I nearly came. No one had ever made me feel so beautiful.

Worshipped.

I tipped my knees farther apart, giving him more room to play with me. His thumb found my clit and applied firm, stroking pressure. Beside me, Parker gripped the toy, turning it to the lowest setting, and my legs tingled as it buzzed to life.

"You have no clue, do you?" The edge of his voice raced through me. "No fucking clue how often I think of you."

I gripped his thighs and squeezed. The soft silicone dragged over my aching pussy. I was slick and ready, but he teased and stroked as he kissed down my breasts.

Finally he sat up. "I want to watch," he said and slowly slipped the head of the vibrator inside me. "Goddamn," he breathed.

The reverence in his voice was empowering. Emboldened, I asked, "You like that?"

"Watching your pussy suck this vibrator deep is the hottest thing I've ever seen." Parker stroked his cock as he watched me. Seeing his large hand wrapped around himself was naughty. Erotic. The buzzing toy pressed against my clit, and my back arched off the bed. Parker planted a hand in the center of my chest, guiding me back down. "Easy, girl. We'll take care of you. Just enjoy it."

A hot, needy ball of desire coiled in my core as his thick voice melted over me. Parker slowly pumped the toy in and out of me as he stroked himself and I watched. Sweat prickled at my hairline as I got closer and closer to release. I wanted—needed—to come. Parker's dick pulsed and strained, his breaths becoming ragged. I angled my hips higher. I was desperate.

"That's it, baby. Tell me what you need."

"More," I panted.

Parker clicked the toy up to intensify the buzzing and gently pressed it deeper. "You take it so well."

I preened at his praise. I wanted to be the woman he thought of years from now. The star of all his dirty fantasies. Lord knows he would forever be the star of mine.

"Fuck. I want to bury this cock inside you."

I smiled, loving how needy and primal his voice was. A dark and delicious thought came to me. "Do it." I wanted to feel him just as badly. Parker started to slowly ease the toy out of me, but my hand stopped him. "Will it fit?"

His eyes paused on my pussy as realization dawned on him. His eyes flew to mine. "Both?" he asked.

I bit my lip and shrugged. "Maybe?"

His breath whooshed out, and something akin to *holy fuck* escaped between his lips. I rolled to my side, holding the vibrator firmly in place as I pushed my ass backward.

Parker nestled behind me. We'd cuddled like this often, but knowing what his cock was about to do was more than intense.

I panted as wetness slid past the toy, coating my inner thighs. The blunt tip of Parker's cock pressed against my opening.

His hot breath was at my ear. "You're in control. You tell me if it's too much."

"I want it but go slow."

Carefully Parker pushed his hips forward, and I adjusted my leg. Willing myself to relax, I opened for him.

The head of his cock stretched me open as he shared my most delicate area.

Through a groan, Parker alternated languid kisses with murmurs of how good, how *right* I felt. The sweetest, grumpiest man on the planet was absolutely ruining my pussy, and I couldn't get enough.

"Talk to me. Tell me," he demanded.

"It's so full. Give me more."

He slid in another inch. "So fucking tight," he ground out.

We were edging the line between pleasure and pain. I wanted to feel all of him, fully seated inside me while my toy vibrated against my clit. Then I wanted him—only him —as he fucked me until I came.

When I told him as much, he stilled. "I can do that for you." My heart leaped in anticipation, and then he gripped my hip and plunged into me until he was balls deep, sharing the tight space with the vibrator. It was intense. Sinfully full. I was one heartbeat away from coming when I reached between my legs and gently pulled the vibrator out.

With only the pulsing rhythm of his cock, Parker fucked me slow and long and hard.

"Be rough," I demanded.

"Is that how you want me to fuck you?" he asked. "Rough and deep until we both come?" One long, deep thrust was all it took before stars were exploding behind my eyes. Parker gripped my hip and pounded into me. Seconds later he stilled as his cock jerked. I pushed my hips back, slamming onto his cock, and he came. His hand shot up, tangling in my hair and gripping it tight as he rode out his orgasm.

His large, muscular frame enveloped me in warmth. Parker was all soft skin, smooth muscle, and *all man*. My limbs tingled, my entire body deliciously sore. I let out a deep, contented sigh.

Parker slipped out of me but hitched his knees up, cradling me in his arms. He nuzzled his nose in my hair, and we lay there, in blissful silence, for a long while.

"Are you okay?" he finally asked.

"Mmm . . . ," I murmured. "More than okay."

Parker stroked a warm hand down my arm. "Did I hurt you?" Concern gave his voice a soft edge, and I warmed at his worry.

"I'm good. More than good. I promise."

"Don't move." Parker planted a kiss on my shoulder before he got up from the bed. He tucked a throw blanket over my naked body, and I was happy to lie there and bask in the afterglow of mind-numbing sex. A few moments later, I heard the bathtub running. One clatter and a mumbled *fuck* through the thin walls of the cottage and he was back at my side. When I lazily shifted, Parker's arms scooped me up. He held me against the expanse of his chest, and I melted into him. My fingertips traced the lines of his tattoos, and I listened to the war drum of his heartbeat.

He carried me into the small bathroom, the smell of his masculine body wash filling the air. "We didn't have bubbles. I did my best."

Instead of setting me on my feet, Parker stepped into the tub with me in his arms. Slowly, he lowered us into the hot water. The tub was small, far too tiny for his large body and mine. We were cramped together, but as the water lapped at my shoulders, I let my eyes drift closed. Parker's heart beat against my back as he held me. He used a washcloth to run hot water down my back and across my shoulders. It dipped low, caressing my thighs and down my legs as far as he could reach.

I stayed silent, not wanting to break the spell of whatever magical bubble we'd wandered into—a place where Parker was my husband and I was his wife. For real. No scary past behind us. No threat of exposing what he'd done. Just us, enjoying the quiet, sated moments it took for my pulse to return to normal.

Parker made me feel adored. Treasured. *Loved.*

I held on to the thoughts that threatened to tumble out of my mouth. I shouted them to him in my mind, wishing I was brave enough to say them aloud.

I love you. All parts of you. Please let me love you.

TWENTY-THREE
PARKER

"How bad is it?" Sienna called from inside the cottage. With my hands in my pockets, I stared at the purple expanse of the sky. Only a sliver of golden orange could be seen just above the buttes in the distance. Dark, rolling clouds had blanketed the sky, and flashes of dusky purple and indigo shone through the thick layer of clouds. We'd be lucky if we didn't get rained on tonight. A light shiver ran through me.

"You'll want a sweater or jacket," I called back to her. Sienna had promised Gemma that we'd go to the Tipp Apple Knocker Festival, so after a long day of work, we got home and cleaned up. Sienna loved working with Chet, but most days she came home smelling like horse shit. *Literally.*

I smiled to myself. My cute little wife was a hard-working badass.

"What are you smirking at over there?" Sienna looped her arm in mine and leaned her head against my biceps.

"Just thinking about you. And horse shit." I dropped a kiss on the top of her head, and she hip checked me. For a moment, we stared off our porch and into the darkening field just beyond the small yard.

Sienna's soft voice broke through the enveloping darkness. "Ma said there'd be a few extra guys there working tonight. Agents."

I nodded. "She's just being cautious." While those of us in witness protection had our freedom, bigger crowds meant unfamiliar faces. Oftentimes Ma would staff a few agents in the crowd as a precaution. Sienna squeezed my arm.

"Are you nervous? We don't have to go." I hated that Sienna still got anxious in crowds. She might always live a life of worry because of me, and there was nothing I could do about it.

"No, it'll be fun. I don't even know what an apple knocker is." She laughed. While she had finished getting ready, I had gone out to warm up the car and have a few minutes to myself. Things had clicked into place with Sienna, and if I didn't take the time to stop and *think*, it was easy to forget. Easy to forget that our marriage was fake— designed to keep her safe and me from prison. The more days that passed, the harder it was to remember that this didn't have a happy ending for us.

Not for me, at least.

Shaking off my dark mood, I placed a hand at her lower back and guided Sienna to the car. I drove, and Sienna sang off-key to the radio. Mostly I stole glances at her profile.

She stopped midsong. "What?" she asked. "Oh, come on. My singing isn't *that* bad."

I shook my head when she rolled her eyes and turned the volume up a notch. Something inside me had shifted over the past few weeks. Maybe it was sharing such a small space with someone. Maybe it was the sex. Maybe it was just *her*. Whatever it was, the typical heaviness that I carried with me had been lightened. I looked forward to quiet nights at home with Sienna. When someone on the ranch offered a friendly greeting, it didn't feel quite as foreign to nod in acknowledgment. I even caught myself smiling. It was a strange and slightly uncomfortable feeling, but I couldn't help but feel more like myself. A *me* that I had never met before. Some of the bitter taste of anger had subsided.

I sneaked glances at her while I wound around the country roads. She chose an olive green, lined flannel work jacket—she called it a *shacket* because it was both a shirt and a jacket. It was functional but cute, and suited her perfectly. Sienna tucked her hands into the oversize arms of her *shacket* as we approached the fairgrounds.

"Look at the trees." Her pointer finger pressed into the glass of the window. In the last week, the tips of the trees had turned. A riot of yellows, oranges, and reds spread across the forest canopy in the distance. More than the pretty landscape, I could hardly look away from her. She was a light—happy and gorgeous and full of life.

I parked the car and turned toward her. "I love—" *You.* I swallowed the words. "Fall too."

Goddamn it.

I clenched my jaw. I'd nearly blurted the words for days now and chickened out every time. Every cute little thing she did lately had them at the tip of my tongue.

We existed together as any happily married couple would, I supposed. Not that I really had any fucking clue, but it felt right. We worked, shared meals, fucked, cuddled, watched movies. She liked it when I read to her. It all felt so normal. Neither of us spoke about our marriage or its expiration date. I still teased her by calling her *wife*. Mostly I just loved the flush of pink on her cheeks when I did it.

It also felt damn good to do it.

We got out of the car and peered through the sea of vehicles to find Gemma. She was supposed to be dragging Evan out of his self-imposed solitude. A few others from the ranch had mentioned coming too. Sienna pulled a hat down over her ears, and I zipped my coat up and met her at the front of the car.

"Definitely glad I wore this." She tucked her hands inside the sleeves of her coat.

"Fucking cold in the valley," I commented.

"I require coffee." Humor laced in her voice, and I threw my arm over her shoulders, pulling her into me, offering my warmth.

"Anything for you, wife."

She smiled up at me, a full, pinched-cheeked smile that squeezed my heart. She looked at me like I was a man who deserved to stand next to her. Not a criminal. Not a cold, grumpy man who pushed away his only family. No, Sienna looked up at me and saw *me*. She looked at me like I was the man I could have been. The man who grew up in a normal home, not a frightened kid scraping by and caring for a younger brother and an addicted mother. Not a man who built walls to protect everyone around him from *himself*. She looked at me like I was a man worthy of loving a woman like her.

But who was I kidding? There was no *woman like her*. She was everything.

I don't deserve this woman.

"Let's do this." She squeezed my middle, and we started off toward the entrance. The closer we got, the more I could feel the excitement radiate from her tiny body. Her steps were swift, and she waved to nearly everyone we passed. I doubted she even knew them, but she found joy in sharing this experience with them.

We passed under a large TIPP APPLE KNOCKER FESTIVAL sign. The county fairgrounds had been transformed. That morning, Tipp had hosted a 5K to kick off the festival, and I was relieved that Sienna wasn't interested in signing us up for that shit. Tents and small booths stretched in long, neat rows. Twinkle lights streamed from one side to the other, creating a soft, glowing canopy. In the main barn, a large stage held a full band, while people danced and lined up for beers. At the far end, carnival rides were silhouetted against the darkening sky.

Children zipped among the crowd as people walked or stopped to check out the various stands. Laughter floated on the autumn breeze, and I thought about how those kids had no clue how lucky they were. As a kid, I'd never gotten to run wild at a carnival or have parents who slow danced to a live band while I sneaked away to find some trouble. Instead, I had wondered where my mother was, if she was coming home, and if it would kill my little brother if our sandwiches had just a *little* bit of mold on the bread.

"This is incredible." Wonder danced in her voice, and her eyes went wide as she took it all in.

"Tipp knows how to throw a party," I agreed. As I scanned the crowd, the flash of Gemma's platinum hair caught my attention.

"Hey, guys!" She bounced toward us, wrapping Sienna in a hug. Evan sulked behind her. I shook his hand, and Sienna gave him a quick, friendly hug.

"How's it going?" I asked him. He looked like shit.

"Fine."

Sienna looked up at him, sadness drooping her features. "Still no word from Val?"

He stiffened and turned away. "Nah. Not yet."

"He's stalking her," Gemma quipped.

Evan pinched the bridge of his nose. "I'm not stalking her." He shot me a pointed look. "I am not stalking her."

"He's emailing her. Every day."

Evan held up his hands and stared at her like, *What the fuck?*

I tried to stifle my laughter. Clearly, he was torn up about her, but I couldn't pass up the opportunity to mess with him. "Dude."

Evan sighed. "It's the only way I can contact her right now. I have a lot to say, so I'm putting it out there. I have no idea if she's even getting them, let alone reading them."

Sienna sighed. "I think it's terribly romantic."

"Can we talk about something else?" Evan's frustration bubbled over as we stopped to order a few hot coffees and continued walking through the crowd.

"Heard anything from your guy?" After working on the books, I was certain something was really off. I didn't want to call too much attention to it just yet, so I'd brought it to Evan. He knew a guy who knew a guy and was trying to get some information.

"Scott's guys can take a while to get ahold of. He said he's on it. We'll hear something if he finds anything new."

Gemma's face twisted into a snarl. I overheard Sienna whisper to her: "Scott? Like Agent Dunn?"

"Scotty is an asshole," said Gemma.

Evan shook his head and turned to reassure me. "Scott's a good guy. He's been nothing but good to us since we came here. I don't know what her deal is."

I tracked my sister and Sienna as they walked a few paces ahead of us, their heads bent down in secret conversation. As we wandered toward the barn to listen to the band,

Evan and I traded our empty coffee cups for beers, while Sienna opted for a coffee spiked with Irish cream liqueur. Her dainty hands wrapped around the cup, and she smiled and winked. My chin tipped up. As I scanned the crowd, it was impossible to tell if Ma had really sent any agents, or if they'd gotten better at blending into the crowd. Maybe I'd even lost my edge and couldn't pick them out anymore.

Small groups of people dotted the barn floor. I recognized many faces from town, including the bartender from the Rasa and Sienna's friend Johnny. An elderly man walked by with a small aluminum pot on his head, worn proudly like a hat. I pointed and looked at Evan in question. "Pothead?"

He laughed into his beer. "Johnny Appleseed."

"Ah." I sipped my beer. "Makes more sense."

Tipp was a weird fucking town, but it was charming. I hadn't thought about Chicago—sure as fuck didn't miss it—in weeks.

"Crap." Sienna huddled into our twosome, dragging Gemma with her. "You guys gotta cover for us."

Before I could react, Sienna was stripping off her jacket.

"Whoa. Wait a minute," I said as Evan and I stepped around the women to block them.

"I'm so sorry, Gem," Sienna said. She turned to me, eyes pleading. "I got bumped and spilled my drink all over her."

Gemma stood quietly, watching as Sienna held out the jacket toward her.

"The bathrooms are too far away, and your shirt is soaked. You can throw this on."

Gemma's eyes bounced between the three of us.

"We got you," Evan assured, closing the gap and blocking anyone's view.

Under the cloak of darkness and two big-ass brothers,

Gemma began removing her long-sleeved shirt. My eyes scanned the crowd, watching for anyone who tried to sneak a peek, but the darkened corner shielded them from view.

"Oh god, Gemma." Sienna's soft gasp had my head jerking to the side. A flash of red, angry scars cut across Gemma's collarbone, chest, and neck. As soon as I'd seen it, I'd looked away, but not before I had taken in the extent of the damage. My gut coiled. I knew she'd been injured in Chicago and had caught glimpses of the scars before, but I had no idea how brutal those injuries were.

Back then, I'd sent Gemma away, telling Evan a half sister was no sister of mine. In reality, it was too painful to even look at her. He got her a low-level job, and when the Family started cannibalizing itself, Evan and Gemma had been caught in the cross fire. They had used Gemma to get to Evan. He'd tracked her and her kidnappers down at an old abandoned house, but in a panic, she'd run through a glass patio door. It had been Val who'd saved her. Gemma never would have been there at all had it not been for my connections to the Mafia. Now she was scarred for life.

Another beautiful woman whose life had been destroyed because of my choices. Pain radiated through my hand, the ache of my missing finger still a present reminder after all this time. I willed myself to stop grinding my molars.

I was stone-still until Sienna's soft touch on my cheek broke me from my dark thoughts. "Hey, come back to me." Her sea glass eyes searched mine. "She's fine."

I refocused to find Evan and Gemma gone. She was off to the side, standing in a new group of people. Sienna's jacket was zipped up high, her scars tucked safely beneath the collar. She was talking to the shop owner, Johnny, as Evan sat by Al the bartender and got lost in conversation. A bright smile slid across Gemma's face. It didn't quite reach her eyes, but it helped to relieve the ache between my shoulders.

"You're in no mood to dance, I see." Sienna pouted.

I glanced down at her. "I don't dance."

She did her best impression of my scowl and then stuck her tongue out between her teeth. I scooped her up in one movement, her legs dangling as my body pressed against hers. I reveled in the surprised squeal my arms teased out of her. Her laugh filled my chest, pushing away the uncomfortable, squeezing pressure.

Looking over her shoulder, I saw a booth set up for fall photos. The line was short, so I pivoted to move her closer. "Come here, wife."

I might not dance, but I knew, based on the sheer volume of pictures Sienna took on her phone, a token to remember Apple Knocker by would make her smile. I wondered, when all this was over, if the picture would be the only thing I'd have to remember her. Or maybe Sienna would take it with her and think of me. Maybe she'd burn it.

The line was quick, and when it was our turn, my hand at her lower back guided her toward the stacks of hay bales and around the smattering of pumpkins. I sat on one of the bales, and instead of letting Sienna sit next to me, I grabbed her waist and sat her right on my lap. She laughed and threw her arm around my neck. As the photographer moved around the hay and centered us in the shot, I palmed and squeezed her ass. The surprise and spark in her eye caused a smirk to curl at my lips.

The shutter clicked as Sienna grinned.

It will never be better than this.

TWENTY-FOUR
SIENNA

"BEST THREE OUT OF FIVE!"

I clenched my jaw to keep from laughing. I couldn't resist the pull of the carnival games. Even knowing they were rigged, I happily handed over my dollars to compete against Parker. After losing time after time, he demanded to pick the next game. Hurling a baseball toward a stack of aluminum milk jugs, Parker assumed he could win that one. But with all muscle and no finesse, he didn't stand a chance.

"Fine. Last one." I ground the ball into my palm, eyeing the tilt and balance of the stack in front of me.

Parker stood, feet planted, legs wide. His shirt stretched across his muscular chest, and I had to steady my breathing. "You're distracting me."

"Just standing here, sweetheart," he mused.

I harrumphed and refocused on my target. I wound up and tossed the ball, knocking over only two of the five jugs. "Dang it!"

Parker eased me out of the way with a playful swat to my ass. "Move it."

The ball was comically small in his hands, and his eyes

were laser focused on the small tower of milk jugs. His throw was deadly accurate, and I knew I'd lost the instant the ball left his hand. The jugs exploded with a crash, tumbling to the ground.

"Winner!" the carnival worker exclaimed.

"You did it!" I jumped up and down in front of him in celebration. "High four!" I held up my hand for him.

A devilish grin spread across his face when my teasing jab dawned on him. He bent down and tossed me over his shoulder. "You are such a little shit."

I squealed and delighted in how weightless I was in his arms, slapping at his back. Parker's booming laugh floated above the noise of the carnival as he wrapped his arms around me. Unrestrained and genuine, his laugh was the most beautiful sound in the world.

For another hour, Parker had humored me, giving in to every whim and whimsy of a small-town carnival. We ate corn dogs and funnel cakes and deep-fried Oreos. I kicked his ass at the rest of the carnival games and even won him a small purple monkey. If it wounded his pride, he didn't show it but rather tucked the stuffed animal in the nook of his arm as we walked through the crowd.

When it was time to go, we found Gemma and Evan back at the barn and said our goodbyes. Parker weaved through the field between parked cars and people walking toward the festival. I wouldn't be surprised if, when the carnival rides shut down, families gave way to rowdy drinkers and dancing.

Once we made it back to the car, my teeth chattered as I warmed my hands in front of the car's vents. "Why is it so freaking cold? It's barely October."

Parker cranked the knob higher as barely warm air brushed over my frozen knuckles. A breeze had picked up, and without a coat, I was chilled to the bone. As the car warmed up, we made our way through the winding roads toward the ranch.

"So, Gemma," I started as he eased the car away from the fairgrounds. "There's *definitely* drama where she and Agent Dunn are concerned. I'd bet my ass something happened between the two of them, but she's not spilling."

He looked at me and his brows pinched forward. "He's old."

A burst of my laughter filled the car. "He's not *old*, Park. He's, like, early thirties or something."

"I'm thirty-three." He shot me a pointed stare that I couldn't help but love. "Trust me, that's old."

"You're thirty-three?" I feigned shock. "Eww." I bit the inside of my lower lip to keep from laughing again.

He swatted at me, and I playfully slapped back at him. He was still annoyed, but a lot less grumpy. "I'm serious. She's *nineteen*. A kid."

I laughed again and patted his arm. "Dear husband, you have no idea how the minds of young women work. Besides, she's almost twenty."

He grumbled something under his breath as the car pulled across the small wooden bridge that led to the entrance of Redemption Ranch.

Home.

We sat in comfortable silence as we made our way across the property to our cottage. It wasn't all that late, but the autumn sun had tucked behind the mountain, casting everything in shadow. In the darkness I could study Parker's profile, appreciating the hard lines and delicious edges. Bit by bit, he was removing his armor. My crack about his pinkie was only a small example of how some of his sharp edges had softened. In those fleeting moments, he let me see him. All parts of him. The silly parts and the vulnerable bits buried deep below the surface. I was convinced Parker had never let anyone see him for who he truly was. Something deep and real inside me glowed at the thought it was *me* who got to see him for the man he was.

"You're staring again." The corner of Parker's mouth tipped up.

"I can't help it. My husband is hot as fuck." I leaned over and pressed a hot, wet kiss at the edge of his jaw. A grumbling, appreciative sigh vibrated onto my lips, and I squeezed my thighs together.

"Who the—" The concern in his voice drew my attention to the person sitting on our front porch. He parked the car and we both got out.

"Something we can help you with, Ma?" I asked, hoping cheeriness blanketed my confusion.

She stood, her moss-green eyes sharp and assessing. "I'm just going to come out with it. We have a problem. Unless you've got some answers and we can get this resolved, you two will no longer be welcome at Redemption Ranch."

My hand squeezed Parker's. "I don't understand. I—"

Ma stood tall. "I told the both of you." She looked between us, cementing me in place. "No bullshit."

Parker's nostrils flared once, but he didn't speak. A thousand thoughts tumbled through me.

Did she know about Chicago? What Park did? That I can't protect him?

My mind wouldn't accept it—there had to be something we could do. This was our *home*. I never expected to, but I had finally found my place. A job I liked. People I cared about. A man I was falling in love with.

"Please tell me what's going on," I pleaded.

Ma suddenly looked weary. "Mr. Davis, I'm going to

need you to tell me why someone would have a problem with your work at the office."

Parker's head tipped slightly as though he was surprised at the direction of the conversation. In fact, so was I. I'd assumed she'd found out about Chicago and our marriage, but this was something else entirely.

"I think you should come inside." Parker strode past her, unlocked the door, and went in. My eyes were saucers, but I gestured toward our door and followed Ma into our small cottage.

HER COOL EYES scanned the room, assessing and cataloging everything she took in, I'm sure. Nerves simmered under my skin. "Can I get you some lemonade?"

On a chair, Ma rested her elbows on her knees, pressing her fingertips against her closed eyes. "Got anything stronger?"

I shot a look at Parker, darkness clouding his features as he nodded at the kitchen. Together we walked toward the cabinets, keeping our backs to her.

"What the hell is going on?" I whispered.

"No idea." Parker pulled three glasses from the cupboard while I grabbed a half-consumed bottle of bourbon. I slid it to him, and he poured three healthy portions. "Just let me do the talking."

I glanced at the glass in front of me, swiped it off the counter, and slammed the dark liquor back. It burned as it slid down my throat, but I tapped the glass on the counter. Parker raised an eyebrow but didn't say anything more as he refilled my glass.

This can't be it. Things were just getting good. He can't go to prison.

Parker sensed my panic and placed a hand over my shoulder and squeezed. I closed my eyes, willing my heartbeat to slow and my nerves to settle. He carried a glass to Agent Brown, and I followed quietly behind him.

Together we settled onto the couch. I wanted nothing more than to find comfort, nuzzled into his body, but he sat rigid and closed off. I held my glass in my hand and concentrated on the warm burn in my chest to keep from crying.

"When your brother came here," Ma started, "he was lost. Angry. Hurt. That boy wanted nothing more than to take care of his sister and disappear."

I looked between the two of them, trying to understand the tense undercurrent filling our living room.

"I've heard of you, you know," she continued. "When Evan and Gemma came here, they were thoroughly investigated, which included a file on you, in fact. Parker Marino." With a low whistle, she shook her head, then took a sip of the amber liquid.

"I asked about you but he wouldn't bend. No matter how I tried to pry information from him, he stayed quiet."

Parker harrumphed. "He planned to testify against me."

Ma swatted a hand through the air. "Ah, he was never going to give them anything of value on you."

Confused, I cut in. "I'm so sorry, Ma. Is there something Parker and I can help you with?"

Her eyes found mine and softened. "Sienna. How you got caught up in all of this is still a bit of a mystery. But I like solving mysteries." Her speculative stare sent a chill through me, and I inched closer to Parker.

Ma brought her attention back to Parker. "Evan told me a story once. How he'd stolen a pack of cigarettes from a bodega and got caught." Parker's jaw flexed as if he recalled the memory in detail. "He said it didn't matter that the store owner saw him swipe them because you insisted on taking his punishment."

Parker nodded. "A broken arm and a couple of black eyes. We both know Evan's too pretty for that," he mused, and Ma laughed while I looked on, horrified.

She looked down her straight nose at him, and she was quiet for a moment. Her sharp green eyes slid down him until they snagged on his left hand. "And what about that?"

Parker flexed his hand, but I grabbed it, wrapping both hands around his. "A little more than a pack of smokes," he admitted.

"I thought only the Yakuza used the pinkie as penance."

Parker's hard eyes stared her down, but she didn't react. Anyone else would have been quivering on the floor at the chill radiating off him.

She sipped the bourbon and watched it swirl in her glass. "See, I'm guessing it wasn't your punishment to take, either, was it?"

Parker broke his numb stare when he looked down and his voice tinged with sadness. "No, ma'am."

Ma rose to her feet. "Didn't think so. Here's the deal, kids." Ma lifted her glass and pointed between us. "Someone's trying to get you in a lot of trouble."

I looked between them. "Us?" I asked. "What do you mean?"

"Illegal drugs—fentanyl, to be exact." She pointed directly at Parker. "In your desk at the office."

"You went through his things?" I shot to my feet.

Parker grabbed my hand, pulling me back to the couch. "It's not a problem, Sienna."

Agent Brown rose, leaving her empty glass, and walked

toward the door. "We had been given reason to believe Parker was using drugs while at work. We'll be doing a more thorough investigation. My affection for your brother is the only reason I'm extending you the courtesy of a warning. If you're bringing drugs onto my ranch, you're done here."

Parker stood and extended his hand. "Appreciated." Ma tried to hide the whisper of a smile before taking his hand, but it was there.

Once she was gone, I turned to Parker. "Tell me they aren't yours."

His jaw ticced, and his hands hung at his sides. "The drugs aren't mine."

Anger bubbled to the surface. "Why didn't you tell her? About the missing money and your suspicions?"

Parker shook his head. "If I told her about the inconsistencies without any real proof and *after* she accused me of having the drugs, it would only look like I was covering my own ass."

I guess it made sense, but fear and uncertainty was rising to the surface.

"Okay," I whispered. Weary and wrung out, I lay beside Parker in the bed, but we barely touched. As I drifted to sleep, doubts clouded my mind. The late-night phone calls, the stitches and sneaking around, the hushed conversations. Was it possible Parker wasn't the man I thought he was? He came from a life of money and crime and secrets. It was possible that it was ingrained in his DNA.

When it came down to it, did I really know my husband at all?

TWENTY-FIVE

PARKER

SOMEONE WAS SETTING ME UP. If that wasn't bad enough, overnight Sienna went from looking at me like I hung the moon to sneaking quiet glances at me with worry creasing her forehead. She looked at me exactly how I deserved to be looked at. It had just taken her this long to realize it.

I had done plenty in my life to deserve her skepticism. I had not lived the life of a noble man. But since being given a second chance at Redemption, I was gifted something I'd never experienced.

Hope.

Hope for a different life. Hope to be the kind of man who deserved a woman like Sienna. I had spent my entire life knowing that hope was a dangerous thing when it came to anything good.

I was filled with white-hot rage when I saw the love in her eyes clouded with confusion and concern. There was a part of Sienna that knew who I was and where I came from. That I was capable of lying to everyone. Her doubts were plain as day, written across her gorgeous face.

She hadn't slept for shit. She tossed and turned and

muttered in her sleep while I stared at the ceiling and plotted.

Someone wasn't happy I was looking into the ranch's financial inconsistencies. Once I figured out who, I'd know who was benefiting and who was behind it.

I woke early, made her a cup of coffee, and left her a note that I wouldn't be home for dinner. She needed her space, and I needed time to get to the bottom of this. I had a plan for her. I needed only a little time. At Redemption, the ranch was crawling with federal agents, and suddenly I couldn't trust anyone.

"Can you walk me through it one more time?" Something wasn't adding up but I was close.

"Jesus, kid. Are you stupid or something?" Ray was a scraggly old man who had little patience for anything or anyone, but he'd been at Redemption a long time and knew how things operated.

"Just walk me through it."

Ray gestured with his hands and slowed his words to help me understand. "Cows come in. They get inspected. We brand 'em. Then they're moved to pasture."

"Do you or anyone else keep documentation on the number of cattle that come through?"

The dark skin around his eyes crinkled as he looked me over. "Why you asking?"

"Just doing my best to learn what I can."

He shook his head. "No. They come in, get the brand, they go out."

"One more thing." I ignored his exasperated grunt.

"The pasture on the far northwest corner—how many head of cattle are up there?"

Ray dragged a hand across the deep lines in his face. "None up that way at all. It's only ever used as a holding spot if we've got issues with any pastures closer to the barns."

I held out my hand. "Thank you, sir. That helps." Ray eyed my hand before holding up his own.

I left Ray to his business and hurried back to the office. Everything Ray had explained confirmed what I had suspected. It wasn't exactly proof, but it was enough to raise some questions and start getting someone to take a closer look at the operations at Redemption.

The ranch had made a reputation for itself. Not only as the secret underbelly of witness protection, but as a fully functional, profitable cattle ranch. Recently they'd shifted toward a single breeding season, but the ranch was in transition. To make up for the gaps, Redemption had been supplementing the herd by purchasing cattle at auction.

Someone was using that, I suspected, to their advantage.

I hopped back into the side-by-side and made the trip back toward the offices. Now that I knew exactly what to look for, I was energized. My strides ate up the distance toward my office. It was getting late, and I knew Steve cut out early and wouldn't be around to ask questions. As I suspected, he was closing the door to his office when I approached.

"Oh. Parker. Still working?"

I ran my hands down my thighs. "Just finishing up." The lie was smooth and casual, but he still paused. "Have a good night, then."

I gave a tight smile and slipped into my office. I stayed behind the door, listening to his steps retreat down the hallway. In my time at Redemption, I was working the books, but it was low level. Receipts and double-checking figures. A few weeks ago a receipt had been stuffed between pages that referenced a herd of cattle in the northwest pasture. After I brought it to his attention, Steve dismissed it as a clerical error and thanked me for finding it.

What I needed was in Steve's office.

I listened another minute before opening the door to my office and slipping it closed behind me. Steve's door was unlocked, and I stepped inside his office. I exhaled a sigh as the door clicked closed behind me.

Looking around his office, I found it was nearly as sterile as my own. A sad cactus was slowly dying in the windowsill, and a chaotic mess of papers cluttered his desk. I shuffled around his office with the practiced ease of a criminal who'd gotten comfortable working quickly and quietly. The comfort of my old lifestyle went to war with a niggling sense of *this is wrong*.

I tamped down my discomfort and continued looking through the files on his desk. The drawers were unlocked, and I fingered through the files. Most were likely digital, but in the era of old-school cowboys, I would bet there was a literal paper trail for some of the ranch's operations.

Within seven minutes, I'd found what I was looking for in a file marked "Saddlehorn Auctions," with paper receipts waiting to be scanned. I moved quickly to the shelves containing the logbooks for all of Laurel Canyon Ranch's activities. There were dozens. I flipped through the pages, unsure of exactly what I was looking for but unable to ignore the itching feeling I was close to finding something important.

Page after page, it was just as Ray said. Cows came in, got branded, then got sent out to pasture. The trouble was, these numbers didn't match the receipts. I fingered through the file folder again. Shuffled between receipts and other documentation was an agreement to purchase and feed cattle on behalf of Smithton Beef Co. . . . cattle that didn't seem to exist, based on Redemption Ranch's veterinary invoices.

I scanned the pages, memorizing as much information as I could so I could bring this all to Ma. Even if the record-keeping wasn't perfect, there had to be documentation of the cattle sales, the branding, all of it. Whoever was responsible knew I was getting too close to uncovering their secret. It was entirely possible they'd planted drugs in my office in hopes of getting me thrown off the ranch before I figured it out. I'd nail that fucker to the wall out of sheer principle.

Then my eyes stopped and I stared at the signature at the bottom of the receipts.

Evan Walker.

TWENTY-SIX
SIENNA

I TRUSTED PARKER, even after he'd killed a man. I couldn't tell you why, but I did. The shock of Ma's accusations had me reeling, but deep down I knew Parker wasn't the kind of man to mess around with drugs. We'd spent too much time in our little cottage for him to be able to hide something like that from me.

It had been a week since Ma's accusations, and while she hadn't kicked us off the ranch yet, tensions were high. The sprawling ranch covered thousands of acres, and I took my time driving one of the work trucks to clear my head. I'd volunteered to check the water troughs at the other end of the ranch. Then I stopped to feed the working horses that the ranch hands used when they were herding cattle, and I visited with Josh before tackling the more unpleasant tasks, like mucking out stalls. The backbreaking work helped ease the tension in my shoulders and clear my mind.

I couldn't shake the thought that meeting Parker when and how I did was completely unfair. I wished we could have met at Redemption, where he wasn't a criminal and I wasn't a woman with a broken past. But the reality was, we never would have found our place on this ranch had it not been for Chicago. That horrible night bound us together, and as senseless as it was, I wouldn't take it back if that meant Parker wouldn't be in my life.

I needed him to know that I would stand by his side. No matter what. Even when I finally told him the truth.

I drove straight to Gemma's house, and in leaping strides I bounded up the steps of her front porch. I knocked swiftly on the door. "Gem! Gemma, you home?"

She pulled open the door. "Are you okay? What's going on?"

"I'm great! How would you feel about makeovers and shopping?"

"Today?" Her nose scrunched up.

"Like"—I pointed down—"right now." Excitement bubbled out of me.

Gemma gave me a wry smile and added, "You need a shower. Give me fifteen minutes."

"You got it!" I raced back to my truck. "Oh! And Gem? I'll drive."

She rolled her eyes as I got in and sped toward my cottage.

"You ARE A GENIUS." Gemma's voice was languid and deep.

"Mmm." It was all I could muster as the masseuse worked her hands deeply into my muscles. The med spa in Tipp was tiny, but we could get massages, pedicures, and waxes, so it was good enough for us. I'd left out the details that I wanted to be buffed and beautified for her brother, but Gemma was eager to join me.

"I called Johnny, and he said to swing by the shop when we're done. He got some new things in the shop this week."

I turned my head and rested it on my hand to look at Gemma. She was also on her tummy, and a towel draped over her shoulders, covering her scars. I glanced away and wiggled my eyebrows at her. "Definitely. I want to grab a few things before we head home."

Gemma snarled. "Gross. That's my brother."

I feigned innocence. "What? A woman can buy sexy things for herself."

We laughed, and she added, "At this point, I'll only *ever* buy things for myself."

"Aww, Gem. You'll find someone someday, if that's what you want." I saw my opening and took it. "With all the tight jeans and testosterone, you're telling me there hasn't been anyone around the ranch you like?"

She stared at me a beat, seemingly at war with how much she wanted to divulge. "Maybe at one time. A crush. But he made it abundantly clear that he wants nothing to do with me."

I reached out to touch her shoulder. "I'm sorry, Gemma. I've been there and it's hard."

"Thanks."

"Scotty?"

Gemma's mouth turned down to a frown. "I don't really want to talk about it."

I pulled my hand back. "Noted. Well, what about Josh? I heard he and his girlfriend broke up a little while ago. Maybe a hot Army vet would do it for you?"

"Josh?" She laughed. "I think he fools around a lot. Plus, he's like a brother."

"A hot one though." I winked at her, and we dissolved in a fit of laughter, only to get shushed by the masseuses. I stifled my giggle and focused on enjoying the rest of the massage.

After massages, pedicures, and a fresh wax, we were as relaxed as we were smooth. The bell to Rebellion Rose tinkled as we pushed through the glass door. As always, Johnny's shop was perfectly staged and smelled of rich oils and fresh linen.

"There's my two favorite girls!" Johnny walked up from the back and gave us each a hug. "You're both glowing."

"Thank you!" We smiled at Johnny, and Gemma dipped into a bow. "Molly at the spa took good care of us."

"Well"—he bowed back—"let's see if I can keep up."

Johnny walked us around, showing off the new blouses, belts, and accessories that had shipped in this week. After I caught his eye, he tipped his head toward the *special* section in the back. A tiny flutter erupted in my belly. I couldn't wait to find something sexy to surprise Parker.

Within an hour, I was loaded down with bags of lotion, a few tops, a new pair of jeans, and the sexiest little lingerie set I had ever seen. After dropping Gemma off, the sun had settled behind the mountain, and I had only a few minutes before I planned to meet Parker for Sunday family dinner. Before heading out, I put on the lingerie and slipped a dress over the top. The autumn air was cool, but the tall boots and fuzzy knee socks helped to ward off the chill as I made my way to the main lodge.

As soon as I pushed open the door, laughter and the smell of dinner greeted me. It was potluck night, so before leaving town, I'd convinced Al at the Rasa to sell me one of Irma's famous apple pies. Steadying it in my hands, I walked toward the kitchen. In the main living room, I immediately spotted Parker stooped in a chair, his head hung down and his voice low as he spoke with one of the agents.

Evan was helping Ma in the kitchen, and he looked only slightly less miserable. Gemma said there was still no reply to his daily emails to Val.

I saw Agent Dunn—Scotty, as Gemma and Evan called him—in the kitchen setting out plates and silverware. I placed the apple pie on the large kitchen island. Scott nodded in acknowledgment, but something over my shoulder drew his attention, and his eyes flared. I looked back to see Gemma hanging her jacket on a hook. When I turned to Scott, he was striding out the back door.

Very interesting.

"Evening, Ma. What can I help with?"

"Is that Irma's pie?" Evan asked, spinning the pie toward him.

Ma swatted his hand away. "Stop that. It's for everyone, you rat."

We shared a laugh and warmth settled over me. Despite the tensions between Ma and Parker, and Gemma and Scott, everyone else seemed content. Settled. I couldn't help but feel like everything could work out. A strong hand on my shoulder had me leaning back into my husband.

He leaned down to whisper in my ear, low and gravelly. "Hello, wife."

A warm blush spread over my cheeks, and I cleared my throat. "This looks wonderful."

Charbroiled chicken, rice with broccoli, roasted potato wedges, and a huge salad had my mouth watering, and a loud growl escaped my stomach.

Ma winked in my direction. "That's our cue. Let's eat!"

The crowd gathered around the island, and we filled out plates before settling around the large farmhouse-style dining table. Scott never did come back, but I noticed

Gemma's eyes still searched for him. Ma's husband, Robbie, said a short prayer, and we all dug in.

Tension pinched Parker's shoulders. Something was nagging him, but he wouldn't tell me what it was. He needed a break—from the crowd, work, the stress of not knowing what was going to happen with Ma.

"Hey," I leaned over and whispered. "Take me for a walk."

Without a word, Parker stood from the table, gathering both our plates and taking them into the kitchen. I hung around, saying polite goodbyes before meeting him in the kitchen and slipping out the back door into the darkness.

As soon as the quiet night washed over us, Parker let out a deep sigh.

"Are you okay?"

"Fine," he grumbled.

I shook my head to myself and rubbed my hand along his forearm as we walked the loop around the big pond. He was carrying the weight of the world on his shoulders and definitely was not *fine*.

Hoping to lighten the mood, I gave him the rundown of my afternoon with Gemma. "We also stopped into the shop, and I got something I'm excited to show you."

His eyebrow tipped up as he looked down on me. "Oh yeah?"

I bit the inside of my lip to keep from smiling. "Yeah."

I turned to face him, walking backward on the path. Before he could react, I playfully lifted the skirt of my dress, flashing him the tiny scrap of lace between my legs. He stopped dead in his tracks as a giggle burst from me, and I took off running down the path toward the pond.

Gravel crunched beneath our feet. My breath was coming out hard, but I made it only a short distance before

Parker's long strides caught up with me. He lifted me from the ground, his strong arms holding my back tight against his front.

"You are so naughty," he teased and placed me on my feet.

I looked around. We were caped in darkness, but the lights from the main lodge were still in view. Anyone walking the same path could stumble upon us. A zip of excitement danced through me.

"You have no idea." I planted my hands against his chest and walked him backward until his back thumped against a large tree. Parker leaned against the trunk, his head tipped back with a cocky smirk as he looked down on me.

"Want to see the rest of your surprise?" I asked, slowly unbuttoning the top of my dress. His eyes traveled down the column of my neck and lower. Slowly, achingly, I revealed more and more of the stone-blue lace that covered the swell of my breasts. "I bought it because it matches the color of your eyes when they get stormy and dark."

Parker reached down and grabbed his cock through his jeans. "Goddamn, my wife is hot." My skin flushed with heat, and my underwear went damp at his words.

Parker placed his hands on my hips and squeezed. "Let me take you home."

I looked around, then bit my lip. "Uh-uh." Pushing him back up against the tree, I sank to my knees. He straightened but allowed me to unfasten his belt and work down the zipper of his jeans. He was thick and hard behind the denim, and I loved the rush of power I got from knowing he reacted to me this way. He was trying to hold it together, but a tortured groan escaped his chest, and it was so fucking hot. I dragged my nails along the hard plane of his stomach, exploring the hills and valleys of abs that flexed under my touch.

Gravel bit into my knees, but it only added to the naughty thrill of kneeling in front of this man. "Take it out for me."

"What?" Parker dragged his hand down his boxer briefs and over his hardening cock. "This? Tell me what you want."

"I want you to pull your cock out." My tongue darted out to wet my lips, and excitement coiled through my abdomen. "Take it out so I can taste it."

Dipping his fingers under the waistband of his briefs, Parker drew up his erection as I pulled his boxer briefs down his hips. Anyone could stumble upon us—me on my knees and Parker's long, hard dick out, ready and waiting to find the back of my throat. My nipples pebbled at the thought, and I reached up to give them a harsh pinch through the delicate lace.

Parker growled as he fisted his cock, and I couldn't help but smirk as I raked my nails up his thighs and moved my mouth over him.

WHAT. The actual. Fuck.

Sienna's lips parted, and her tongue swirled over the tip of my cock, licking the drop of precum from the head. I had to brace one hand against the rough bark of the tree to keep from falling over when she wet my cock with long, slow strokes of her tongue. Sienna slid my cock into her mouth, guiding it with one hand until it reached the back of her throat. She worked the muscles there, moving her soft palate over the head of my cock, and I nearly lost it.

In the darkness, with only the moonlight in the crisp autumn sky illuminating us, Sienna was a goddess. On her knees, but in complete control, she swirled her tongue and stroked me with one hand as she sucked. My hands moved to her hair, brushing it back so I could see her lush mouth as it stretched around my cock. Sienna's low moans had me barreling toward the edge of release, but as much as I wanted to experience coming with her mouth on me, I needed more.

More of her.

"Sienna." I gently tugged her up, but she protested with

a grunt and took me deeper in her throat. My eyes rolled back, and my head hit the tree behind me.

Jesus, fuck.

I could feel my release gathering low in my balls, and I needed to stop her if I was going to draw this out any longer. I cupped her cheek and eased her head back. Her eyes were wild in the moonlight, and her swollen lips were soft and kissable. I pulled her against me and crushed my mouth to hers.

"I need you all to myself," I snarled into her ear. Tucking myself back into my pants, I then smoothed Sienna's dress as she buttoned the top. Tiny bits of gravel clung to her knees, and I knelt to brush them away. I let my hand slide up her smooth thigh and grip her muscular flesh.

Murmurs of people walking down the path had a giggle erupting from her. "Good timing," she whisper-laughed.

I pinned her with a stare. "Not funny," I warned. "Get over here." I hauled her up and swung her around, onto my back. Her rich belly laugh floated on the air, and I took off in a run as she bounced behind me.

"You're wild."

"What's that?" I called behind me.

"You're wild!" Sienna raised one fist into the air as we laughed and rushed toward our cottage. After bounding up the stairs to our home, I set her down to unlock the door.

"How are you not even winded?" She pressed her body against my back as I fumbled with the key.

I pushed open the door, desperate to feel her again. "To the bed. Now."

"Ooh, I like you grouchy." I slapped her ass and she yelped and added, "Yes, sir."

As she sat, Sienna tucked her hands under her knees, pushing her tits together. I knew the gauzy lace beneath her dress would taste like heaven. I took my time, reaching behind me to peel off my shirt as she sat on the bed, removing her shoes and the fuzzy socks that went all the way up to her knees. The tiny indents from the stones were red against her creamy skin, and I glowered.

I stalked toward the bed but lowered to my knees. Moving slowly, I kissed up each calf to her knee, careful to plant gentle kisses across the indented skin.

"Does it hurt?" I asked.

"No. Park, you feel so good." Sienna had started to unbutton her dress when I stilled her hands. "Let me."

She groaned, and her head tipped back, her arms supporting her weight. One by one I slipped the buttons through my calloused fingers until the entire dress spread open, revealing her soft curves covered in delicate blue-gray lace.

"Christ, Sienna. You're luminous."

Her hand brushed down her chest and across her flat belly. "I'm glad you like it."

"Like it? I could live a thousand lifetimes and never find anyone as beautiful and full of light as you." The blush on her cheeks deepened, and my cock thickened as I kicked off my jeans and boxers. My hands found her slim waist, and I hooked my fingers into her panties, pulling them down her thighs and past her ankles. I stilled on her bare, puffy pussy, and my eyes locked on hers.

"You like?" Any hint of shyness vanished as she tipped her knees open.

I slid my hands up her thighs, dragging my nose along the thin skin. My hot breath danced over her pussy, already slick and wet.

"I like you any way I can have you, but this . . ." I teased soft kisses around her clit. "This is heaven." Pushing her knees farther apart, I devoured her. Sienna's hips rose to meet my eager mouth as she alternated between clutching the sheets and tugging at my hair. Every tingle of pain the pulling caused drove me mad. I couldn't get enough of her. Still teasing her clit, I ran one finger down her seam, and her thighs quivered around my head.

"I know how full my wife likes to be. Don't worry, baby," I said as I slipped one finger into her heat. She was dripping wet, so I slid a second finger into her and licked up every drop of her arousal.

Sienna's voice was raw and strangled as she cried out: "That goddamn tongue. Holy shit."

I knew she was close, and I needed to feel her squeeze and pulse around me as she came. Slowly I dragged my fingers out of her and hiked her farther up on the bed, then settled my hips in the cradle of her thighs.

Her nails raked up the back of my neck and into my hair. "Park . . ."

I lowered to give her a few gentle, sweet kisses. We've fucked rough and hard, but this time I needed to savor her. I needed to remember every inch of her, because when she was gone, it wouldn't just be her body I missed. I'd miss her laughter. Her dancing. Her sunshine.

I slid my hands between her breasts and gripped my fingers around her throat and lightly squeezed, feeling her rapid pulse beneath my fingertips.

"Yes, yes. Park, yes."

I centered myself and moved, bit by bit, inside her until I was fully seated in her wet, hot pussy. Her thighs wrapped around my hips as her body shook. Languidly I took us closer and closer to the edge, savoring every drag of my cock through her slick center.

I was losing her. It was only a matter of time, but it

didn't matter, because with her I had already completely lost myself. As panic built in my chest, I drove deeper into her wet, sucking heat. A snarl ripped from my chest. I'd be damned if I didn't make sure she was set up for life, and whether she knew it or not, she'd always carry a piece of me with her. Stroke after stroke I poured my heart and soul into her.

The words I needed to say burned at the back of my throat. Stuck. So instead of giving voice to the growing love I couldn't seem to control, I used my body to show her.

Worship her.

"You are so fucking beautiful. My wife. My love." The words, low and rough, tumbled out of me as I buried my face in her hair. Her body shook as she moaned and rode out her release. The tight squeeze of her pussy tore mine from me, seconds behind her, as my cock pulsed and I pushed deep inside her.

I held my weight off her with my forearms, but she pulled me down to her. "I like to feel your weight on me."

I stroked the hair from her face and kissed down her jaw and across her chest. One pert, pink nipple poked through the lace of her bra, and I teased it with a drag of my teeth. She hissed in a breath, and I soothed the sting with the flat of my tongue.

"Let's get you cleaned up, beautiful girl."

After a quick shower, I walked her back to our bed and wrapped her in my arms. I had no fucking clue how I was going to live without that woman. It would absolutely destroy me. I had decided a long time ago that the most important thing was to protect Sienna. If that meant she led a life without me, then so be it. If her safety meant I had to rot in a prison cell for what I had done in Chicago, I'd go willingly. All that mattered was that Sienna could lead a long and happy life. Our days were numbered, and the insistent urge to memorize every curve and freckle had me tucking her closer to me.

As my breaths grew heavy and deep, I kissed her flaxen hair. "Sweet dreams, darling wife."

TWENTY-EIGHT
SIENNA

Tears pricked at my eyes as I stared out the bedroom window, wrapped in the arms of my husband. After his strong hands smoothed cleansing bubbles over my body in the shower, he'd laid me down, wrapped me in his arms, and soothed me with his warmth.

But I couldn't sleep.

I recalled every demanding stroke, and I knew exactly what had happened.

You are so fucking beautiful. My wife. My love.

His words clanged around my head in an incessant loop as my heart squeezed. I knew those words for exactly what they were.

A goodbye.

But it was too late. I had fallen in love with my husband, and I couldn't let that go just yet. Listening to his measured breaths, I whispered into the darkness.

"Park, I'm not ready to leave here yet." My voice was thick with emotion.

He nodded against me and pulled my back tighter

against his chest. I sighed. Emotion built behind my ribs and grew bigger and bigger, inflating like a balloon until the tiniest breath would make it burst.

My mind raced to lay out the facts, find the silver lining. *Anything to make him understand.*

Parker had saved my life. I had spent a surprising, intoxicating few weeks discovering the man behind Parker's stoic facade. I looked forward to his daily gripes and grumbles, only to tug a smile from him. I'd crushed on that version of him but fallen madly in love with the man who loved to read spicy romance and cleaned when he was stressed out.

Suddenly our cottage felt too small. Despite his warmth seeping into me, I felt cold and alone—the worst kind of lonesome, where you're not even by yourself.

It couldn't wait until morning. I had spent too many nights sad and alone in Chicago, desperate to have someone to share my feelings with. Parker cared for me. I felt it in every touch and lingering stare.

I gently bucked my hips backward to rouse him.

"Mmm." Parker ground his hips into me, and I felt the hard steel of him press into my back.

Mistake.

I stifled a soft giggle and rolled to face him. "Husband," I whispered as I brushed the hair from his forehead.

"Wife." Sleep laced in his voice as I kissed the tip of his nose.

"I can't sleep. I'm worried."

"The cleaning bucket is in the closet."

I rocked toward him. "No." I laughed. "I need to talk to you."

His eyes blinked open as they tried to focus on my face in the dim light. "Talk to me, babe. What is it?"

"I don't want us to have to leave the ranch."

He lifted to his elbow and propped his head on his hand. "I'm working on that. Let me take care of it. Trust me."

Trust.

So often I'd given my trust freely and openly. That was never the problem. No, it was the aftermath of picking up the pieces of my broken heart once that trust left me alone. Again.

"What are we going to do about Ma?"

"I've been thinking about that." Parker rubbed the sleep from his eyes and sighed. "Sienna, we need to tell her. About Chicago. Evan and Gemma too."

Fear clutched my throat and I shook my head. I couldn't bring myself to accept it was our only option.

"Someone is trying to get us kicked off the ranch. I'd bet anything it has to do with the finances not adding up and me poking around. Asking questions."

"What if she doesn't believe you? She may force us to leave anyway."

"I will always take care of you. But if she's going to trust us, we need to trust her."

The threat of tears burned behind my eyes. Once Parker knew the truth, that our marriage couldn't protect him like we'd thought, I'd lose him. But maybe there was a small chance that Ma Brown could help us. Maybe we'd proven ourselves worthy of redemption.

I nodded and swallowed past the thickness in my throat. "You're right. It's time."

"Tomorrow." He kissed my hair and tucked a hand under his head, drifting back to sleep.

"Tomorrow."

~

"You ready for this?" Parker wiped down the kitchen table as I arranged a plate of freshly baked chocolate chip cookies.

"Hell no," I admitted as I wiped my hands against my outer thighs and plastered on my sunniest smile. "Let's do it."

Parker stopped me midstride. His large palms smoothed over my arms and shoulders. "We came here to keep you safe. If that's not possible, then . . ." He paused as though the words were painful to admit. "Then we need help."

I looked into his eyes, searching for the right answer. "If they know the truth. If they know what happened."

He shushed me. "I know."

I shook my head. I needed to get it out. "No, Parker. You don't understand. I was wrong—about not being forced to testify against you. It's TV bullshit. If everyone knows, I can't protect you."

A small smile teased his full lips as he looked down on me. "I know."

I blinked at him, struggling to understand. "You know. You know?"

"One trip to the library and I figured it out. While it sounds good in theory, the whole marital privilege thing is bullshit."

"But you—then why did you—"

"Believe it or not, I don't mind being married to you. I'm in it for more than your ability to keep secrets." Then he winked, fucking *winked* at me.

I pushed his arms down. "How can you joke at a time like this? I am *literally* freaking out."

He walked over to the plate of cookies and popped a whole one into his mouth. "Dunno. Guess your optimism is rubbing off on me."

I growled at the knock at the door. "It's all those romance novels. I think I liked you better when you were crabby," I grumbled as I stalked toward the door.

After I pulled the door open, I saw Evan standing on our porch with his arms crossed over his broad chest. Gemma peeked behind him and waved, and Agent Ma Brown offered me a sad smile.

"Please come in." I stepped aside, and they filed into our small cottage. "I made cookies." I infused as much positivity in my voice as I could, but it still fell flat.

Smooshed on the couch, Evan, Gemma, and Agent Brown sat shoulder to shoulder, waiting.

"Are you pregnant?" Gemma beamed up at me.

"Jesus, Gem." Parker sighed. "No."

She looked at Ma Brown and shrugged.

Parker stepped up next to me and grabbed my hand. "I want to start by saying we're telling you this because we trust you. That's a hard thing for me to admit, but it's the truth. And we want you three to trust us too."

"Something happened in Chicago." I tried to sound brave, but my voice wobbled.

Gemma's eyes went wide. Evan's jaw ticced once, and Ma's head tipped back in a slight frown, assessing each of us in the cramped space.

Parker stepped forward, shielding me from the brunt of their stares. He looked toward Evan. "Once you fell off the grid, people started asking questions. Getting nervous. It wasn't long until everyone assumed I knew more than I was letting on. The Family wasn't happy with my silence, so one night I was set up. I was able to fight myself free. I ran. I ran to a place I thought was empty and only I knew about."

He squeezed my hand and continued. "Sienna and her uncle were closing up the restaurant when I broke in. I thought I could hide. In the shuffle I'd lost my gun, and everyone in the city knew my face. I had nowhere else to go. When I saw she was there, I tried to leave, but her uncle shouted. They must have heard and broke in behind me."

"Is that how he died?" Gemma asked.

I tightened my grip on Parker's hand, willing to steal some of his strength as painful memories of that night came flooding back. "He couldn't get another word out. They shot him."

"Fuck," Evan said under his breath.

"Keep going," Agent Brown urged.

Parker's jaw tightened as though he could recall each detail too. "There were two of them. I was fighting them both, but at one point, one left to find where Sienna had hidden."

"And then what?" Gemma leaned forward, her eyes glued to me.

Parker stiffened at the memory of what came next. I straightened. I could get through it. I'd done it a thousand times in my mind.

"The guy came into the kitchen where I was hiding. He didn't see me at first, but he found my purse. Dumped it all over the floor and grabbed my ID. He snapped a picture of it and texted it to someone, I think." I swallowed hard and willed my voice not to shake at the next part. "The guy found me huddled under a cabinet. He dragged me out by my leg. I kicked and screamed and scratched at him the best I could."

"Good for you." Agent Brown nodded in my direction.

I swallowed thickly, not wanting to remember but knowing I had to continue. Just this once. "He was really strong. His hands were all over me, and I couldn't stop it. He squeezed and laughed. I did what I could to fight, but he was so much bigger than me. He tore my skirt."

Parker and Evan sat stone-still, backs stiff and straight. Gemma's hand flew to her mouth. Ma Brown shook her head, sadness etched on her face.

"When I kept fighting, he slapped me in the face. Screamed at me to stop resisting."

That was how Parker found me. Helpless and pinned to the floor as a strange man slapped me across the face and tore at my clothing. I could still recall the look of horror and disgust on Parker's face after he stalked into the kitchen.

"I saw red," Parker interjected. "I grabbed him by the collar and dragged him off her." He closed his eyes and dropped my hand to drag both of his through his thick hair. "I hit him. I couldn't stop. I didn't *want* to stop."

"And you killed him. The both of them?" Ma Brown spoke matter-of-factly.

"Yes."

One word and our secret was gone. The truth was out there. Parker had torn the man off me and beat him to death as I'd screamed in horror. Sirens had wailed in the distance —the neighborhood had likely heard the screaming and gunshots. Once Parker's arms had gone limp, I had scrambled toward the body of my uncle and sobbed until I was wrung out. Until Parker had stood over me, telling me we had to leave.

"I'd do it again too."

I looked up at him as his eyes traveled over my face.

"You couldn't have let him go," Evan added. "They'd

have just sent someone else. And then you had Sienna to think about. They had her face and address."

Gemma wrapped her arms around herself. She'd been through a different hell, but she knew fear like I did. Her voice turned hard, much harder than should have been possible for her nineteen years. "They deserved it."

Ma Brown sighed. "You're both lucky to have gotten out of that restaurant alive, let alone the city."

"Parker knew we had to leave. I could barely walk, but I followed him until we could figure it out."

"I got in contact with the cop I used to help out." He nodded toward Evan. "Val's partner. He alluded to where you were, but I wasn't certain. Figured I could shoot my shot and hope for the best. I doubted anyone would suspect I would wind up in Montana."

A long silence filled the air. Our arrival in Montana wasn't without consequences. Unknown to us, we'd been followed, and it had put Gemma and Val in grave danger. As a result, Val had returned to Chicago, and Evan hadn't been the same. Tension clung to the air, and my heart pounded in my ears.

"I never intended for you to get caught up in this." Parker looked between his siblings. "For either of you. We didn't know we were followed."

"We know." Gemma's voice was small but strong. She was still working through her own emotions regarding her brothers, but it was progress.

"We got here, and it wasn't exactly a warm reception," I added. "I kind of freaked out and told Evan we were married."

"You're not even married?" Gemma's shock rose above the tension.

"We are." I raised a hand to quell her question. "But not

until we were already in Montana. I was terrified that Parker would go to prison for what he did to save me. I said the first thing that came to mind and blurted it out, and it was too late to take it back, so we did it. We were the only two alive after the restaurant, so I thought it would mean if we were questioned, I wouldn't have to testify against him."

"You watch too much television." Ma was slightly amused, but her eyes were still hard and assessing.

"I know." I smiled and tucked a hair behind my ear. "Turns out I tricked poor Parker into marrying me, and there isn't a damn thing I can do to protect him."

"Poor Parker?" Gemma scoffed, and it eased the tension in the room as everyone joined in a quiet laugh that died in the autumn air.

"Fuck." Evan ran his hands across his face. "You should have told us sooner."

"I know." Parker nodded but continued to study his little brother.

"Is that everything?" Ma asked as she stood.

I looked toward my husband, waiting. He nodded and my mouth hung open.

"So that's it then." Ma slapped her hands on her thighs and rose from the couch. "I need to think about this. We'll talk later."

"What do we do till then?" I asked.

Ma looked around at all of us. "You keep your mouths shut."

We all nodded in solemn agreement.

"I'm drained," Gemma groaned and pulled Evan to his feet. "Let's go. It's been a heavy night for everyone."

She turned toward me and pulled me into a hug. "I'm sorry for you."

I squeezed her back. "I'm sorry for you too."

We broke apart, and I walked her toward the door as Evan and Parker finished a hushed conversation with a shake of their hands.

As the door snicked shut behind them, I was too stunned to move. Parker had the opportunity to tell everyone what he'd discovered with the books, and instead he'd remained silent, destroying our chances to stay.

TWENTY-NINE
PARKER

I couldn't do it.

The plan was to tell the truth about our marriage and then expose what I'd found with the books, but I couldn't bring myself to do it. With Evan's name still attached to the purchase receipts, I couldn't muster the courage to call him on it.

Drained from the tense evening, I slinked to bed like a coward and ignored the pleading looks of confusion Sienna sent my way. I also sneaked out early the next morning because I was an asshole.

Four weeks went by, and we all pretended like I hadn't admitted to killing two men and that Sienna and my marriage was bullshit. It didn't matter that she had become the most important thing in my life. But when a thick white envelope addressed to me, but intended for Sienna, finally arrived, I knew it was time.

I made arrangements for Ma to come by. Our time was up, and I would give her what information I could while trying to protect the life my brother had created for himself. I asked him to meet with us, and he agreed without hesitation. I'd give him the opportunity to speak his truth, but I wasn't about to force his hand.

The envelope was heavy in my hands, and I knew, beyond a shadow of a doubt, that this was the right thing for Sienna. She deserved this. It gave me strength and comfort to finally make the right choice in my life, especially for her.

The knock at the door jumbled my nerves, and I let out a shaky breath. My eyes darted to Sienna. She was wiped after a long day at work, and I urged her to take a hot bath and a nap. Plus, it gave me a little while to work things out in my head while I straightened up the cottage.

"Dude. I can hear you thinking in there and smell the Pine-Sol. Open up." Evan's voice floated through the front door of the cottage.

I pulled the door open wide. "Asshole."

He smiled and shook my hand. "Dickbag."

"Sienna's sleeping in the back, so let's keep it down, but thanks for coming." I looked him over. His eyes were bright, and he was clean shaven. *Happy*. "What's up with you?"

His smirk widened. "She wrote back, man." Like a giddy teenager, he grabbed my shoulder and shook me as he squealed like a twelve-year-old girl. "She fucking wrote back!"

I smiled, so happy for him. "That's great, man. Congratulations. So what's next?"

He slapped me on the shoulder. "Time to get my girl."

"Well all right." I shook my head. Everything falling into place for Evan. I wasn't about to ruin that. If it meant covering for him, so be it.

"So what's up? What do we need to talk about?"

I ran my hand down the scruff at my jaw. "You know what? It's nothing. Just have a beer with me." I walked to the fridge and pulled out two cold ones.

He eyed me. "Don't do that."

I tipped my hand. "What?"

He grabbed his beer, popped the top, and took a long pull before answering. "*That* thing." He pointed his bottle at me. "The thing where you think you know what's best for everyone, and so you let the shit pile onto you."

I opened my own beer and drank a third of it. It burned in my chest and did nothing to allay the pounding in my skull. "I'm not."

Evan set his bottle on the table with a snap. "Parker, let's not do this."

"It's good, man."

"What the fuck." He was exasperated but I wouldn't budge. "You cut your own finger off, and you're going to tell me that you *don't* take on too much shit?"

I looked down at my hand and flexed. "I told you. I don't ever want to talk about that."

"Well, I do!" He raised his voice, but when my eyes sliced to Sienna's bedroom, he quieted. "I fucked up. I was ready to take my punishment, but you wouldn't allow it."

My back straightened, and bile burned at the back of my throat. "You were twenty-two. It wasn't right."

"I was old enough to know better."

I laughed a humorless laugh. "Well, that may be true." Evan had gotten tangled up with a stripper, and one night they'd taken her tips and lost it all on blackjack. *Thousands.* He hadn't realized she was up to her glittery tits in debt to our associates.

He was better than that, whether he realized it or not. I'd be damned if he ended up another club-hopping *bro*, flashing his money at the club, who wound up dead in the back of a car before he hit twenty-five. So I took his punishment and froze him out. He was stubborn, and he didn't leave the life altogether, but thanks to my influence, he never had the chance to climb the ranks.

"I didn't ask you to take the punishment for me."

I looked at my little brother. It was never a choice. "I'd do it again though."

He walked to me and gripped my shoulder. "I know you would. So let me in this time."

The weight of it—the Family, Sienna, Montana, the books—finally felt like too much. So I told him. Everything from the numbers being off to the questions I'd been asking, even the file on Smithton Beef Co. I'd found, but I didn't mention his name attached to the purchases.

Evan drained his beer. "Does Ma know?"

"She knows someone isn't happy with Sienna and me showing up here. Someone planted drugs in my office. I didn't want to tell her about the books until I had something to give her. Anything."

"Give her the copy of the purchases."

I swallowed more of my beer and shook my head. "That's not an option."

"Why the fuck not?"

I looked him over. In all the time I'd spent with him on the ranch, he was finally happy. It killed me to take that away from him, but I was so tired of the lies. I'd still cover for him, but maybe he'd tell me the truth—anything I could go on. I handed him a copy of the receipt.

He scanned the page, then paused to stare at his name scrawled across the bottom. "This is unreal. That's not me."

I sighed. "Dude. It's a signature."

Evan flipped the paper onto the table and paced across the floor. "And it's not mine."

I took a long, hard look at him. His face was chiseled and scruffy now, but I could still see the baby with the cleft lip who'd turned into the rambunctious little kid who'd turned into the brother I'd promised myself I'd always protect. Our mother had turned her back on us. The foster care system had failed us. When the dust settled, it was only two scared kids holding on to each other and hoping to survive.

How had we gotten so far off track?

Evan filled the tense silence between us. "I'm a lefty. Look at the tilt of the letters. I didn't sign that shit." He poked his finger down hard on the paper, wobbling the table beneath it.

And then he spoke them—the two words we used with only each other when there was no one left to trust and we needed to hear it straight. "No bullshit."

The pinch in my shoulders released. I held my hand out to him and nodded as we shook. When a knock sounded at the door, Evan grabbed the paper from the table.

"Ma," I said in greeting as Agent Brown entered the cottage.

She looked between us. "Boys."

I smiled at that. Two grown-ass men reduced to boys in the presence of this tenacious woman.

"Whaddaya got for me?"

Evan and I exchanged a charged look before I stared hard at the closed bedroom door. We'd trusted Ma with the truth about Chicago. I had to believe I could trust her with the other information I had dug up.

For her.

The cottage was pristine but it was cramped. Without a lot of places to sit, we scattered around the living space. Ma sat on the couch, her hands clasped in her lap, waiting. Evan sat on the end table next to her. I leaned against the armrest of the living room chair. For a moment we let the quiet move over us like fog.

Finally I sucked in a deep inhale and took the first step. "I still don't know who planted the fentanyl, or why, but I think it has to do with something I stumbled across."

Ma's eyebrow tipped up as though she was surprised there may be something going down on her ranch she didn't know about. "I'm listening."

Evan relaxed and nodded in encouragement as I started from the beginning.

"I was just doing my job. Checking balances, running numbers. Just like you told me to. It was a mess."

Ma nodded, knowing exactly what kind of mess I had been trying to organize.

"In one of the piles there was a receipt that couldn't be accounted for. At first I didn't think much of it. I put it aside and kept working. Then it happened again. When I asked Steve about it, he seemed unfazed and said he would handle it." I shrugged. The first few times it happened, I had assumed he had taken care of whatever inconsistency it was. "By the time I learned what the jargon on the receipts and logbooks meant, I understood what I was looking at. Then it *really* got interesting."

Ma sat straighter. "What were they for?"

"Cattle. A lot of them."

"That's not unusual," Evan added. "As we're adjusting the breeding program, we've had to make purchases to fill in the gaps. The breeding program isn't self-sustainable to meet our demands just yet."

I stood to pace, my mind zipping in a thousand directions as I tried to recall just why it had bothered me so badly. "I get that." Frustration gnawed at me as I tried to articulate the ominous feeling I'd gotten that day at the office. I looked toward Ma. "I was learning. I wanted to do a good job. It felt *good* to be doing what felt like honest work. So I started asking questions."

"What kinds of questions?" Ma's eyes were unfocused, like she was working out the invisible puzzle right in front of her.

"Stupid ones, according to Ray." That got a wry laugh from them. "Operational. Where the cattle came from. Where they grazed, how they rotated through the pastures. I didn't think much of it."

"Someone did." The muscle in Evan's jaw moved as he crossed his arms.

"But here's the thing." I paused my pacing to look at them. "They existed on paper, but there is no evidence of those herds anywhere on Redemption Ranch."

Ma lifted her hands. "All right. Let's walk through it."

Evan's back went straight. "Maybe the cattle do exist, but somehow the logs were screwed up. They didn't get counted in the books."

Ma looked over her glasses directly at me. "You're not even going to mention Evan's name in the books?"

I steeled my gaze. "No, ma'am."

A ghost of a smile slipped across her features, but she looked away and it was gone. "And why's that?"

"Because it has nothing to do with him." With my anger rising, my voice was hard. "You knew about that?"

She smiled then. "You're not the only one who's been asking questions." Then she lifted both hands. "I just needed to see where you stood on the matter."

"So if these cattle exist," I started, willing the conversation to get back on track, "then why forge Evan's signature?"

"Fuck. Yeah, you're right. If it was a legitimate purchase, it wouldn't be unusual for me to sign off on it."

"And," I added, "according to Ray, cattle come in, get branded, and go to pasture. There'd be a dozen eyes on the cattle themselves. No one could hide a herd that size without raising some eyebrows."

I waited a beat before I added, "Unless . . . Could it be Ray? He's branding cattle but not logging them?" I thought back to the wily old bastard. It didn't seem likely, but I had a sneaking suspicion he hadn't always been a ranch hand. A criminal can smell his own kind.

"I don't think so. Ray is an asshole but he's not crooked. Least not anymore." Ma shook her head, dismissing the idea.

"What about someone else? Another ranch hand?" I looked between them, hoping maybe the suggestion would spark a memory of some disgruntled employee.

"That's a stretch," Ma countered. "They wouldn't have access to the accounts or the documentation to cover it up."

Evan ran a hand over his face as I rested my forearms on top of my head and sighed.

What a fucking mess.

Ma tapped a finger on the wrinkle just above her lips. "Steve?"

I frowned. "I don't think so. After working with him, I'm not sure he's smart enough. I'm almost certain he's involved, but . . ." I sighed and slapped my hands on the outside of my thighs. "I don't know. It would have to be someone who's smart. Close enough to intimately know our operations and how to exploit them."

A small gasp floated over my shoulder, barely audible, and I turned to see Sienna standing in the doorway of our bedroom with her hand over her mouth and her owl eyes shining with tears. "Oh my god. I know. I know who it is."

THIRTY

SIENNA

I SAT WRAPPED in a blanket between Ma and Evan as Parker paced across the floor.

"Now you can't go throwing accusations around here." Ma's eyes were intense, but I was certain.

"Yes, ma'am. I understand." Emotion clogged my throat as I thought of Chet being responsible for the logbook inconsistencies. Trying to get rid of us. My stomach knotted. The possibility he was involved was a niggling pinch in my side.

"Tell us what you know." Parker's voice was cold and hard, but when my eyes met his, he softened. "Please."

I cleared my throat. "I don't have proof." I looked between the trio as they scrutinized my every syllable. "But after hearing you tonight, some weird things that nagged me make a lot more sense."

"Weird?" Ma prompted.

I turned my hips to face her. "I'm always trying to learn. Figure people out. He's always been a fun little mystery wrapped up in an old-school cowboy package. The old man charm, his wealth of knowledge. But he's definitely not from here. Josh mentioned he has a daughter he doesn't like to talk about. His favorite football team is the New York Giants."

"Lots of people like the Giants," Evan added.

I chewed my bottom lip. "Yeah. That's true. But he's, like, *really* into them. My dad used to always say, 'Love your city, love your team. It's where you'll find your roots.'"

"Is there anything else?" Parker walked behind the couch, placing his large palms against my shoulders and massaging. His touch centered me and encouraged me to go on.

"He keeps notes. A *lot* of them. Usually he has a little leather-bound notepad when we're checking the herds. It's always with him. But then there's the black notebook he keeps in his office. He keeps it locked in a safe. I've seen it a few times—he takes it out, writes something, then immediately locks it back up. If everything he documents is in the one he keeps with him, what's in the one from the safe?"

Evan paused, mulling everything over. "So let's lay it out. In the file Parker found, there was a purchase agreement. Someone, presumably Chet, is making purchases for Smithton Beef Co. They provide the up-front cost for the purchase and feed, thinking these cattle will pasture here at the ranch until they're ready for slaughter."

"Only he never actually purchases any cattle at the auction. The money from Smithton gets deposited in some separate account, and he pockets the money." Parker nodded as it all started to unfurl.

"What happens when it's time to sell and Smithton Beef Co. wants their cut?" A thousand questions rattled around in my head, but how Chet ever thought he could get away with it was the most curious.

"Sell a few excess cattle, get Steve to fudge the numbers,

report some cows died of natural causes, move some money around. There's all kinds of ways to explain it." Parker rounded the couch and settled into a chair, resting his elbows on top of his knees. "It's how we kept under the radar in Chicago. If you keep moving the money, no one can find it."

Parker reached back to knead the thick muscles at the base of his neck as he looked at me. "But why would Chet want you off the ranch? He adores you."

"I'm married to you, and you've been asking too many questions. If something is off and he's behind it, the last thing he needs is someone snooping around."

Evan turned. "So he or Steve planted drugs, hoping that would be a quick way for Ma to throw you out on your ass."

Parker's fists clenched at his sides. "Only it didn't work because Ma didn't believe the drugs were mine." He looked at Ma. "Why didn't you?"

A small smile floated across Ma's face like she was enjoying us fumbling around and trying to figure it all out. "See, when you first came here and I did all that digging into your past? I remembered." Ma tapped her temple and looked at me as I stared in awe. "Were you aware that your husband here has had 'moderate persistent asthma' since he was a child?" I looked at my husband. I had no idea, and his only admission was the tiniest nod.

"And fentanyl," she continued, "is a synthetic opioid whose side effects include suppressed breathing and bronchospasms. Fentanyl is more than fifty times stronger than heroin. If it was his and he was using, he'd be a dead man."

"Someone wanted me gone. Off the ranch so I'd stop shining a light on the operation." The hard tone of Parker's voice sent a nauseating tingle through me. "They assumed the fastest way was to get Ma riled up, and she'd throw me out. When that doesn't work, the only thing left is to up the stakes. He'll make a move."

"It all adds up to Chet being at the center of it." The truth was bitter on my tongue.

Ma Brown let out a deep sigh. "Chet has a history. He came to Redemption a long time ago and has been a loyal employee—at least we thought so. But it's not uncommon for those in witness protection to fall back into old habits. It's much more common than you think."

"We don't even *really* know what he's up to. Only a file —which we're hoping still exists after all this—a theory that it has to do with the herd numbers, and that he's trying to keep it under wraps." It was Evan's turn to burn a path across our living room floor.

"He's smart. Smart enough to pull something like this off on a ranch full of federal agents." Anger and betrayal tinged Ma's voice, and I placed my hand on her knee in comfort.

"Which also means he's got balls," Evan added.

"Or he's getting reckless. Desperate." Parker stilled as we all looked at each other and waited.

We sat in strained silence. I knew what to do. "I can find out. Get him to tell me what's going on."

"No fucking way," Parker ground out.

Evan shook his head. "Not a chance."

"It's the only way. If Chet is behind this, or he *knows* something, who better to let in than his protégée? If he's behind this, he's too smart to take chances. He trusts me." I looked to Agent Brown to be the rational one. "Ma?"

She looked weary and a bit beaten down. "A confession would certainly make things easier, and me approaching him or asking questions would only raise his suspicions."

"I don't like this." Parker's voice was laced with

concern. "A man against a wall will lash out, and I will not have my wife in the cross fire." My heart raced at the intensity of how his gravelly voice danced over the words *my wife*.

I had to do it. For him. For us and this random, insane life we'd stumbled on. My heart splintered thinking that the kind old man who'd welcomed me so openly had been tangled up in cattle fraud and was desperate enough to get us kicked off the one place that had kept us safe after Chicago. I trusted him. I felt sick just thinking about it.

My mouth was dry, and nausea did a slow roll in my belly. "I know what we need to do."

THIRTY-ONE
SIENNA

"You keep your chin up and stay alert." Parker looked down at me, his scowl deepening as his cobalt eyes moved over the planes of my face. His hands moved to cup my cheeks as he dropped his forehead to mine. A low grumble radiated from his chest.

He pulled his head back to study me. "I could always beat it out of him."

A light laugh escaped me, and I wound my arms around his waist, resting my head against his chest. His heartbeat pounded against my ear.

I took a cleansing breath. "I can do this."

The plan was to get Chet talking, like he tended to do, when we were out checking cattle in the pastures. Ma made sure Josh was busy with other tasks, leaving Chet and me alone. I was going to do what I always did—ask too many questions and poke and prod until something knocked loose. I couldn't raise his suspicions, but I could play the sunny, silly woman rattling off questions only a city girl would ask. It was a long shot that he'd spill any of his closely guarded secrets, but it was the only thing we had to go on.

I knew in my gut he was hiding something, and the "ghost cattle" theory was the only thing we had to go on. He wouldn't reveal everything—I knew that for sure—but if I could get something, any little nugget that made sense of what was happening, maybe we could stay. Parker could be safe. The thought of Parker's secret being exposed was gut-wrenching. If anyone else knew about Chicago, there'd be no way Ma could protect him, and he would go to prison for the rest of his life.

Fuck that noise.

I steeled my shoulders, convincing myself that I could pull this off.

Just another day at work.

I swallowed down the nausea that threatened at the back of my throat. I fluffed my hair and hoped that I looked normal despite how liquid my insides felt.

"Stay on your horse. Be careful. Watch his hands, and if he tries to grab—"

"I'll be fine." I squeezed my eyes closed and willed myself to believe my own words. "I'll be careful. If something goes wrong, I'll take off on the horse and find you. I promise."

"We could loop Josh in. See if he can get it out of him."

Last night we talked about a thousand options, including asking Josh for help. The trouble was, we weren't certain he wasn't in on it, and we'd determined that it wasn't worth the risk of showing our hand before we could get more information from Chet. Without information or hard evidence, we were stuck.

The fewer people involved the better.

Ma's words hung around my shoulders. This up to me.

"Josh is too close. It makes sense that I'd be asking questions. Even if he wasn't in on it, Chet would know if Josh started poking around. He's too smart to fall for that."

"If you can't get anything from him, we don't have enough to prove anything I've found. There's nothing more than some numbers that don't add up and a couple of threats. If he knows about Chicago, you're not safe with me."

I steadied my eyes on his. "Then we run. Thelma and Louise style. Only maybe we stay away from tall cliffs."

"I can get behind that. Dibs on being Louise."

I swatted his arm. "Why do I have to be the sad housewife?"

Parker lifted his hand to cup my face and stroke his thumb across my cheek. "You're right. You are far too vibrant for that. You should just be you. Strong-willed perfection wrapped in sunshine. As long as I'm breathing, you will always be taken care of. You have my word."

He pulled me closer, and I drew his spicy, masculine scent deep into my lungs. Wrapped in his arms, I felt strong. Steady. Parker had a way to light me up from the inside and amplify the glow that nestled in my chest. Since losing my parents, I had searched for a true and deep connection, someone to understand that I needed roots but still wanted my limbs to climb high enough to feel the sun and sway in the breeze. With him, I was special. I belonged.

He's the home I've been searching for.

A knock at the door broke our bubble, and reality came filtering in. I untangled my arms from around Parker's waist as he moved to open the door for Ma. Overnight she'd transformed from Redemption Ranch's caring matri-arch to government special agent. Two additional men, dressed in common work clothes but clearly trained agents, followed silently behind her. One had a gun tucked into his waistband, and he adjusted his flannel to hide the bump.

Ma's eyes were hard and assessing and telegraphed that this whole operation was serious business. Even in the dim predawn light, I could see her analyzing, mulling, and making a thousand tiny decisions as we stood in my living room.

"You know what to do?" Ma asked me.

I gulped hard but tried to stifle it. I spared a glance at Parker and pressed my tongue to the roof of my mouth to keep my emotions in check. I was doing this for him. For *us*. When all this was over, we'd have proven ourselves worthy and earned our place at Redemption.

"You'll have a mic." She held up a tiny microphone connected to a wire and battery pack. I stepped forward, and she tucked the pack into the small of my back. Another agent stepped forward to tape it into place as I held my undershirt up and squeezed my eyes closed. Ma gently wove the wire up my shirt and secured it on the inside collar of my flannel. She adjusted my shirt to help it lay correctly as I patted the pack and fussed with the hem of the shirt.

"If you could test it, ma'am." The taller agent held a small box to his ear.

I cleared my throat. "Um . . . testing? One, two—"

"That's fine," he said as the other stifled a laugh.

Jesus. It's not like I know what I'm doing here.

Parker's hard eyes sliced to him, cutting off his laughter, and he choked it down.

"I can hear you loud and clear. It'll record everything you say. It's not too windy today, but environmental factors won't be in our favor. Stay as close as you can."

I can do this. I can do this. Fake it till you make it, right?

"Okay. I got this!" I offered a wobbly smile that didn't

quite reach my eyes. I let out a deep sigh. "Don't want to be late for work."

Parker grabbed my shoulders and squeezed. "I have to go to the office. I don't want Steve getting suspicious either. But I'll be here." Parker tapped my chest, right where my heart hammered against it. "Always right here."

I fought a fresh round of tears as emotions tried to claw their way out of me. Parker tipped his chin up and flashed a cocky smirk. "Now get to work, wife."

"You bet." I stepped toward our front door, and my eyes paused on the knob for a fraction of a second.

It's time.

I cranked open the door and held my shoulders straight as I headed into work, just like I would any other day. The barn seemed to have grown overnight, looming dark and ominous in the early-morning light. I waved and smiled at each ranch hand as I passed and walked directly to the coffee maker outside of Chet's office. I poured a half cup and threw it back.

"Ugh, god. I hate black coffee," I whispered to myself. "Okay. Okay. Okay." I was looking around, hoping no one was witnessing my mini meltdown when I remembered the wire tucked beneath my shirt.

Act normal. Ask questions. Lie your ass off.

I knocked a happy rhythm on Chet's office door and waited as my heart beat wildly.

"It's open." Chet's warm and familiar voice had goose bumps erupting on my forearms.

"Morning, boss!"

Chet flipped the black notebook open as his eyes flicked up to me. "Morning." He quickly scrawled something before flipping it closed and spinning his chair toward the safe.

"Whatcha working on?"

Jesus, Sienna. Could you be more obvious?

He spun back to me. "Same ol'."

I tapped my hands against my thighs and looked around the small office. "No Josh today?"

Chet stood to gather his coat from the hook beside the door. "Called away, so it's just us today. We'll make the rounds. See what's what."

"Fantastic!" My voice was an octave too high.

Chet shook his head. "I can see you don't need another cup of coffee. Let's go."

I followed Chet out of his office and toward the stables. We mounted our horses, and I was careful to keep my back away from him. In the layers I wore, I was fairly confident the pack was hidden, but I couldn't take any chances.

As we eased into the morning, the familiarity of the day soothed my racing mind. Day after day I'd done nearly the same routine. Check the cattle. Make sure they'd been rotated to the appropriate pasture. Look for signs of disease or distress. Document any concerns.

As we ambled across the rolling fields, I pressed a finger to the microphone at my lapel. The vast expanse of Montana lay before me, and I had to remind myself that I wasn't alone. If things went sour and I needed help, they would hear me and come running.

I sneaked a glance at Chet. Despite my suspicions, I also believed in my bones that he wouldn't hurt me. Maybe it was naivety, but there had to be more to his story. Somehow he'd managed to find his place at Redemption Ranch. A second chance. A home. And he was throwing it all away for money.

As the rising sun chased away the morning chill, I let it warm my face. When I glanced to my left, Chet was studying me. I held his stare for a moment and forced myself to smile.

"Do you have kids, Chet?"

Talk about a cold opener. Shit.

The soft wrinkles around his eyes went flat as his smile melted off his face. "Funny you should ask me that. I was just thinking you remind me so much of my daughter Jennifer. Or at least how I think she might have turned out."

I made a noncommittal but surprised *hmm* in my throat. "You never really talk about her. Does she live nearby?"

Chet rested his hands on top of the saddle horn and looked past the grazing cattle to the mountain in the distance. "New York."

I didn't know where I was going with the small talk, and I was outmatched. I didn't have a clue what I was doing.

"Is that where you're from?"

He raised an eyebrow in my direction. "I'm from a lot of places."

"Funny." I smiled. "You don't have a New York accent. I never would have guessed."

"You lose a lot of things when you come here. It's one thing no one tells you about." An edge of darkness crept into his voice, but I saw my opening.

"It's different here. That's for sure. I'm just thankful I have someone like you to help me navigate everything."

He offered only a noncommittal shrug as he slowly moved his horse down the pasture. I followed closely, maneuvering my horse by his side.

I needed to press harder.

"I've been thinking about it a lot, actually. The whole setup here. It feels a little stifling sometimes—all the agents around acting like normal stockmen and ranch hands. Sometimes it hurts my brain to think about."

"You get used to it." He thought for a moment. "But you also shouldn't get complacent. That's my advice to you."

I leaned in so the microphone could catch his voice, and I hoped it looked like I was enthralled by what he was saying. I felt the minutes tick by, and a bead of sweat dripped down my spine despite the autumn chill in the air. He was used to my off-the-wall questions, so I decided a surprising and direct approach was best.

"So how do you make any money around here?" I asked directly. Chet paused his horse, but I barreled through my plan. "I mean, think about it. Ma gives us a leg up with a place to stay and a job, but let me be honest. Ranch hand money isn't Chicago money, right?" I winked in his direction and hoped it didn't look like I was having a stroke.

The air was thick as he stared at me. His burst of laughter jolted a surprised laugh from me as he shook his head. "You are somethin' else, kiddo."

I continued to laugh with him and hoped he'd take the bait.

"If you're struggling with money, I can help you out."

Got him.

"You'd do that?" I feigned innocence. If it was a daughter he was missing, it was a daughter I could give. Play the part. Let him think he was helping me like he couldn't help her.

"You're a pill, Sienna. But yeah. I can help you. There's a few things on the side that'll get you some extra spending cash."

"Oh yeah?"

"Sure," he continued. "I recall a time a gal made soaps and sold them to that Porter boy who owns the shop in town. Al at the Rasa also hires some extra servers. I could put in a good word."

My shoulders fell. That was not what I needed.

"But if we're talking *Chicago* money," he continued, "then maybe you could work for me."

My belly clenched. Excitement danced over my skin.

Holy shit. This is it.

I smiled up at him again, willing warmth to reach my eyes. "I'm so lucky to have you, Chet. Thank you. Chicago money is *exactly* what I need."

He nodded, seeming to mull over what to say next.

"I've got a side project or two. It's not exactly 'official ranch business,' but it's lucrative."

I widened my eyes and nodded eagerly.

Chet pinned me with a hard look. "Now if I tell you any more, you gotta be with me or I'd have to kill you. Lots of places for a young lady to go missing around here." He finished with a wink that I suspected was intended to be playful, but my stomach twisted.

The plan was to make him believe I was on his side. That he was helping me and would confirm anything that proved he was running an illegal operation under everyone's noses. I could see the undercurrent of confidence as he spoke. If I pulled that thread, fed his ego, maybe he'd completely unravel.

"No one gets hurt, right?"

"Nah," he said. "It doesn't even hurt operations here on the ranch, so it's a win-win. Only time someone would get hurt is if they got in our way." He looked me over again. "Like that big husband of yours. Is he going to be a problem?"

I smiled a genuine smile as I thought of my husband. "Park? Definitely not. I've got him wrapped around my finger."

Chet laughed. "I have no doubt. That's a good thing. I know about that nasty business in Chicago."

My blood went cold, and I could feel the color drain from my face. I opened my mouth and tried to stammer a response, but Chet lifted a hand. "I know, Sienna. It was all over the news. When someone new comes to Redemption, it becomes a fun little game to figure out what they're running from. Couple of Mafia guys and a restaurant owner are found dead with witnesses saying they saw only a man and a woman leave? It's not that hard to put together when you know what you're looking for."

My eyes lowered in shame. As much as I wanted to forget it had ever happened, there was no outrunning what happened that night.

Chet leaned back in his saddle, stretching his back. "Truth is, sometimes I miss the thrill."

I eyed him. All at once it was clear that he was a man who thrived on control. It was a game, and it didn't matter to him that the players were real people who were doing their best to start over.

I needed to remember the plan. I might not be able to forget Chicago, but it had happened and we were here now.

My pulse thrummed through me as I found my voice. "He won't be a problem. I promise."

He patted my knee, and I had to will myself not to recoil. "I believe he came across some information that is best left undiscovered. Forgotten. Maybe you can help me with that."

He leaned closer, his leg brushing mine atop our horses. If Parker could see how close Chet was, he'd be fuming. I kept my eyes steady, eager to learn more. I couldn't breathe, couldn't blink. Even if he didn't fully admit to swindling the Smithton Beef Co. into paying for cattle that didn't exist, he'd admitted to running a side operation on the ranch. Right under Ma's nose. I knew she would never let that go.

I hated that a man like Chet didn't see the opportunity Redemption Ranch provided people. A safe haven. A second chance. He'd taken advantage of Ma and her generosity along with everyone else who pretended our muddied pasts didn't exist so we could move on.

I pitied him for it.

"Parker did mention seeing something odd at the office. Some kind of log and receipts for cattle that are unaccounted for." I hadn't intended to call Chet out on the full operation, but resentment and anger rose in my gut, and I had to know.

Chet hardened right in front of me. The lines on his face deepened as darkness swept over his features. "That's exactly what I'm talking about. He needs to forget that ever existed."

I eased my body back at the intensity of his voice. His hand snapped out and gripped my wrist. "Sienna," he warned. "That file does not exist."

I swallowed hard, and tears pricked at my eyes as his grip squeezed me tighter. "Okay. I understand."

"Good. That's good." His grip eased, and as he settled back into his saddle, his features returned to the calm, kind man I thought I knew. "Day's wasting. Let's get back."

I nodded and followed behind him toward the barn. With his back to me, I felt for the small microphone, praying that it caught our exchange and that it was enough. The panic of being alone with Chet was visceral. I felt sick knowing this dark, deceitful side of him was hiding beneath the surface of who I thought was a kind and compassionate man. Chet's thinly veiled threat clanged in my head. I was alone with him in the middle of the pasture, where no one would hear me call for help if I needed it. If we could get to the barn, maybe I could signal someone that I was done. I needed out. The wind whipped my hair as I stared, the barn growing closer.

Nothing out of the ordinary. My heart sank.

Maybe no one is coming.

THIRTY-TWO
PARKER

THE PLAN WAS to have Sienna charm as much information out of Chet as she could without raising his suspicions. At the lodge, I passed Agent Scott Dunn relaying information to a small group of agents. My skin felt tight and hot. I couldn't stand by and do nothing.

When he finished and turned, I was waiting for him. "What's going on? Where is Sienna? It's been too long."

His eyes flicked down my front, unaffected by the harshness of my glare. "It's being handled."

When he tried to step around me, I blocked his path. "Handled? What the fuck does that mean?"

Scott tipped his head and led me back toward my office. "Shut the hell up." Once the door closed behind us, I stepped forward, and he backed up to pace the room.

He lowered his voice. "Steve's gone. No one has seen him today. We've got guys out looking, but, Parker, she did it. Got more than we thought. It's enough to bring him in."

I wanted to pump my fist in the air.

Fuck yeah, she did it.

"So what now? Where is she?"

He flicked his head in the direction of the pastures beyond the lodge. "Still out there, but they're headed back. We're rounding up a team to take him in for additional questioning."

"She's still with him? Get her the hell out of there."

"We're working on it. It's vital the day appears as normal as possible so he doesn't get spooked. He's on horseback. If he bolts, it would be damn near impossible to find him again. Ma wants him detained."

"He touches her and she won't need him detained. He'll be a dead man." Hot rage burned in my chest.

"You really want to go there? I may be Evan's friend, but I'm still a federal agent." We both stiffened.

A sharp knock ratcheted up the tension as Gemma's insistent voice came through the door. "Parker! Open up! I need to talk to you." She knocked again before I could make it to the door. "Parker!"

I pulled the door open. "Jesus. What?"

Gemma's eyes sliced to Scott the exact moment his jaw ticced and he looked down, avoiding her eye contact. Her nostrils twitched and she huffed a breath. "What the hell is he doing here?"

At her harsh words, Scott pushed past us. "I was just leaving."

"What the hell? I can't deal with whatever is going on between you two."

A sound of disgust erupted from her throat. "There's absolutely nothing going on between us. He's a hothead and a liar."

I shook my head at my little sister. "Whatever. I need to leave." I had to get to Sienna. Make sure she stayed safe.

"That's why I came to get you. I was driving toward my place when I saw agents descend on the main barn like locusts. They sent everyone home. I went to your place to get the scoop from Sienna, but she's not there. I wanted to know if you'd heard from her."

"Gemma, listen to me very carefully." I gripped her shoulders and leveled my eyes with hers. "Go home."

"What? Parker, what is going on?"

I closed my eyes and steadied my breathing. "Gemma. I have been a terrible husband and an even shittier brother. I didn't do my job of protecting you in Chicago, and it will always be one of my greatest regrets. Please. I cannot worry about her and worry about you."

I opened my eyes to see Gemma's face shining with tears. She stepped forward into my arms. "Thanks, jerk. Now I've cried twice today."

I gave her a quick squeeze. "Why'd you cry twice? Need me to kick the shit out of some punk kid?"

Her eyes flicked to the doorway. "No," she said. "It's not anyone worth my tears."

I tapped her shoulder. "You're tough. It's no wonder Sienna is crazy about you."

"Is she going to be okay?"

I grabbed my jacket from the hook by the door. "I won't let anything happen to her. Go home. We'll come find you after."

She nodded and smiled, and I had to trust that she'd do what I asked and go straight home. Tearing through the lodge, I ignored anyone who tried to stop me to ask questions. I was determined to get my girl.

My wife.

Inside the barn was total chaos. Ma was barking low orders, and agents were moving quickly to prepare for Sienna and Chet's return to the stable. Everyone hunkered down, and a hushed silence rippled through the large space.

I was supposed to be at work, but there was no fucking way I wasn't going to be close when Sienna returned.

My mood darkened as two agents tried to stop my forward progress. Ma's head whipped up, and she nodded for them to let me in.

With quick strides I moved to her side. "What the hell is going on?" I whispered. "Where is she?"

"They're coming over the ridge now. It doesn't appear that he knows anything out of the ordinary has happened. Once they get here and dismount, I'm going to talk with him." Tension and nerves radiated from every inch of me. Ma narrowed her eyes at me. "If I tell you to go home, will you listen?"

"No."

She shook her head. "Then stay back and keep your cool."

"Yes, ma'am."

Minutes crawled along like hours as we waited, crouched behind the low walls of the stalls and tucked behind equipment in the barn. Finally Sienna's lyrical voice floated on the air as she laughed at something Chet had said. It was strained and tight, but I doubted he noticed. The wide barn doors were open as Chet rounded the corner with Sienna at his side. He instantly stiffened, sensing something was off.

The barn is too quiet.

When Ma stepped forward, revealing herself, confusion flickered over his face. When she didn't smile, the light in his eyes dimmed, and his eyes darted around the open space.

"Morning." He tried to sound casual, but the word was strained. "What brings you around here this morning? Where'd all my workers go?"

"I sent them home early."

He scoffed and Sienna eased away. He caught the movement, and the reality of what was happening hit him. A guttural growl tore from Chet's chest. "You fucking bitch."

He spat the words in Sienna's direction. As she took a slight step backward, he wound his arm around her neck, dragging her back against his chest. I stood to my full height but was blocked by an agent with a gun.

"Is that what this was?" He bared his teeth at her ear as he roared the words. "Always poking around and asking questions. I should have known."

Ma approached slowly with the practiced calm of a federal agent. "Chet, now calm down. You and I need to talk."

"So what was it? She was wired?" Chet cranked on Sienna's neck, and my fists clenched at my sides. If it weren't for a barn full of agents with guns drawn, I would have ripped his head from his fucking shoulders.

Chet's hands roamed over her body, and she cried out. From the small of her back, he pulled the battery pack and smashed it into the ground. "Unbe-fucking-lievable. You know, I almost trusted you. Looks like you fit in with the liars and the cheats after all. Stupid fucking girl." His sneer dripped with betrayal and venom.

Ma never raised her voice but remained calm and steadfast. "It's over, Chet. It's over."

The confident calm of her voice made his lip twitch, but his eyes cooled. "Nothing's over. You won't get a damn thing out of me."

He had betrayed his employer and his friend and he knew it, but he couldn't give up the lie. He released his grip on Sienna only enough to shove her forward. Her hands and knees smacked the ground with a crack and she cried out. My gut twisted as I watched her scramble, trying to get her bearings. Before he could retreat out the door, an agent came up behind them and tackled Chet to the ground. They landed with a sickening thud.

Sienna scooted away as they struggled, and once she was on her feet, she looked around in panic. I stepped forward, and when she spotted me, she ran straight into my arms, crashing into me. I held her close, winding her legs around my waist and pressing my face to her neck.

By the time all hell broke loose, Chet was subdued. With all the commotion, a crowd started to draw, and it took several agents to push them back. Ma barked orders at several men, and they scurried off.

She walked toward us with a serious look on her face. "You did good." She gently squeezed Sienna's shoulder. "I wasn't sure you could pull it off, but once he started talking about his daughter, I knew that was it. You got him."

"Was it enough?"

A small smile passed over her features. "It was enough to raise some serious questions. Ones that will be much harder for him to avoid. We'll take it from here. Are you all right?"

Sienna was still a bit shell-shocked, but she swallowed hard and tried to smile. "I think so? My palms hurt from hitting the ground, but other than that I think I'm okay." The way she shook told me she was definitely not okay.

Ma looked at me over Sienna's head. "Take your girl home."

I nodded once and bundled her closer to me.

Despite knowing she was safe, panic coursed through me as we made our way home and reality settled in.

This is it. The end of us.

~

Dread, low and tight in my chest, built and swelled. Sienna deserved so much more than a life of criminals and secrets. I had known it for a while. It was why I went behind her back and did what I had to do to be sure that she could live the life she deserved.

Sienna's perfect future certainly didn't include me, but if I had been completely honest, I had zero regrets. In the months I'd had her, I'd found peace. Connection. Acceptance for who I was and not who I was expected to be. I'd take her leaving wet towels on the bathroom floor and her terrible taste in music if that meant I could fall asleep with her head on my chest and our legs tangled together. Sure the sex was fantastic, but it was the unbridled connection that I had never had with another soul.

I lamented the bastard who would have her after me. I fucking hated him. The faceless dickweed who dared to think he was good enough to breathe the same air as Sienna.

But what was the alternative? Selfishly keep her with me—a weight chained to her neck, keeping her anchored when she was destined to fly? I could never do that to her.

We had made it back to the cottage, but I was wound tight, unable to relax. My hands trembled, and I dragged them through my hair to steady the shake, hoping she didn't notice. Deep breaths sawed in and out of me as I struggled for control.

"Hey, husband."

I couldn't even look her in the eyes.

Fucking coward.

"Park. I'm okay. I promise. Come sit with me."

I finally gained the courage to risk getting lost in her cerulean eyes. Despite the weariness, they still glowed.

I gently cleared my throat. It was time. "I've got something for you. A gift."

A smile lit her face. "A present?"

I left her to get the thick white envelope that had been tucked away at the bottom of my drawer. I smoothed the paper between my palms before handing it to her. Confusion flickered over her face as she looked at the envelope.

"What's this?"

"I realized I can give you something no one else can."

Her dainty brows furrowed as she looked at me but didn't open the package.

"Freedom."

"Park, I—I don't understand."

"Read it."

Her fingers pulled on the flap, and she removed the thick stack of paper. She began to read aloud, *"Dear Mrs. Davis—"* She looked at me and smiled, and my heart broke a little more. *"Congratulations! On behalf of the Undergraduate Affairs Department of the Mark and Robyn Jones College of Nursing at Montana State University, I am pleased to inform you that you are accepted to the Bachelor of Science in Nursing program. We are looking forward to working with you in the upcoming semester."*

A sad smile crossed my face as I imagined Sienna thriving at nursing school—making friends, laughter and sunshine surrounding her.

"Parker, this is crazy! How is this possible?" She couldn't hide the excitement in her voice.

I forced a smile for my gorgeous wife. "When Gemma mentioned you checking out the flyer at the library about the nursing program, I looked into it. Applied. You got in. They want you. You can start as early as the January semester."

"But what about *before*? Don't I need records? Transcripts or something?"

"I've worked it out with Ma. A benefit of witness protection is the ability to pull a few strings. Getting fake high school transcripts wasn't a problem. She took the liberty of assuming you were a pretty good student and didn't feel too bad fudging a document or two for the greater good."

Her clear eyes went wide as the information settled over her. "I could really go back to school?"

"You will," I assured her. "As Sienna Davis, you have to start from scratch, but I know you can do it. It's all paid for. All you have to do is show up and do the work."

A small squeal erupted from her tiny body, and she launched herself at me. "Parker, this is incredible!"

I wrapped her in my arms as her feet dangled. I breathed her in—salt water and summer breezes, always. My heart fractured as I wondered how many of these moments I would have left. I set her on her feet, and her hands rested on my forearms, her face flushed with happiness.

"My mind is racing to a thousand places. What about the ranch? I'll miss it, but this opportunity is something I never thought I'd have again." Her hands cupped her own face as she raced through her thoughts and paced around the living room. "Where will we live? What about work for us? I'm sure we can find you something. And for me there's always another restaurant. College kids have to eat, right?"

I ignored the tumble of questions as a sharp pang stabbed under my ribs. I tried to memorize the happy glow of her face.

I put that there.

"You can live on campus or have an apartment. I wasn't sure what you'd prefer, but the choice is yours."

"Live on campus?" She scoffed. "We couldn't live—" She paused midstride and looked at me. Her pert mouth popped open. "Parker, what are you saying? What did you do?"

As realization dawned on her, I accepted the burn in my gut. She needed this. To move on. Live her life without me holding her back. "Sienna, for as long as I can remember, I struggled. Struggled to care for my brother when my mother couldn't. Struggled to live up to the expectations of a dangerous family who turned their backs on anyone who didn't fall in line. Struggled to keep Evan and Gemma away from that life by destroying any connection they tried to make with me. It was an endless loop."

I smiled at her despite the tears welling in her eyes. "And then you showed up. The first day I saw you in your uncle's restaurant, I couldn't believe someone could glow from the inside out. I enjoyed the warmth of that glow any time I could sneak away and sit in your section. But I stole that glow when I brought my troubles down on you. You deserve so much more."

"I don't want more. I want you."

I shook my head. She didn't know what she was saying. "Sienna, you're leaving, but I'm not going with you."

THIRTY-THREE
SIENNA

THIS ISN'T HAPPENING. This cannot be happening.

"No." Fuck everyone telling me what they thought was best for me.

"Sienna. It's done." Heaviness weighed down his shoulders. I didn't know if it was from the weight of the conversation, or the last few months, but I could see he didn't want this any more than I did.

"And if I don't go?" Defiance glowed in my eyes as I tipped my chin in challenge.

"That's your choice. Ma said you've earned your place at the ranch. But if you go—and you should—I've got enough money to set you up for the rest of your life. After bringing so much pain into your life, it's the least I can do. Please, let me do this for you."

I couldn't believe how easily he could talk about us no longer being together. "And what about us?"

"Ma knows the truth. We both know being married can't save you from being forced to testify against me if it were to ever come down to that. It's time for you to move on."

I shook my head. He knew as well as I did that we'd stopped pretending a long time ago. My eyes scanned his large frame—the expanse of his chest, the cut of his waist. I tracked down the corded muscles of his forearms as Parker wrung his hands.

"Parker Davis, I never thought you would stitch me up only to break my heart all over again." I'd used his new name on purpose, to show him that he had a choice and he was choosing wrong.

"Sienna, I'm hanging by a thread here. I'm trying to do the right thing."

Anger flared in my chest. I stormed toward the door and ripped it open. "Well, you're fucking it up!"

"I HATE to break it to you, but most men are idiots." Johnny Porter reached across the café table and patted my hand.

"Pshh, ain't that the truth." Gemma raised her coffee cup to clink it against Johnny's.

Anger swelled in me, and I was so afraid to lash out at Parker that I stormed out the cottage door and went straight to Gemma's house. She took one look at my splotchy, tear-stained face, loaded me up in her truck, and headed to town. It was midday, but Johnny had no qualms about leaving the shop to his employees while he met us at Brewed Awakening.

My knees were pulled to my chest as I settled into the soft, broken-in loveseat by the fire. It was a cozy setup with plush chairs and the small couch nestled around a low table. Perfect for both romantic dates and wallowing. "I just don't get it. Why? Why does he think that I would want to leave without him? I thought things were going really well."

"Parker has always been a bit of a loner." Gemma shrugged, reluctant to hurt my feelings. "Maybe being married and *so close* to someone was harder than he expected."

"Loner? I think the word you used before was *skank*."

Johnny laughed, and a smile teased at the corners of her mouth as she wrinkled her nose. "I did call him that, didn't I?"

"You did."

Gemma let loose a heavy breath. "I don't know, Sienna. The guy I thought I knew in Chicago and the one who showed up in Montana are so different. Even in the last few months he's completely changed. For the better. I know that has to do with you."

I offered her a sad smile. Parker *had* changed. He'd let me, and other people, in. Allowed others to see a fraction of the glimmer that I knew was inside him.

The warm coffee washed over my tongue as I took another sip. I couldn't make sense of it all. "I feel like an idiot. When he handed me the envelope and I read the acceptance letter, all I could think about were the possibilities. For *us*. It didn't even occur to me that he wouldn't come with me." I shook my head. "So dumb."

Johnny looked at me from across the small table, his kind eyes serious. "It's never dumb to be hopeful."

"Sometimes people just let you down." Sadness had crept back into Gemma's voice, and I leaned into her, resting my head on her shoulder.

"Do you want to talk about it?" I asked. Johnny looked on with sad, knowing eyes.

She cleared her throat. "Definitely not. This is your wallow. I won't ruin it for you."

We all chuckled, needing the levity when everything felt so wrong and off-kilter.

The three of us sat in companionable silence and enjoyed the crackle of the fire and the warmth of our coffees.

I swiped at the tears that gathered on my lower lashes. "Guys, I'm a mess. I ran away with a total stranger, told everyone that we were married, then *actually married* his grumpy ass and went ahead and fell in love with him when I knew it would end in heartbreak. I trusted a man who, as it turns out, was lying to everyone and stealing people's money. I spent my whole adult life doing anything I could to prevent being alone. Not even a fake husband could do it, because look at me." I tossed my hands up. "I'm a joke!"

Across from me, Johnny sipped his latte and set the mug down with a snap. "Are you about done, then?"

I sank farther into the couch and crossed my arms. "I think so."

"Good." He nodded. "I'm about to give you some advice, whether you want to hear it or not. So buckle up."

I sat up a little straighter and blinked at him. Gemma gripped my hand in solidarity.

"I have sat in a room, surrounded by people who were supposed to be there for me and love me, and felt completely, utterly alone. Love isn't 'I love you but' or 'I love you if you just change this.' You breezed into this town, not knowing a soul, and you still managed to charm every single person who's ever met you. You are enough. You don't have to be perfect or say the right things or have all the answers. You just have to be you. But the more you try to accommodate and bend and meet people in the middle, the further you get away from *you*. And I say fuck that."

The lump in my throat had grown with every word. All I had ever wanted was true, pure love, but it always came at a cost. Change a bit here, take a bit there. I was so concerned about taking up less space and accommodating everyone else that I hadn't really thought about what I truly needed to be happy.

"You are pure sunshine," Johnny assured me.

"But"—I sniffled—"he doesn't want me."

Gemma rolled her eyes. "You know that's not true. That man watches you like you're the most precious thing on this earth. He's in love, and it scares the shit out of him."

"If he loves me, then why push me away? Why not go with me? Or we could stay here!"

Johnny cut in. "The man is in love with you. He wants to give you everything, but it sounds like he doesn't believe that there's room for him too."

I pressed my fingertips into my eyes. I was so tired.

"The nursing school application was terribly romantic." Gemma smiled up at me.

I pouted. "It was, wasn't it?"

"So what are you going to do, sunshine?" Johnny's eyes sparkled with mischief.

THIRTY-FOUR
SIENNA

After pulling into Laurel Canyon Ranch, Gemma dropped me off at the main lodge. The afternoon air was still buzzing with frenetic energy after Chet's arrest. They'd taken him off the ranch for questioning, but hushed conversations and sidelong glances continued. Agents moved in and out of the building, handling tasks and mitigating the blowback from the news about Chet getting out to the rest of the ranch.

I paused at the entrance to Ma's office and stared at the cheap brass name tag: Special Agent Dorthea Brown. I glanced down the hallway and wiped my sweaty palms against the seat of my jeans. When I raised my fist and knocked once, Ma Brown's voice immediately answered. "It's open."

I pushed through the door. Ma was behind her desk, her glasses perched at the tip of her nose as she flipped through handwritten notes and typed into her laptop.

She glanced up as I entered. "Sienna." The lines of her face deepened when she smiled. "Please come in."

I returned her smile. "Thank you. I know you're busy, and I don't want to take up too much of your time."

"Honey, please. After what you did for us today? I've got all the time in the world for you." She moved from behind her desk and circled to sit at the edge of it. "I don't think I had the opportunity to thank you."

"I tricked a man who was nothing but kind into trusting me and ruined his life. Feels pretty crummy." I offered a sad smile.

"We're all given choices in life, my dear. Chet made his, and now he has to live with them. That's on him. Not you."

I nodded. "I came by to thank you. As surprising as it was, I feel like I've found myself here."

"Thank you. People call it Redemption Ranch for a reason. It's a place for second chances. I've always believed in it."

"It's a very special place." I knew the next part would be hard. "I think I might be leaving for a while. I have an opportunity to go to nursing school in Bozeman." I shook my head. "I still can't believe I'm saying that out loud. I've wanted to be a nurse for a very long time, and after Chicago I assumed that dream was over."

Ma gave me a knowing smile. "I'd heard that was a possibility. I'm happy for you, but I will be sad to see you go." She reached to pull me into a hug. "And what about that husband of yours?"

"I'm still working that out."

"You do that. In my experience, when men who are used to power feel powerless in the presence of a woman they love, it's a very frightening feeling. Most live their whole lives denying any good feelings because they've seen how quickly it can be taken away. If I was a betting woman,

I'd say you've knocked Parker on his ass, and he doesn't know what to do about it."

A small ember of hope flickered in my chest. I knew she was right about Parker. I'd found my footing in Montana, and I'd be okay. But I wanted more than okay. I wanted shout-from-the-rooftops,   can't-believe-this-is-my-life, blissed-out happiness.

I deserved that and so did he.

Parker's car was parked in front of our cottage as I walked up to the porch. I huddled against the crisp fall air as oranges and reds splashed against the darkening sky. In the distance between the main lodge and our home, my confidence began to wane. Maybe I had imagined the intent of his lingering glances and the warm affection of his touch. Maybe I had pushed him too far, too fast, and he wasn't ready for the level of commitment I needed.

With every step, worry pinched my shoulders. I needed to be brave. I needed to be strong. If Parker had made his choice, I would leave the ranch alone. But I was sure I could help Parker see that he deserved the goodness inside his crusty, crabby exterior. In fact, his grumpiness was a part of his charm.

I took a deep, steadying breath before pushing open the front door. Eerie quiet settled over the house. Only the smell of Pine-Sol greeted me as I entered. I scanned the living room and kitchen, but Parker wasn't here. The cottage was small. It didn't take any time at all to walk through, but I couldn't help but pause at the dining room table where we'd played cards and laughed, the bookshelf that held his historical romances. I stood at the entryway to our bedroom. My eyes stilled on the bed where he had explored every inch of my body and where together we had discovered new and delicious ways to bring each other pleasure.

"You came back."

I jumped at his voice, and my hand flew to my chest. "Jesus! You scared the shit out of me." A nervous laugh teetered out of me. Parker stood with tousled hair, like he'd dragged his hands through it and pulled at the ends. His gorgeous blue eyes were clouded with doubt and sadness. I wanted nothing more than to run to him, wrap his giant shoulders in my arms, and comfort him. My feet were rooted to the ground.

Aching silence filled the cottage. Parker moved one hand over the other, smoothing his fingers over the scars. Finally he spoke. "I told you that it was a payment." He turned his hand over, examining where his pinkie had once been. "But what I didn't tell you was that it was also a reminder. A reminder of the choices I had made and that I would never be whole again."

Tears burned in my eyes as I stared at my broken husband. "I don't believe that."

He shook his head, his inner grump making a reappearance. "You have the opportunity to start a new life with nothing and no one holding you back."

I squared my shoulders and tilted my chin. "Maybe I like my life just fine."

"Stubborn woman."

Challenge gleamed in my eye. "You have no idea."

He scoffed and dragged a hand across the rough edge of his jaw. "What do I have to do to convince you to leave this place? To leave me behind and start over?" I watched his frustration stack and build as his breaths lifted his pecs and strained the fabric of his shirt. A thrill coursed through me, knowing what delicious things hid beneath that T-shirt and they were all mine.

I stepped forward, closing the distance between us, and tilted my head to look him in the eye. "I'm. Not. Leaving."

His nostrils flared. "Then I'll divorce you."

A shotgun laugh burst out of me. "Liar."

Hot, steaming tension radiated between us. His temper was a cracking whip ready to lash out, but I didn't care. I had seen his heart and all the love he had to give, and I wouldn't allow him to do this to himself. To us.

His jaw flexed, our bodies so close I could feel the heat pumping off him. "This isn't real."

I pushed his arm. "Well, it is to me!"

In one swift movement, Parker grabbed my arm and crushed his lips to mine. His tongue invaded my mouth, and I stretched up to my tiptoes to get more of him. My arms wound around his neck, and I moaned into him.

His hands clenched the fabric of my shirt. Tangled in each other, we poured every broken part of ourselves into that kiss. Relentless and unforgiving, Parker devoured me in the quiet of our living room.

When we came up for air, his voice was throaty and rough. "You will never kiss another man."

"Never." His lips moved down the column of my throat. Heat pooled low in my belly.

Parker released me, but I used his arms to steady my wobbling legs.

"Sienna," he said on a growl. "You need to know something."

I waited as he struggled with the words.

"You married an asshole."

A smile spread wide across my face. "I married a marshmallow."

He reached down to tuck a strand of hair behind my ear and cup my face. Tilting my head, he looked into my eyes. "I am an asshole, but I'm trying to be better. For you. I'm standing in front of you, telling you I've made a mistake. Forgive me?"

THIRTY-FIVE
PARKER

I DIDN'T DESERVE Sienna's forgiveness, but when she'd given me a second chance, I ran with it. After some late-night talks and a few tears, we agreed to leave Redemption Ranch.

Together.

Sienna had an opportunity at her feet, and I'd be damned if anything would get in her way.

When Christmas Eve rolled around, Ma had planned a big gathering. In the main lodge, a wood fire crackled in the fireplace. The entire space was decorated for the holidays, and garlands of pine and fir hung on the mantel. The stuffed moose mounted on the wall wore Santa hats, and a deer sported a fake red nose. A single candle flickered in each window, illuminating the space in a warm glow. Evan had cut down a huge tree, and it was decorated with lights and ribbons. Presents were stacked on the tree skirt.

In all my thirty-three years, I had never been a part of such an elegant Christmas celebration. The smile that tugged at my mouth spread quickly, and I let it happen— something I was still getting used to.

"Pretty impressive, right?" Evan walked up behind me and clamped a hand down on my shoulder.

I looked over the tree. "It's nice. The tree's kind of small though . . ."

"Dick."

We laughed, and I turned to wrap him in a hug. Emotion rose in my throat, but I cleared it away and whacked Evan on the back.

As we stood apart, I looked at his sweater, then down at my own. I gestured between us. "I guess this is their doing?"

As our heads turned toward the trio of women giggling in the kitchen, I did my best to look annoyed. Dressed in matching reindeer sweaters, Evan and I looked fucking ridiculous.

Gemma howled with laughter, no doubt the ring leader in their debauchery. Sienna was doubled over, and Val's chin was raised as she looked at my brother, her eyes wild with mischief.

Anyone could see that those three were trouble, and Evan and I were in the thick of it.

"When do you leave?"

"The week after next. We want to get settled before her semester starts."

Evan nodded. "Is she excited?"

I tracked my wife as I thought about his question. "She is, but I know she'll miss it here. If she could have both—a nursing degree and still live here—she would. But like I told her, you can't ride two horses with one ass."

Evan laughed. "Look at you, cowboy."

I grinned again. "Got that one from Ray. If you listen long enough, he says the weirdest shit."

Ma and her husband, Robbie, were setting up food in the kitchen, and our women started to set out the dishes and silverware. When we moved to help, Sienna swatted at the air, telling us to leave them be.

"You and Val staying around here?" I asked.

"Yeah. Something about it feels kinda permanent." He tucked his hands in his pocket, and I knew exactly how he felt. Since Evan went to Chicago to win Val back, he'd been a changed man. Lighter. Happier. It wasn't long before he'd proposed, and they were married in a simple ceremony that I was proud to be a part of.

It was everything he deserved.

A few more guests showed up, and old-school Christmas music crooned from the speakers. I thought back to the barren, presentless Christmases Evan and I had grown up with—something I rarely allowed myself to do. More and more those sad memories were being replaced with new ones. Sienna was always at the core of them.

I was moody and difficult. She was still radiant and carefree, but we made it work. When I caught her eye and she dazzled me with a full, white smile, my heart stuttered.

"Let's come together and say a few words." Ma's voice cut through the crowd, and we all fell in line. Sienna tucked in beside me, and I inhaled a quick breath of her hair before dropping a kiss on the top of her head.

I still didn't deserve her, but I was damn sure to try to be the man she needed every day.

"Why?" Sienna moaned into my shoulder. "Why did I eat that last slice of pie?"

I chuckled and rubbed her feet as we both sat on opposite ends of the couch. "Because it was Irma's, and no one can resist her apple pie."

She rubbed her too-full belly. "I'm dying."

"Well, don't die yet. I have something for you."

Light danced in her eyes. "An early present?"

I smiled at her and lifted a finger. "One. Only one early present. Don't think I didn't notice you trying to sneak around your gifts."

Her guilty smile flushed her cheeks. She was so damn cute. "I've got one for you too." Sienna leaped from the couch and dug through the small pile of presents until she found the one she was looking for.

She shoved the rectangular box in my lap. "You first! I'm too excited to wait."

Her gift was carefully wrapped in simple craft paper, but on top was an extravagant red glitter bow. She had tucked a piece of pine in it. Without even opening it, it was already the nicest gift anyone had given me.

I held the small rectangular box and was careful when I slipped off the pine and bow. When I unwrapped the brown craft paper and lifted off the top of the box, I paused. It was a key chain with a retro pinup girl on it with a grumpy face and the words *This is my happy face.* A belly laugh rumbled out of me as I held it up.

"It's perfect."

Sienna beamed at me. "I thought it was fitting."

That woman was something else. Despite being irritable, she loved me anyway—just as I was. I didn't need to change or be anything other than who I was around her, and it was the most freeing thing in the world.

"There's one more thing," she added.

I looked down into the box, and under the key chain was a pair of gloves. I lifted an eyebrow in her direction.

Sienna lifted her hands. "I'm not being a smart-ass this time, I promise."

Still skeptical—she'd taken to poking fun at my missing finger. I didn't admit it to her, but she was right all along. By her treating it like it was no big deal, the significance of it was lightened. I could accept my hand for what it was, and it didn't have to mean more than that. The weight of it and its power over me was a self-imposed prison.

When I lifted the gloves, I saw the left hand had only four fingers.

"I got to thinking . . . ," she started. "All winter you've been saying that your hands are cold, but you can't wear gloves comfortably. So I made some adjustments!"

My chest was tight. "You made these?" I slipped the glove on. It fit perfectly.

"I did." Her smile was radiant. "Johnny said there are places that make custom gloves, and he can help us with ordering if we need him, but I decided to make a pair. Kind of like a trial run. If you like them, we can order as many as you like!"

It was homemade. Thoughtful. I couldn't believe I was spending the rest of my life with a woman who not only saw me but loved me despite my flaws. Maybe even because of them. It was unreal.

I couldn't wait any longer. I hauled her up against me and kissed her hard, pouring my rising emotions into her. When I broke the kiss, she was flushed and breathless.

Her gift was tucked away, so I walked toward our bedroom. Behind two boxes and under a blanket in the closet, I got the package, wrapped in Christmas paper.

"Hey! You hid it."

I pointed at her. "Damn right I did. You snoop."

Sienna poked her tongue out at me as she tucked her legs under herself and cuddled into the couch. "Do I get to open it?" She could barely contain her excitement, and my heart beat against my chest.

I handed her the box, still standing at her feet. I tucked my hands into my pockets to hide my nerves.

"To: My wife. From: Your husband." She read the tag and smiled at me, her blue eyes dancing with anticipation.

As she slipped off the ribbon, I started talking. "Sienna. It was a Tuesday afternoon when I walked into your uncle's restaurant. The moment I saw you, I knew. You were different. I tried to deny it, but every part of me calls to every part of you." She slowed her unwrapping as she looked at me. I had to keep going. "Somehow, one of the worst nights of our lives turned out okay." At that, she smiled and shared a quiet laugh. "You are my wife. You were always meant to be my wife. Wherever you go, I go."

"Parker," she whispered.

"Keep going." I nodded toward the half-opened gift. She looked down and tore the paper off, and I lowered to one knee.

"Sienna Davis. I cannot give you my last name, but there is something I can give you. We took the name of the man who helped raise you. I promise that I will honor his name every day. I will love you and protect you and never stop trying to be the kind of man who deserves to stand in your light."

With tears in her eyes, Sienna opened the small box to reveal a sparkling diamond ring. The center stone was a large oval that gleamed, even in the dim lighting of our cottage. Petite stones trailed down the slim band in dashes and dots.

"Parker. Oh my god, Parker, it's beautiful."

"Sienna, I love you more than any living soul on this earth. Will you be my wife?" I smiled at her. "Again?"

Crushing the box between us, Sienna leaned forward and grabbed my face with both hands. Her mouth moved over mine, and I held her close as we kissed.

She peppered kisses on my face.

"Yes."

Kiss.

"Yes."

Kiss.

"Yes!"

My laugh was rich and deep.

We were on the precipice of a brand-new life. Leaving again, much like we had in Chicago. Only this time, when she took my hand, we would still be running toward the unknown, but we'd be doing it together. Side by side.

A grump and his ray of light.

Husband and wife.

EPILOGUE

Parker

Two Years Later

Miriam tilted her chin—a tingle of excitement tittering down her spine—she had never dared to argue with a gentleman, let alone the man who reported directly to her father, the Baron. As she assessed the smooth skin at his jaw, she saw no trace of shame at being discovered.

Lord Pemberton watched her for a moment. The muscle in his jaw twitched. His gaze dropped to her mouth, and when her lips parted, for an endless second she forgot how to breathe. Abruptly he took her hand and bowed, brushing his lips over the thin skin of her knuckle.

"Lady Hatten, it is quite unfortunate you have discovered my secret place." A devilish gleam danced in his eyes. "What might we do about that?"

"Order up!" The ding of the bell at the counter ripped me from the pages of *The Scoundrel's Intent*. I swiped my glasses from my face and rubbed my eyes. It was late, but Sienna was working a shift at Reba's Diner, and I happily sat in a corner booth, reading and watching life in Bozeman unfold around us.

Making her rounds, Sienna appeared dressed in her work uniform—a traditional waitress shift dress. I smiled to myself. A rush of heat coursed through me. I had plans for that little outfit later. She was radiant as she walked toward me, carrying a refill of my Dr Pepper.

"Hello, husband!"

I nodded. "Darling wife."

Sienna beamed at me as she slipped next to me into the booth.

"On break?" I asked, inserting a bookmark into the paperback she had picked up for me. Our neighborhood had an incredible used bookstore. Sienna had let it slip that I couldn't help but love my historicals, so the shop owner set aside a few interesting titles every week.

"Mmm." Sienna closed her eyes and rolled her shoulders.

"You should quit. You know you don't need to work."

Sienna bumped my arm with hers. "Yes I do." Her voice quieted. "We can't always rely on a duffel bag full of money. It's got to run out eventually."

I shrugged and lifted my eyebrows. She knew as well as I did that we had plenty of money. Not only was her tuition paid for but our monthly rent was as well. For the past two years we had accessed only the money from my former life when absolutely necessary, but it would be a very long time until that money ran out. I had provided testimony in court and negotiated a stipulation to access a few accounts. It was probably illegal and had gone mostly under the radar, but once the money had been transferred, I had given the prosecutor everything she needed to win a landmark case. My testimony alone had catapulted her career—she didn't give a flying fuck about some mobster's "missing money" when they were sitting behind bars.

In the meantime Sienna and I lived a modest life in Bozeman. She attended nursing school full time during the day, only taking a few shifts a week at the diner because she said she liked it.

I didn't mind. I loved sitting in the corner, reading a book and remembering the days I was too stuck in my own bullshit to even talk to her. Now my new identity afforded me the opportunity to do consulting work for businesses, mostly word of mouth. I took a look at their books and logs and let them know where there were weaknesses, opportunities for bad guys like me to take advantage of them. A time or two I even found money was already going missing. I was paid often and paid well.

"Are you looking forward to Sunday?" We'd made plans to make a trip back to Tipp for family dinner.

"I can't wait. Ma is going to be so surprised. I can't believe it's already been seven months since we've been to family dinner."

I smoothed my hand over hers, my rough, inked skin a stark contrast to her softness. "She understands. Everyone does. You're busy with school and work. Already halfway done." I gave her a quick squeeze. It had taken only a few months away from Tipp to realize we both missed the weird little town. Sienna and I decided that after her nursing program, we'd do what we could to move back.

"Gemma said that there's a new woman there that's got everyone in a tizzy—I guess she's a celebrity or something."

"Wow. That's big news for around there."

"Right? Gemma couldn't share the details, but I am

dying to know who it is. She swore I would know her when I saw her. I already made a list of possibilities."

I laughed, pulling my wife close. Sienna shifted on the bench seat, resting her head on my shoulder and her hand on my thigh. We'd been alone in Bozeman, and with her long hours and my standoffish demeanor, we hadn't made real friends while we had been there.

I missed Evan and Gemma.

When we could, we drove the long hours back to Tipp and visited our friends and family at Redemption Ranch. Evan and I had never had a true family, but we'd found one in Tipp. Sienna was committed and focused on finishing her degree, and I would do anything in my power to make her dreams come true.

Every moment that passed, I was grateful that Sienna had chosen me. People gravitated toward her, circling the sunshine and leaving better because of it. She'd taught me the value of connection. It was something I planned to instill in our children.

My hand moved to the subtle swell of her belly. I stilled and waited, hoping to feel something.

Sienna's sweet breath hit my ear. "I told you it's too early to feel anything."

A grumble rolled around in my chest. "I know. But he's in there."

Three weeks ago, Sienna had come to me with tears in her eyes and told me that her period was late. I had shot to my feet and wrapped her in my arms as I bawled like a baby. Creating a life with Sienna was the greatest joy I had ever felt. Boy or girl, I was going to give that kid the best life. The life I had dreamed of as a kid.

She looked up at me. "He, huh?"

"Or she." I winked at her. "Maybe both."

Her owl eyes went even wider, and she slapped my arm. "Parker Davis, don't you put that juju on me!"

I feigned shock. "What? You wouldn't want to carry my twins?"

She fluttered her lashes at me and teased the bottom of her lip. "I want all your babies, but maybe we start with just one."

"Okay." I lowered my mouth to hers. "We'll start with one."

Every day since finding out she was carrying our child, I had hoped our babies would have my grit and Sienna's sunlight. But the one thing I knew for certain was they would each have the name I was sure to honor every single day of my life.

∼

WANT MORE of Parker and Sienna? Get your exclusive bonus scene by visiting:

https://www.lenahendrix.com/get-parker-and-siennas-bonus-scene/

SNEAK PEEK OF THE REBEL AND THE ROGUE

She's a princess—Hollywood royalty to be exact. When cool, hard-hearted Effie Pierce steps one high-heeled foot on my property, she proves to be a temptation I can't seem to resist.

As an Army vet, I'm used to challenges, but working on a ranch that's a cover for Witness Protection is no easy feat. I keep my head down and my hands clean—figuratively speaking.

Now I'm in charge of showing Effie the ropes. One problem: she's also the girl who stole my heart—and my first kiss—when we were kids. Effie's got secrets of her own and once those threads begin to unravel, I start to realize there may be more to her than the aloof heartbreaker everyone's made her out to be.

Effie is smart, successful and sexy as hell—I can barely sleep knowing she's *right down the hall*. And when the chemistry between us ignites, it's hard to deny that there's more to the sultry starlet than she lets on.

She may play the rebel, but this woman makes me want to go rogue.

Pre-order The Rebel and the Rogue on Amazon!

SNEAK PEEK OF FINDING YOU

CHIKALU FALLS, BOOK 1

Lincoln

Three Years Ago

The jolt from the blast rattled through the truck, blowing out the front window. All of the doors flew open. Unlatched, I was ejected from the vehicle—thrown onto the open road. I slid before coming to a grunting halt against a nearby building.

I remember every second of it. There's no way to describe how it feels when you think you're going to die. No white light, no moment of clarity. The one thing that crossed my mind was that I wanted to kill the mother-fuckers who did this.

With so much adrenaline pumping through my veins, I couldn't feel a thing. The blast from the IED into the truck as we were leaving a neighboring village also meant that I couldn't hear shit. I knew from his anguished face Duke was screaming, writhing on the ground, but as I stared at him, I heard nothing but a low ringing between my ears.

Smoke swirled around me as I fought to get my bearings. My eyes felt like they were lined with sandpaper, and my lungs couldn't seem to drag in enough air.

Get up. You're a sitting duck. Get. The fuck. UP.

Dragging myself to my knees, I patted down my most tender places, and except for my right arm, which hurt like a bitch, I was fine. I looked back at Duke, whose face had gone still. Although I already knew, I checked his vitals, but it was pointless. Fanned out around us were eight or nine other casualties—some Americans, some villagers. One set of little feet in sandals I just couldn't look at.

Ducking behind another car, I drew my gun and swept the crowd. *Come on, motherfucker, show yourself.* Civilians were getting up, walking past like nothing had happened. Those affected by the blast were screaming, begging. It was a total clusterfuck. My eyes darted around the area, but I couldn't find the trigger man. He'd melted into the crowd.

I ran back toward the mangled, smoking remains of our Humvee. Fuck. It was a twisted mess of metal and blood. Crouching around the base of the truck, I moved to find the guys. Lying in the dirt, knocked halfway out of the doorframe, was Keith, hanging on by the cables of the radio, his left leg torn at a sickening angle. He was dazed, staring at the pooling blood staining the dirt around him and growing at an alarming rate. Without my med kit, I had to improvise. I ripped his belt from his waist and using that and a piece of metal, successfully made the world's worst tourniquet around his upper thigh.

Over the constant, shrill ringing in my ears, I yelled at him, "I got you! FOCUS. Look at me . . . We got this!"

His nod was weak, and his color pallid. He probably only had minutes, and that was not going to fucking happen. I grabbed the radio mic. The crackle of the speaker let me know we weren't totally fucked. Calling in a bird was the only way we were getting out of this shithole.

"This is Corpsman Lincoln Scott. Medevac needed. Multiple down."

"10-4. This is Chop-4. Extent of injuries."

"We've got a couple hit here. Ah, fuck, Wade took two in the chest. At least four down."

"Roger that. Let's get you men onboard."

Leaning back on the truck, weapon across my legs, I felt warmth spread across my neck and chest. The adrenaline was wearing off, and I became aware of the pain in my neck, shooting down my ribs and arm, vibrating through my skull. Reaching up with my left arm, I traced my fingertips along my neckline and felt my shirt stick to my skin. Moving back, I found a hot, hard lump of metal protruding from my shoulder and neck. It had buddies too—shrapnel littering my upper torso, arm, and neck. My fingers grazed the pocket of my uniform, and I held my hand there. I could feel the outline of the letter I kept in my pocket. Its presence vibrated through me. Touching my right forearm, I thought about my tattoo beneath the uniform. Looking down, all I could see were shreds of my uniform and thick, red blood.

Hold steady. Breathe.

My fingers explored. My vest was the only thing that kept the worst of the blast from reaching my vital organs. This neck wound though . . . damn. This wasn't great.

The cold prick of panic crept up my legs and into my chest.

Calm the fuck down. Stop dumping blood because you can't keep your shit together. Breathe.

I focused on Keith's shallow, staccato breathing next to me. I tried to turn my head, but that wasn't fucking happening. "You good, man?"

"Shit, doc. Never better."

"Hah. Atta boy."

We sat in labored-breathing silence. Listened for the medevac helicopters. As the scene around us came into focus, I realized how easily the lifeless bodies of the Marines around me could have been mine. I counted six members of my platoon killed or badly wounded. Our machine gun team, Mendez and Tex, had been among the dead. Mendez was only twenty.

Already struggling to breathe, I felt the wind knock out of me. Just last week, in a quiet moment outside our tent, Mendez told me he was afraid. He missed his mom and little sister and just wanted to go home to Chicago. Becoming a Marine was a mistake, he'd said.

"Doc, I don't wanna die out here, man."

In that quiet moment, he'd revealed what we all felt, but never spoke aloud. Instead of offering him some comfort, I'd stared out into the blackness of the desert by his side until he turned, stubbed out his cigarette, and walked back inside.

Leaning my head back, I let my own thoughts wander to Finn and Mom. His easy smile, her lilting laugh. I wondered what they were doing back home while I was slowly dying, an imposter in the desert.

When I walked off the plane, the airport had an eerie feeling of calm. I could smell the familiar summer Montana air over the lingering stale bagels and sweat of the airport. I hoisted my rucksack over my shoulder and began to walk toward the exit when a small voice floated over my right shoulder. "Thank you for your service."

My whole body shifted, I still couldn't turn my head quite right, and I peered down at a little boy—probably six or seven at most. "Hey, little man. You're welcome."

Then he clipped his heels together and saluted, and I thought I'd die right there. He was so fucking cute. I saluted back to him and dropped to my knee.

"You know, they give these to us because we're strong and brave and love our country." I peeled the American flag patch off my shoulder, felt its soft Velcro backing run through my fingers. "I think you should have it."

The little boy's eyes went wide, and his mother put her hand over her heart, teared up, and mouthed, "Thank you." I tipped my head to her as I stood.

"Linc! LINCOLN!" I heard Finn yell above the crowd and turned to see my younger brother running through baggage claim. His body slammed into me, and we held onto each other for a moment. I ignored the electric pain sizzling down my arm. Over his shoulder, I could see Mom, tears in her eyes, running with a sign.

"Damn, kid. We missed you!" Finn laughed, his sprawling hand connecting with my shoulder. I braced myself, refusing to wince at his touch. But Finn was huge, a solid two inches taller than my six-foot-one-inches. He'd definitely grown up, reminding me that he wasn't the same gap-toothed fifteen-year-old kid I'd left behind when I enlisted.

"Kid? Don't forget I'm older and can still beat the shit out of you. Hey, Mom." I engulfed my mother in a hug. Her tiny frame reminded me why everyone called her Birdie.

"Eight years. Almost a decade and now I get to keep you forever!" We hugged again, her thin arms holding onto me tighter, nails digging into my uniform. Mom was a crier. If we didn't get this under control now, we'd be here all afternoon with her trying to fuss all over me like I was eleven and just wrecked my dirt bike. But the truth was, while I'd been home for the occasional holiday leave, Chikalu Falls, Montana hadn't been my home for over a decade.

She finally released the hug, holding me at arm's length. "I'm so happy to have you home," she sighed.

"I'm happy too, Mom." It was only a small lie, but I had to give it to her. I was happy to see her and Finn, and to put the death and dirt and sand behind me. But I'd planned on at least another tour in the Marines. I was almost through my second enlistment when the IED explosion tore through my body. The punctured lung, torn flesh, and scars were the easy part. It was the nerve damage to my right arm and neck that was the real problem.

Unreliable trigger finger wasn't something the United States Marine Corps wanted in their ranks. In the end, after the doctors couldn't get my neck to turn or the pain radiating down my right arm to settle, I'd been honorably discharged.

I glanced down at the poster board that Finn scooped off the ground. "Oh, Great. You Somehow Survived" was written in bubble letters with a haphazard smattering of sequins and glitter. Laughing, I adjusted my pack and looked at Finn. "You're such a dick." I had to mumble it under my breath to make sure Mom didn't hear me, but from the corner of my eye, I could see her smirk.

"Let's go, boys."

It was a four-hour trip from Spokane, Washington to

Chikalu Falls, Montana—but only out-of-towners used its full, given name. Saying Chikalu was one way to tell the locals from the tourists.

The drive was filled with Mom's updates on day-to-day life in our small hometown. Finn eagerly filled me in on his fishing guide business, how he wanted to expand, and how I could help him run it. I listened, occasionally grunting or nodding in agreement as I stared out the window at the passing pines. Ranches and farmland dotted the landscape as we weaved through the national forest.

I was going home.

"You know, Mr. Bailey's been asking about you. He heard you were coming home and wants to make sure that you stop in...when you're settled," Mom said.

"Of course. I always liked Mr. Bailey. I'm glad to hear he's still kicking."

Finn laughed. "Still kicking? That old man's never gonna die. He's still sitting out in his creepy old farmhouse, complaining about all the college kids and how they're ruining all the fishing. I saw him walk into town with a rifle on his shoulder last week like that's not completely against the law. People straight up scatter when he walks through town. It's amazing."

Changing the subject, Mom glanced at me over her shoulder and chimed in with, "The ladies at the Chikalu Women's Club are all in a flutter, what with you coming home this week. You make five of our seven boys who've come home now." A heavy silence blanketed the car as her words floated into the air. No one acknowledged that three of the five who'd returned came home in caskets.

Clearing her throat gently, she added, "And you got everyone's letters?"

I nodded. The Chikalu Women's Club was known around my platoon for their care packages and letters. Without fail, every birthday, holiday, and sometimes "just because," I would get a small package. Sometimes because we'd moved around or simply because the mail carrier system was total shit, the packages would be weeks or months late, but inside were drawings from school kids, treats, toiletries, and letters. I'd share the candies and toiletries with the guys. We'd barter over the Girl Scout cookies. A single box of Samoas was worth its weight in gold. For me, the letters became the most important part. Mostly they were from Mom and Finn, young kids or other mothers, college students working on a project, that kind of thing.

But in one package in November, I got the letter that saved my life.

I idly touched the letter in my shirt pocket. Six years. For six years, I'd carried that letter with me. After the bombing, it was torn and stained with my blood, and you could hardly read it now, but it was with me.

"The packages were great. They really helped to boost morale around camp. I tried writing back to the kids who wrote when I could. Some of them didn't leave a return address," I said.

Mom continued filling the space with anecdotes about life around Chikalu. My thoughts drifted to the first time I'd opened the package and saw the letter that saved me.

In that package, there had been plenty of treats—trail mix, gum, cookies, beef jerky, cheese and cracker sandwiches. When you're in hell, you forget how much you miss something as simple as a cheese and cracker sandwich. Under the treats was a neat stack of envelopes. Most were addressed to "Marine" or "Soldier" or "Our Hero" and a few were addressed directly to me. I always got one from Mom and Finn. When I got the packages, I shared some of the letters with the guys in camp. The ones marked "Soldier" were always given to the grunt we were giving shit to that week. Soldiers were in the Army, but we were Marines.

On the bottom of this particular box was a thick, doodled envelope—colored swirls and shapes covering the entire outside. It was addressed directly to me in swirly feminine handwriting. Turning it over in my hands, I felt unsettled. An uncomfortable twinge in my chest had me rattled. I didn't like not feeling in control, so rather than opening it right away, I stored it in my footlocker.

I couldn't shake the feeling that the letter was calling to me. I spent three days obsessing over the doodles on the envelope—was it an art student from the college? The mystery of it was intoxicating. Why was it addressed to me if I had no idea who had written it? When I finally opened it, I was spellbound. The letter wasn't written like a traditional letter where someone was anonymously writing notes of encouragement or thanks. This letter was haphazard. Different inks, some cursive, some print, quotes on the margins.

It became clear that the letter had been written over the course of several days. The author had heard about the town letter collection and decided to write to me on a whim. It included musings about life in a small mountain town, tidbits of information learned in a college class, facts about the American West, even a knock-knock joke about desert and dessert. I read that letter every day until a new one came. Similarly decorated envelope, same nonlinear ramblings inside. A voice—her voice—came through in those letters.

There were moments in the dark I could imagine her

laughter or imagine feeling her breath on my ear as she whisper-sang the lyrics she'd written. Her letters brought me comfort in those dark moments when I doubted I'd ever have my mom's buttermilk pie again or hear Finn laugh at a really good joke.

Over the years, she included small pieces of information about who she was. Not anyone I'd known pre-enlistment, but a transplant from Bozeman. She'd gone to college in Chikalu. "The mountains and the river are my home," she wrote. Her letters were funny, charming, comforting.

The one I carried with me was special. News reports of conflict in the Middle East were everywhere, and she'd assumed correctly that I was right in the thick of it. She told me the story of the Valkyrie she'd learned about in one of her courses.

In Norse mythology, Valkyrie were female goddesses who spread their wings and flew over the battlefield, choosing who lived and who died in battle. Warriors chosen by the Valkyrie died with honor and were then taken to the hall of Valhalla in the afterlife. Their souls could finally rest.

Reading her words, I felt comfort knowing that if I held my head high and fought with honor, she would come for me. I carried her words in my head. Through routine sweeps or high-intensity missions, her words would wash over me, motivate me, and steady me. She connected with something inside of my soul—deep and unfamiliar. At my next leave, I'd gotten a tattoo of the Valkyrie wings spread across my right forearm so I could have a visual reminder of her. I could always keep her with me.

Glancing down now, I slid my sleeve up, revealing the bottom edge of the tattoo. It was marred with fresh, angry scars but it was there. My goddess had been with me in battle, and I'd survived.

Pulling into town, I knew I had to find her—the woman who left every letter signed simply: *Joanna.*

❧

Continue reading Finding You

ACKNOWLEDGMENTS

To my grump of a husband, thank you for letting me be your ray of sunshine and annoying the shit out of you. A secret part of me is glad I'm the only one who sees your tender heart. I promise to always keep it safe.

Leanne–you are my daily check-in and (better) half of the Dream Team. I appreciate your faith in me–more than you know. I also couldn't do any of this without your help and gentle reminders. Over time you've become so much more than a PA. I'm honored to call you my friend.

Special shout-out to Elsie for being the ultimate sprint partner, critiquer of blurbs, and strategizer. I am so blessed to have someone in my corner that knows and understands the ups and downs of this business. I can't wait until we finally run away together–we're going to be blissfully happy, I just know it.

Nicole–I love that you were shocked to hear about my books but then quickly became a trusted confidant and reader. I can't thank you enough for your love and support. One of these days we're going to be in the same state and I'm going to never let you leave!

James and Laetitia–thank you for always giving my stories the love and polish they need. Your individual insights help bring my stories to life and I couldn't do it without both of you. Combined make an editing and proofreading powerhouse and I am so thankful to work side-by-side with you!

To every reader who gave this book a chance–THANK YOU! When I originally had the idea of a "mafia cowboy" for Redemption Ranch, a lot of people thought I was joking. Ha!

Thank you for reading Parker and Sienna's love story. You are the reason I can write and bring love into this world.

You are everything.

ALSO BY LENA HENDRIX

The Chikalu Falls Series

Finding You

Keeping You

Protecting You

The Redemption Ranch Series

The Badge and the Bad Boy

The Alias and the Alar

The Rebel and the Rogue

(coming fall 2022!)